# The
# Eighteenth

The Eighteenth

Edited by Watch Jane Write - www.watchjanewrite.com

Formatted by Tim Gabrielle

Cover design by Coverquill.com

ISBN:  978-1-9992340-0-3


authortimgabrielle.com

To Pop

# CHAPTER ONE

It took the Valley Ridge police department three months to discover that Walter David Scott had been the one responsible for the murders of seventeen students from Valley Ridge High School in Loudoun County, Virginia. During the long months of his killing spree, Walter had roamed the hallways of the school where he worked as the day shift custodian, plotting his course of action in secret. Police had repeatedly combed the school grounds, looking for evidence and interrogating anyone of possible interest; Walter himself had been questioned three times before his final showdown with Sarah Prince, the eighteenth name on a list of victims he wasn't able to complete.

The list was one of the most important pieces of evidence the police had discovered when they raided Walter's home after his capture. Eighteen names, seventeen of which had been scratched out in dried blood, were scrawled neatly down the middle of a tattered piece of notebook paper:

Scott Freeman — The Quarterback
Stacy Smith — The Prom Queen

Meghan Stern — The Addict
Johnny Park — The Basketball Star
Dana Bagley — The Cheer Captain
Trevor Flax — The Gay Kid
Bethany Platt — The Valedictorian
Rachael Borden — The Nerd
Kyle Greene — Mr. Moneybags
Katie Greene — Ms. Moneybags
James Lampton — The Comedian
Marisa Jamison — The Bitch
David Braddock — The Loner
Michael Chan — The Chinese Kid
Molly Thomas — The Whore
Kara Stein — The Ugly One
Derek Long — The Black Kid
Sarah Prince — The Orphan

Seventeen murdered teens, all laid to rest under tombstones with their names neatly etched across the front. Each gravestone was a grim reminder of the events that transpired during the spring of 2009 in the small Virginia town. Walter had attended most of their funerals, taking time to console the families with the rest of the staff, a fact that was met with shock and disgust once he had been revealed as the one responsible. Valley Ridge had been a quiet, soft-spoken town, but that all changed with the first stroke of Walter's knife.

The first name to be crossed off his list had been Marisa Jamison (The Bitch). Marisa had been an avid runner and star of the school's track team. Long after her murder, her name would remain etched on medals and trophies in the school display case from the many events she'd dominated, but the thing many would remember her for was the cruelty she displayed toward people outside of her social circle. She was, in every way, the bully-bitch of Valley Ridge. The night Marisa was murdered, she'd been on a running track surrounding one of the town's public soccer fields as the sun set over the horizon. She had been a junior at Valley Ridge High and ran nightly with her teammates, but on the night of her murder, she'd been alone. Walter watched from the tress that surrounded the track, his bowie knife held tightly in his hand. In the months leading up to the murders, he'd sat the knife on his bedroom dresser so that he could see it every morning. He had smiled at it daily, fantasizing about when he'd be able to use it for the first time. There were no smiles as he crouched in the shadows, though; only a fierce determination to complete his task.

He had waited, knowing at some point that she would stop to check her text messages, which she always did. He had watched Marisa and her teammates long enough to know it was just a matter of time before they stopped and zoned out on their cellphones. Walter had often fantasized about running out of the trees and slicing their throats before any of them took the time to raise their eyes from their wretched machines. It was a nice thought, but he restrained himself. The others weren't on his list...Marisa was.

Her running that night had gradually slowed until she stopped and pulled her phone from the back pocket of her running shorts. She had been typing furiously, completely lost in whatever message had been sent to her, as Walter emerged silently onto the track. A heavy black hood hung over his forehead, shadowing a black fabric mask that covered his determined face. The hood had been sewn onto an ankle length trench coat, the bottom torn and shredded. He took the appearance of a ghostly spectre as he moved toward her in the harsh lights of the track field. His sleeves were torn to bits as well, falling in strands around a pair of black leather gloves. He looked like a reaper in the night, which had garnered him a name from the local media.

The Reaper Grim of Valley Ridge.

He had been close enough to see the glowing words on Marisa's screen when he reached forward and grabbed her thick, blond ponytail. A gasp escaped her mouth as he pulled her head backward, feeling the tension as she tried to pull away from him. He slid the knife across the softness of her neck and breathed in her sweet, fearful scent as blood began to spew onto the running track. She fell like a pile of laundry onto the track, grasping at her neck in a vain attempt to stop the bleeding. She died in a fit of bloody, terrified gurgles, as Walter stood above her in silent excitement. Her blood formed a thick pool around her body that marked the beginning of a three-month manhunt.

Walter had preferred to kill his victims one by one, but if the occasion warranted it, he would stray from the course. The fact that the handsome, alpha-male quarterback had been secretly fooling around with the school's only openly gay student was a fact that Walter saw with disgust, but also great potential. Both Scott Freeman (The Quarterback) and Trevor Flax (The Gay Kid) had been on his list long before Walter had caught them together in a bathroom stall at the town's bowling alley, but once he discovered them together, he decided they had to be killed together.

Trevor and Scott had been his seventh and eighth victims, following Marisa, Dana, Kara, David, Johnny, and Stacy. Walter had spent almost every Thursday evening practicing for his Friday night bowling league. His bowling team was possibly the only thing he cared more about than the sacred list he kept tucked away in his pocket. Each Thursday night, Walter walked into the alley with a smile and made small talk with the cashier. The cashier's name was Nick Smith, another student at the school. Walter had grown far too attached to him, which meant his name was nowhere near his tally of victims.

Walter hadn't expected to see any of his potential victims at the bowling alley on practice night, but he'd been pleasantly surprised to see Trevor and his group of friends already set up at a lane, throwing balls haphazardly between fits of obnoxious laughter. Walter had requested a lane near their group so that he could secretly watch, hoping to take advantage of the evening and cross another name off his list. He kept his kill suit in a duffle bag in his trunk, so no matter where he was, he could be ready at a moment's notice.

Walter had been a well-loved figure at the high school prior to his capture and the group of teens lit up seeing him set up a few alleys down. Water had thrown strikes and spares with almost every throw and found himself becoming increasingly irritated with Trevor's careless approach to the game. Trevor was thin, almost sickly thin, and the way he danced around to celebrate almost picking up a spare made Walter's stomach turn. Each ball that crashed hard on the lane, followed by their boisterous laughter, had brought Trevor one step closer to Walter's knife that evening. He'd taken a break and sat with a cold bottle of beer, thinking of how he would end Trevor's life, when Scott Freeman walked through the doors of the alley and sealed their fate.

Scott stood nervously near the entrance, glancing at Trevor with fidgety hands stuffed into his jean pockets. Scott made brief eye contact with Trevor before disappearing into a small arcade near the shoe return. Trevor's group of friends got up to leave, and to their surprise, Trevor said goodbye and let them leave without him. He waited for them to leave before disappearing into a washroom at the opposite end of the building, followed soon after by a very nervous looking Scott. Walter stepped away from his lane and smiled at the front cashier, who had been hopelessly lost in the glow of his cellphone.

What Walter had discovered when he walked through the swinging door of the men's room had changed the course of his plans for both Scott and Trevor. He hadn't been able to see at first, but the sounds that had echoed out of the lone stall were enough for him to know what was happening. He silently made his way into the washroom and knelt down, looking under the gap between the floor and the bottom of the stall. Trevor's bright pink flip-flops stood firmly on the ground, his toes wiggling comically as they popped out from underneath his crumbled khaki-shorts. A pair of expensive-looking blue jeans knelt in front of him, the folds creasing slightly as the two of them engaged in the behavior that would eventually lead to their collective demise.

Walter had observed their secret encounters on numerous other occasions after that night as he waited for the right time to end their lives, but while he waited for the right moment, he made time to kill Kara Stein (The Ugly One) and David Braddock (The Loner). By Walter's judgment, David didn't have a single friend in the school other than Kara. There wasn't anything strange about David, other than the fact that he seemed to just exude an unwillingness to connect with his peers. By most standards, he was handsome, but there was something about him that kept him from growing close to anyone. Kara, on the other hand, had a large nose and big, coke-bottle glasses. Her hair was unnaturally thinning for her age and her figure was borderline anorexic. In the superficial world of high school cliques, David and Kara simply did not fit in. Walter had caught the two of them fooling around in the back of David's car in a grocery store parking lot. In all the time he'd spent watching them, he'd never realized they'd been an item, which in the end didn't matter to him. He'd swung open David's door and stabbed them both in the neck before either of them could call for help.

David's father, Harvey Braddock, was a local police officer and a member of Walter's bowling team. As luck would have it, Harvey would be the one to find the two of them the next morning.

After David and Kara's deaths, the town was in an uproar. Parents were keeping their kids at home as much as possible, which made Walter's plans much harder to execute. On a rainy Tuesday night, Scott had invited Trevor over to help him study for a coming math test; at least that's what he had told his parents. Trevor had been known as a popular math-whiz at the school so his parents never thought twice about it. At 1:15 am, Walter slid into the Freeman's home by simply opening the back door. He'd brought everything he'd need to break in but by some twist of fate, nobody in the house had thought to check their back door. As Todd and Miranda Freemen slept in their second-floor bedroom, Trevor and Scott laid naked together in Scott's basement room. Walter eased himself into the room as the two of them rolled together, twisting and moaning quietly as Walter approached in the dark.

The screams of Todd and Miranda Freeman had echoed through the neighborhood the next morning when they went downstairs to wake their son. Trevor was on top of Scott, their bodies stuck together from the sticky, drying blood. Walter had been in and out without making a sound.

Bethany Platt (The Valedictorian), had been found slumped over her bedroom desk, her face and hair in a pool of blood on the desktop. Walter had nearly decapitated her with his knife. Her bare feet had become stuck to the floor in a pool of sticky blood and the sound of them tearing away from the hardwood would haunt the dreams of everyone in the room for months. In the immediate struggle when Walter had grabbed her from behind, Bethany had panicked and sent most of the items on her desk onto the floor, including the valedictorian speech she had been writing. A group of her friends had tearfully read the speech to a chorus of sobs at that year's graduation.

Meghan Stern, (The Addict), had been close to death by the time Walter had snuck into her basement bedroom in the middle of the night. Her single mother had been working late as a bartender at one of the town's only bars, unknowingly leaving her daughter in Walter's eager grasp. He had slowly opened the door to her bedroom as her television blared from inside. Meghan had been a tall, heavyweight, outspoken girl, and he had expected to have a struggle with her before ending her life. His concern washed away as he slid into her bedroom to find her barely conscious with a needle still injected into her forearm. She woke slightly as he plunged his knife deep inside her heart, a glimmer of fear and confusion on her face before she gasped and slipped away.

Derek Long (The Black Kid) had been found hanging from the orange rim of a secluded basketball court, his stomach sliced open with his insides in a steaming pile below him. The morning his body had been discovered had been warm, prompting the middle school basketball team to practice outside at the behest of their coach. They'd met at the school and jogged to the nearby court, which was slightly secluded in a patch of trees close to a popular playground. The kids screamed in horror as they came through the thinly treed area to see Derek's body, swaying slightly in the morning breeze as his engorged tongue peeked out from behind his dry, cracked lips. The coach and his assistants would never take the kids off campus for practice again.

Kyle and Katie Greene (Mr. and Ms. Moneybags), Michael Chan (The Chinese Kid), Molly Thomas (The Whore), James Lampton (The Comedian), and Rachael Borden (The Nerd) had all been killed at a party at Michael's house. The murders at the house party had become Walter's greatest accomplishment; he considered them to be the apex of his murderous plot. He had expelled more patience and cunning than he'd known he was capable of as he killed each of them before slinking away into the night, unnoticed.

Michael had been murdered first, his stomach nearly gutted in his damp basement. Michael had alerted Walter to the party in the first place when he jokingly asked him to come, sealing his and the other teens fate with a simple joke. Walter had crept into the basement before the party had started and waited, hoping Michael would have to come downstairs for more beer for the party-hungry teens. Walter's heart had almost exploded from his chest when, halfway through the night, the basement door opened and Michael came waltzing down alone. Michael opened the door of the fridge and smiled at the glowing sight of all the beer in front of him as Walter slowly ascended from his dark corner of the unfinished basement. He had screamed against Walter's gloved hand as the knife plunged repeatedly into his stomach; his intestines spilled onto the floor in front of the fridge as Walter dragged him back to the dark.

After finishing with Michael, Walter crept through a basement window to keep watch of the other kids inside the party. Kyle Greene was sitting against the back of the house with his pants pulled down to his ankles and a giant penis drawn across his forehead in thick, permanent marker. Walter had looked down at the inebriated teen as he debated whether or not to take advantage of the drunken idiot in front of him. It seemed a disappointingly easy kill for him, especially after Meghan's, but in the end Walter had flung Kyle over his shoulder and moved him to a shed in the back of the large backyard. He tossed him down to the floor and slid his knife into Kyle's bottom jaw and into the base of his brain. Kyle's eyes didn't even open, leaving Walter slightly frustrated over not being able to soak in his final moment.

The party continued as Walter disappeared into a patch of woods in the back of Michael's property, leaving Kyle's corpse to bleed beside the Chan's riding lawn mower. The house was well lit as the teens continued to fill themselves with alcohol, unaware of the mayhem that was transpiring around them. Walter had known that any of his victims could be found at any moment and send the party into a panic, but the teens were far too involved with themselves to notice, and with Michael's parents negligently away for the night, he knew he was in the clear. He watched with a set of binoculars as Molly whispered softly into James' ear before she disappeared up the stairs with a smirk. Walter flew across the backyard in a flash, his tattered trench coat flying in his wake.

A light illuminated in the upper level of the house as Walter leaped into an old tree that sat just outside the second-floor windows. He waited in the branches for a moment to make sure nobody had seen him before he jumped from the tree and landed on a section of the roof that led to a set of bedroom windows. He had been worried that the sound of him landing would have drawn attention, but the music had continued to blare, mixed with the laughs and cheers of the teens on the main floor as they moved about their evening, still unaware of his presence.

From the window, he had watched discreetly as Molly undressed and laid on the bed to wait for James. The night was cool, so most of the windows in the house had been opened by Michael before his guests had arrived. As Walter scanned Molly's naked form underneath the white bedsheet, he climbed through the double-paned window and silently slid inside. Molly remained unaware as she laid naked on the bed, tapping on her cellphone as he slinked toward her. In the second before he got to her, she turned and saw him beside the bed. She opened her mouth to scream but his hand quickly covered her mouth as her eyes bulged with fear. Her blood had soaked through the mattress to the floor as James entered the room with a smile on his face and a drink in each hand. The sight of her mutilated body had barely registered in his mind before Walter leaped from behind the door and kicked him to the ground. Walter closed the door and plunged the knife into the confused teen's heart.

His last kills of the night had occurred down the long, dark driveway that led to the road. After he had finished making a mess of Molly and James, Walter left through the window and escaped to the front of the house, keeping watch beyond the front fence in a long field adjacent the house. He had decided his evening was finished, but with one last look through his binoculars, he had spotted Katie preparing to leave the party. He made his way down the driveway and removed his kill suit, knowing he'd have no play on her dressed in his murderous disguise.

He watched the front door from afar as he strained his eyes through his binoculars. His heart began to race wildly as Rachael joined Katie outside and got into the passenger side of Katie's BMW. He surprised himself as a soft moan escaped from his mouth, followed by a chill that radiated through his core. It was as if the moan had come from something inside, something not completely part of him; something primal and hungry...and very much in control.

Walter walked down the driveway as the car approached, giving a smile and a wave as the headlights illuminated him. He was nervous they'd keep driving, effectively making them witness to the fact he'd been at the party, but the car had slowed as they recognized the custodian they had all loved during their years at Valley Ridge.

"Mr. Scott, is that you?" Katie had said as she rolled down her window.

"It is indeed!" he had said with a laugh. "Michael invited me tonight as a joke. I thought it'd be funny to actually show up and surprise him! I'm afraid I've been a bit lost trying to find my way though and I'm starting to wonder if this was a bad idea from the start. Is that his place down yonder?"

"Yep, that's his place back there," Rachael had said.

"Oh goodness. Look at these directions he gave me. He must have really not wanted me here tonight!"

Walter reached into his back pocket as Katie leaned out of the open car window with a smile, which had stayed on her face for a moment as his knife entered her head through her right ear. It was a smile that he wouldn't forget; it filled him with wonderful, unending joy. Katie grabbed her ear as her face grimaced in confused agony. Blood began to drip through her long blonde hair as she slumped back into the car while Rachael began to scream wildly. Katie's head hit the steering wheel as Walter reached in and pulled his knife out of her head, sending her sideways onto Rachael's lap. Rachael exploded into a fit of hysterics as her friend's blood spurted thickly onto her lap.

Walter moved in front of the car, his knife reflecting off the headlights as Rachael kept her petrified eyes locked onto his. After a moment of being frozen in fear, she opened her car door and flung herself off of her seat. Her foot caught the doorframe and she fell to the ground, knowing her chance to escape had passed. Walter's fingers entered her hair and pulled backward, exposing her neck to him in the harsh moonlight.

"Please, No, Mr. Scott!" she sobbed as she locked eyes with the crazed man above her.

Another moan escaped his mouth as her words filled him with vicious excitement. His knife ran across her throat just at it had Marisa's, sending a spray of blood in front of her and onto the moonlit gravel drive. The sound of her blood hitting the gravel had been interrupted slightly by the sound of Katie behind them as she let out a gasp as her body went through the final motions of death. He continued to hold Rachael in his arms as she bled in front of him. Much to his surprise, she hardly fought back; instead she slid backward into his embrace as the life slowly drained from her body.

Walter looked back toward the house to find that everyone was still entranced in their music and merriment, clueless to the growing collection of bodies around them. He took a moment to inhale the metallic sting of her escaping blood as he looked down at her in the soft moonlight. Her eyes looked up at him, filled with confusion as she died in his murderous embrace. Her pupils dilated as the last of her life escaped, which had sent a shiver through Walter's body as he let his gaze continue to lock onto hers long after she'd left him. Katie and Rachael's murders had been the most intimate of his kills, which he'd named his beautiful kills. Their memory would bring him endless joy as he sat alone in a jail cell, awaiting his execution.

Walter was long gone before the police turned down the long driveway to find the lifeless bodies of Rachael Borden and Katie Greene. Walter had slept like a baby that night, secure in the fact that his list was almost complete. He'd watched the news coverage the next day while eating an omelet with a large glass of orange juice, chewing loudly as the footage on the television flashed images of the petrified partygoers from the night before.

After the house party massacre, he only had one victim left on his list. It was a name he'd left for last and on the day of his execution, it hadn't been his beautiful kills that he had thought about, but instead how Sarah Prince (the Orphan), had bested him in the town's library. On his dying day, he'd concluded that he had been overconfident, given that in three months he'd been able to murder seventeen teens, completely undetected. The excitement of a fulfilled list had driven him to the point of insanity, and with only one last name to cross out, he had rushed his plans, had rushed his delivery, and had written himself into a no-win situation.

As the sun set on the night of Sarah's would-be murder, Walter had donned his kill suit and snuck into the town's library. The building was a reader's dream, with a parking lot made of cobblestone that led to the old stone exterior of the building. The inside was dotted with comfortable couches and easy-chairs, always ready to accept a reader and take them away to another world. Just as she did every week, Sarah walked into the library and made small talk with the elderly librarian. She had a soft spot for librarians, so much so that she had given endless amounts of thought toward becoming one herself. Walter listened as the librarian brought up the murders in an attempt to make sure Sarah stayed safe. His fingers twitched with reserved excitement as he thought about the librarian's face when she found Sarah's lifeless, mutilated body in the biography section later that night. Sarah was supposed to have been his last kill, and he had intended to make a mess of her; a tribute to his glorious venture, constructed out of her insides, but the librarian wouldn't find Sarah that night. There would be news coverage, both local and nationwide, but not detailing the beautiful finale of his work.

The library had been set to close within an hour as Walter watched Sarah from the deep shadows in the back of the old building. The librarian, who Walter had estimated to be well into her seventies, did her rounds dutifully, but unbeknownst to her, her absence from Sarah was part of his masterful plan. During what he knew would be one of the librarian's final sweeps of the night, Sarah closed her laptop and stretched her hands high above her head. She slid the laptop into her side-bag before disappearing into the non-fiction section, ready to return the books on the Civil War she had used to supplement her online research. Even with all the murders, Sarah made sure to dutifully keep up on her school assignments, which filled him with glee over the futility of her actions.

She disappeared in between two tall isles of books as the familiar darkness settled over Walter's mind.

It was time...

The librarian was at the opposite end of the building, giving him plenty of time to make his mess and leave before she hobbled her way back. He sprinted toward Sarah with tunnel-like focus, leaping over a table before launching himself into the musty isle while she replaced a book on the shelf. Just before his strike, she had seen him moving toward her like a phantom shadow. She had fixed her eyes on the knife in his hand and flung her bag in front of her. The laptop accepted the knife in a loud, crushing sound; the impact sent them both backward onto the floor. Walter landed beside her, taken aback by her defensive action as he looked frantically for the knife that had been lodged in the metal and plastic of her laptop. His face exploded in agony as Sarah smashed the spine of a large, hardcover book flatly against his face. Blood gushed from his broken nose as he cried out in pain, followed by Sarah's shriek of fear as she wiggled away from him and fled the aisle. Dazed and barely able to see through the pain, Walter clumsily made his way after her. His ski mask had become saturated with blood, impairing his ability to breathe. Blood bubbled and spat from the mask, dripping down onto his kill suit as he accidentally plowed into the senile librarian as the front doors swung shut from Sarah's escape.

"Fuck," he angrily yelled as his eyes fixed on the now motionless door.

"Please don't kill me!" sobbed the woman from the ground.

"Don't worry, you old bitch. You're not on the list."

If he had chased after Sarah, he wouldn't be able to make a show of her insides like he'd planned, but his list would be complete. If he allowed her to escape, killing her later could be a problem, as she'd be living under a microscope with her parents and the police. He had stood in the library, the librarian still crippled with fear on the floor as he weighed his options. The red and blue flashing lights reflected in the front windows made the decision for him.

Walter had darted to the back of the library, hurdling over the librarian as she shrieked in fear. He catapulted himself down a small flight of stairs in one bound before his vision became laser focused on the dimly lit backdoor. His eyes throbbed with mad anticipation as the blood from his nose continued to bubble and gush into his saturated mask. His heart pounded in his chest as he neared the door, but quickly sunk into his stomach as it flung open. A police officer stepped inside, a gun raised directly at Walter's chest.

"HANDS UP! DROP THE WEAPON!" screamed the officer. Walter dropped his knife to the ground as a second officer scaled the steps behind him. "ON YOUR KNEES! HANDS ABOVE YOUR HEAD!"

The officer stepped further into the door way and flicked on the light switch. Walter's heart sank deeper into the pit of his stomach as he realized the police officer standing in front of him was Stanley Wilkes. Stanley was a thirty-year member of the Valley Ridge Police Department, who'd served his years without a single smudge on his record. He was beloved by everyone in the town, without exception. Even the troublesome teens in the area minded their manners out of respect for the gentle, helpful police officer.

He had also been on Walter's bowling team for the past ten years.

"Stanley...I'm so sorry," Walter said, falling to his knees and placing his hands behind his head.

Walter had indeed been sorry, but not for his crimes. He had always liked Stanley, and Stanley had liked him. The two of them had gone for beers together dozens of times, most of those nights ending on Walters's porch with a deck of cards. Yes, Walter had been sorry...but only because Stanley would now know his secret. It broke his heart that at the end of his reign, it would be Stanley Wilkes, probably his only true friend in the world, that would bring him to justice. Stanley stepped forward and kicked the knife away from Walter's feet. He pushed back the hood of Walter's kill suit and tore off the blood-soaked ski mask.

"No..." Stanley said, looking down at his friend with as he head swam with confusion. Walter diverted his eyes from him as the officer from the stairs stepped forward and handcuffed him.

Sarah's aunt Hannah had flown into the parking lot in her PT Cruiser as Sarah stood silently with an officer. Walter had watched Sarah run to her with tears in her eyes as Stanley deposited him into the back of his police cruiser. Walter's eyes had met Sarah's as they drove slowly passed her. She had looked back at him with shocked confusion as he smiled, and without any thought or reason, he winked at her before Stanley pulled onto the main road.

"Please tell me this is some weird prank, Walter," Stanley said. "I know you; this couldn't have been you the whole time."

"I'm sorry, Stan. I'm so sorry you had to be involved like this."

"Oh God, Walter! How could you do this? Do you understand what you've done? What got into you?"

Walter spent the rest of the ride in silence as he cursed himself inwardly while replaying the events of the night. None of the others had given him any trouble at all, and given Sarah's small stature, he had never thought she would have been the one to give him trouble. He felt incomplete, like a part of himself was left in the library, never to be gathered again. He couldn't believe that Sarah Prince, the orphan of Valley Ridge High School, would be the one to end his reign and leave his work unfinished.

Stanley parked his cruiser and opened the door for Walter. Walter stood in front of him as they looked at each other in silence. Stanley couldn't come to terms with the suddenly unfamiliar man that had stood in front of him. He'd never met this person, and as he stood in front of him, it had scared him deeply.

"This may be the last time we get to speak for a very long time, Walter. Please, try and explain to me what happened."

"I'm sorry, Stanley," he said as he looked at him with dead, sorrowful eyes. "Tell the boys on the team I'm sorry too."

"That's what you're worried about? Walter, do you understand what you've done? Did you ever stop to think that you killed Harvey's kid? He's been your friend for years!"

"Harvey Braddock has been on our bowling team for years, Stan, but he's not a friend."

A pair of FBI agents dressed in matching black suits came out of the precinct, glaring at Walter as they approached him and Stanley. The bureau had been in Valley Ridge for weeks while they helped the local and state police try and stop Walter's killing spree.

"Goodbye, Walter," Stanley said as he handed him over to the two men. He watched them led Walter inside as he tried to fight back tears welling behind his eyes.

In the weeks after Walter's capture, the rest of the town would struggle to understand, just as Stanley had. The trial had been incredibly turbulent, each day filled with tears and outbursts from the parents and relatives of the murdered teens. Sarah had sat through much of the trial and watched in stunned disbelief as Walter stood trial for the murders of seventeen of her classmates. She remembered her first day of freshman year, when the friendly custodian had helped her to find the school library. He had happily walked her to the library with a smile before going on his way as she disappeared inside. She couldn't help but wonder at what point she had been added to his list...and why.

The list had been displayed at the front of the courtroom daily, each named blotted out in dark crimson, with the obvious exception of Sarah Prince. Walter watched her intently each day, hardly listening to the proceedings going on around him as he tried to come up with possible ways that he could end her life before he was locked away. He knew he was heading to death row, so one more murder in front of the courtroom would be of no consequence to his sentence, but with no weapons at his disposal and an armed bailiff at the ready, he knew he'd lost his chance that night in the library.

Even when the jury passed down the verdict of guilty on all seventeen murder charges, attempted murder, and aggravated assault, Walter sat firm as he stared at Sarah with a coy smile on his face. The courtroom erupted into a chorus of tears and applause as the bailiff led Walter David Scott out of the courtroom, off to spend the rest of his days on death-row as he awaited his date with the lethal injection chamber. It would be seven years before his execution; the time would fly for Walter, but for Sarah it would feel like an eternity, living in the shadow of the Reaper Grim of Valley Ridge, Virginia.

\*\*\*\*\*

Sarah had gone through the entire ordeal of Walter's killing spree without the care and support of her mother and father. Laura and Michael Prince had been kind, loving, and thoughtful parents, giving Sarah the stereotypical, small-town life that most people only dream of. Every Friday night had been game night around their kitchen table and every Sunday evening was ice-cream night at the town's only ice-cream shop. Laura spent Saturdays teaching Sarah how to bake, serving up cookies or slices of pie once Michael returned home from work. Sarah's life before Walter was as typical and All-American as you could imagine.

Laura had found a small amount of local success as a writer, having self-published two books that had garnered state-wide fame but nothing more outside of that. Michael owned and operated a successful gas station just outside of Valley Ridge, which had been handed down to him from his father after he passed. Being one of the only gas stations before the West Virginia border a half hour away, the pumps were never without a car and the beer fridge was constantly in a state of restocking. Sarah and Laura spent most nights together, having dinner and watching television as Michael worked late hours to make sure his business was running properly. Most nights, Michael would walk in after 9:45 pm and eat a warmed-up plate of food as Laura kissed him goodnight and retired to their bedroom for the evening.

A year prior to the night that Walter ran his knife across Marisa Jamieson's throat, Michael Prince stood in the store of his gas station, counting money and filling out order forms. Michael's regular stock-boy had called in sick, so Laura had to come in to help with the nightly duties. The two worked without speaking, listening to country music as they got closer to closing the store and heading home for the evening. At 9:04 pm, the gas station exploded into a ball of orange flames and black smoke.

Laura, Michael, and six patrons who had been refilling their vehicles died in the explosion, which the authorities found suspicious but ultimately labeled an accident. The authorities had found the source of the blast to be at one of the pumping stations, but without any cameras watching the old pumps, there was no way to tell if there had been any foul play. The Princes' last will and testament had named Sarah as the executor of their estate and the main beneficiary of any property, including their home and business assets. The insurance payment from the gas station was paid directly to their estate, giving Sarah a sizeable nest egg to sit on as she silently mourned her parents. Laura's sister Hannah moved into the Prince home and stayed there until Sarah's eighteenth birthday. Prior to the deaths of Laura and Michael, Hannah and Sarah had been relatively close, but their time spent after the explosion was mostly quiet, both of them co-existing and supporting each other from afar.

Sarah had only been a freshman the year she stopped Walter's killing spree. Her grades had been above average all year and the school had offered her to take the remainder of the school year off to heal, but just a week after Stanley Wilkes took Walter into custody, Sarah was back at the school library, reading and studying for her year-end exams. She had always been a bit of a loner at school, choosing to spend her lunch breaks reading in the library as opposed to sitting with her classmates in the cafeteria. After the murders had ended and life slowly began to go back to normal, she fell back into the same routine, happy with a pile of books and a hot tea.

For the first six months after Walter's capture, her phone and social media had been alive with activity as reporters from local and national television stations reached out to her for comment. Money had been offered for her to do numerous appearances, all of which she had declined. Shortly after the murders had ended, an up-and-coming film director had knocked on her door and begged her to cameo in a script based on the murders. Sarah slammed the door so hard that the windows of the house rattled as the shocked director stepped awkwardly away from her door. She applied the deadbolt with as much gusto as she could manage before disappearing into her house in a fit of frustration.

Hannah moved out after she met her boyfriend, Robert. Sarah was just shy of graduating school and was fairly well adjusted, given the trauma she'd endured since the death of her parents. They spent their final week together, reminiscing and saying goodbye before the day Hannah drove away with Robert. She wasn't moving far away, but neither of them had been apart from each other in years. Even though they'd spent a lot of those years in silent companionship, the two of them both shed their share of tears as Robert drove her away in his pickup truck.

Sarah graduated from Valley Ridge High School in the spring of 2013. Her class was the last of the students that had been at the school during Walter's killing spree, meaning news reporters and press were there to film some of the afternoon's events. Although members of the press were granted permission to film the events of the ceremony, including a moving tribute to the seventeen murdered teens, the staff had barred them from interviewing any of the students while on school grounds. It was a somber ceremony, just like the previous three had been. In each of the previous ceremonies, the parents of the victims who would have graduated walked hand in hand and collected an honorary diploma on behalf of their murdered child. They had each been met with a standing ovation as they accepted the diploma and left the stage in tears. Sarah was treated in the same manner, which brought tears to her eyes as she awkwardly waved and made her way off the graduation stage.

While most of the senior class spent graduation night partying, Sarah sat at home with Hannah and Robert as they watched a movie and ate pizza. After their movie had finished and the pizza was done, Hannah hugged Sarah and drove home with Robert, leaving Sarah alone in the quiet house she had once shared with her parents. She went to bed early, shedding tears as she imagined the site of her mom and dad sitting together in the high school auditorium, watching her walk across the stage with pride, but it didn't take long for Walter to enter her mind and chase their memory away. She didn't sleep until long into the night, her mind firing image after image of the time when Walter had terrorized her and the community. She finally fell asleep at 4:15 in the morning in a sea of nervous energy.

# CHAPTER TWO

On the night of August 6, 2016, at 9:00 pm, Walter David Scott sat alone in his cell on death row, waiting for his turn to have his name added to the state of Virginia's death list. As he sat in the silence of his cell, he could still taste the special meal that had been provided to him two nights before. It had begun with a can of Chef Boyardee ravioli, which he had eaten straight from the can with a plastic spoon, then an entire box of Ho Ho's. He washed it all down with a cold bottle of Wild Cherry Pepsi. His taste in food was simple; the prepackaged delights, coupled with the vivid images of his beautiful kills, were enough to keep him calm and content as he awaited his final moments. A door opened and closed down the hallway followed by the sound of footsteps on the clean, echoing floor. Two guards appeared at the door of his cell, each with an emotionless look on their face.

"Walter, it's time." A small rectangle opening slid open, waiting for his hands to reach through.

Walter rapped his knuckles on the frame of his bed for the last time before standing to face the two guards. He placed his hands through the opening, letting one of the guards secure his wrists with a pair of cold handcuffs. "I suppose it is. Time to pay the piper, as they say."

The guards guided Walter down the whitewashed hallway that lead to the execution chamber. They stood behind him, each with a hand on his arm as they gently maneuvered him toward the chamber. The guards were calm and reverent, knowing that no matter the crime, they were responsible for leading their prisoner to death. Even with seventeen kills to his name, they treated him with the same reverence as any other death-row inmate.

Walter walked with no fear, still reminiscing over Rachael and Katie's deaths as the guards ushered him toward his final destination. The image of Rachael in his arms as her blood coated the ground filled him with a sort of euphoria, but his dreamy state was washed away as Sarah's face flashed before his eyes when the reached the chamber door.

"Let's get this over with," Walter said as the guards opened the door and ushered him through.

The injection gurney sat empty in the middle of the room, its arms outstretched to the side, ready to accept him. Walter had hardly noticed though; his eyes were drawn to the newly waxed floor. The speckled tile distorted his image; a blurry, unfinished version of himself, which was exactly how he had come to think of himself for not completing his list.

The warden stood in the corner with a smile on his face as Walter was led inside. He was a cold, calculated man with a dry sense of humor and a dislike for most of the inmates in his prison. He took pride in the fact that none of the inmates knew his first name, each of them referring to him only as Warden Crawford. He wasn't a tall man, well under six feet, with thick, receding brown hair, brushed backward in a wispy style that revealed his broad forehead. The day of the execution, he had worn an expensive-looking designer suit; black from his shoes all the way up to his tie. His satisfied grin did not waiver in the least as the guards walked Walter to the gurney.

Walter's eyes fixated on the witness gallery, hidden behind a thick black curtain. He had no family to come visit him and all his friends weren't interested in the final moments of the calculated serial killer he'd become, but he had a feeling *she* would be there. The Orphan...the one that got away. She would want to see his final moments played out like a macabre show.

"Tick, tick, tick," Warden Crawford said as he stepped in between the witness gallery and Walter. "Time's almost up, Walter."

"You can go to hell."

The Warden had cocked his head sideways, his hands resting in his pockets as he turned to walk away. "The final words of a dying man. How poetic."

"See you on the other side, *Fletcher*."

Warden Crawford froze in place at the sound of his first name. Hearing the name come out of Walter's mouth filled him with rage.

"I believe you may, brother. I look forward to it!" His final statement to Walter came with a touch of bravado as he motioned the priest into the room to offer his services to Walter. Walter hadn't even noticed the priest's presence, but when the man approached, he put his hand up from the arm constraint.

"Father, I appreciate it, but I do not require your services. The warden, however, could use a little Jesus in his life."

Silence hung in the air for a moment before Warden Crawford opened the door leading to a hidden room that housed the equipment that would end Walter's life. "Let's get this show on the road, shall we?"

A doctor came into the room as the warden disappeared.

"What's the prognosis, Doc?" asked Walter as the doctor set up beside him.

"Not good." The male doctor swabbed his arms and placed the IV lines into his skin. "Not good for you, anyway. The rest of us are gonna be right as rain as soon as you're gone."

"Friends with the warden, I assume?"

"No, not at all; between you and I, I hate the guy. He makes my skin craw, but you...you're a whole different kind of monster. I hope you rot in hell."

"Alright then," Walter said, glancing at a female guard standing in the corner. "Is it me, or did everyone wake up on the wrong side of the bed today?"

The guard tried her best to conceal her smile as the doctor wheeled his cart away. Walter's body craned upward as the gurney raised him to face the witness gallery. There was a moment of complete stillness before the black curtain slowly slid away to reveal the six required witnesses to view his final moments. Two of them were people he'd never seen in his life, but judging from the notepads they were holding, he had assumed they were members of the press. Sitting in the front row in the middle seat of three chairs sat Stanley Wilkes. Walter hadn't expected anyone of value to him to be at his execution and seeing Stanley had brought a small bit of happiness to his final moments. Stanley looked at Walter with sad, tired eyes, exhausted by the days leading up to the execution. His attention was quickly drawn away from Stanley and the reporters as he focused on the remaining three witnesses.

Sitting together in the second row of seats had been Sarah's aunt Hannah and Harvey Braddock. He fully expected Hannah to be there but the sight of Harvey staring back at him with vicious hatred shocked and unnerved him. Any normal person would have felt a cold chill from Harvey's focused gaze but Walter simply stared back for a moment before turning his eyes to the person he'd been waiting to see since he had been locked away. Her eyes hadn't left his since the curtain had been pulled away, and even when he had been looking elsewhere, he had felt her gaze boring into him with furious hatred.

"Hi, Sarah," Walter said with a sideways grin.

"You'll have your time to speak, Mr. Scott," said the female guard as she turned toward the group of witnesses. "Can everyone hear me?"

The group sat with their gaze fixed on Walter, so focused on him that nobody but Stanley acknowledged her.

"Walter David Scott, you have been sentenced to death for the murder of Scott Freeman, Katie Greene, Kyle Greene, Meghan Stern, Jonathan Park, Dana Begley, Trevor Flax, Bethany Platt, Rachael Borden, James Lampton, Stacy Smith, Marisa Jamison, Molly Thomas, Kara Stein, Derek Long, David Braddock, Michael Chan, as well as one count of attempted murder and aggravated assault. I would like to give you this time to make a final statement."

The walls seemed to close in around them all as they waited for Walter's final words. For a moment, it almost seemed as if he wasn't going to say anything until he opened his mouth and let out something barely louder than a whisper.

"The woods are lovely, dark, and deep. But I have promises to keep, and miles to go before I sleep...miles to go before I sleep."

"Robert Frost," whispered Sarah. The sound of one of her favorite poems coming out of his mouth brought a grimace to her face. "You son of a bitch..."

Before his eyes were forcibly removed from hers by the lowering gurney, he winked at her one final time. The satisfaction of his final words and his last glorious wink was soon washed away in a sea of silence as Warden Crawford stood in the small room inside the chamber, speaking with the governor over the phone to get the final go ahead to proceed. Walter had felt the eyes from the witness gallery on him as he laid strapped against the gurney, helplessly waiting the first of three drugs that would put him to sleep, stop his muscle functions, then finally stop his heart.

He winced as an icy sensation erupted in his right wrist, snaking its way up his arm. It tingled slightly, and if it hadn't meant that his death was seconds away, he would have even possibly enjoyed it. He felt his eyelids become heavier and heavier, and before long he was completely unable to keep them open.

"So long, my friends," he whispered as his eyes closed softly and his body relaxed.

"Wait; something doesn't feel right," Walter said. It only took him seconds to realize he hadn't actually said anything at all, but thought it behind his closed eyelids. He heard a door open and shut, followed by footsteps to the side of the gurney. A hand wrapped its fingers around his forearm and squeezed hard, sending blistering pain up and down the deadweight of his arm.

"Walter, can you hear me?" said the doctor, still squeezing tighter and tighter. "Walter, I need you to respond to me if you can hear me."

*"OH, I HEAR YOU, YOU SACK OF SHIT! FUCK YOU! FUCK YOU! FUCK YOU, YOU PIECE OF SHIT! THIS IS ON PURPOSE!"*

"The inmate is unresponsive," the doctor said, before giving a final squeeze and disappearing back into the hidden room.

Walter felt another sensation begin at the point of his IV as the second drug entered his system. His mind swam with searing pain as the new drug worked its way into his veins, setting his mind and soul ablaze with fiery, explosive pain.

# CHAPTER THREE

"The inmate is unresponsive," the doctor said, his voice distorted slightly through the speaker in the witness gallery.

"Are you okay, honey?" Hannah asked, leaning forward and giving her niece a hug around her neck.

"Yeah, I'm fine. Just ready for this all to be done." Sarah reached her hand over and placed it on Stanley's forearm. "How are you doing, Stanley?"

"I'm okay. I'm just tired and ready to move on. It's been a hard week. I've played this moment over and over in my head leading up to today. I almost didn't come."

"Couldn't have stopped me from being here," Harvey said, his eyes still fixed on Walter. "I need to see this through to the end."

"He was your friend, right?" Hannah asked.

"He was more Stan's friend than mine. We just bowled together."

"I wish that he hated me for catching him and bringing him in but the only thing he seems remorseful over is the fact that I know his secret. I hate him for making me feel conflicted like this. It makes me sick to my stomach to sit here and watch him with anything other than satisfaction."

"Don't sweat it, brother," Harvey said. "It'll all be over soon."

"He was your friend," Sarah said, watching Walter through the glass. "I think you were his only friend in the world. Nobody's going to be blame you for the way you feel."

"Something's happening..." said one of the reporters as she leaned forward in her chair to get closer to the glass. "He's moving."

"That's impossible," Harvey said, watching as Walter's fingers began to slightly twitch.

His chest began to rise, up and down, like the beat of a drum. The doctor and warden came into the execution chamber as Walter released a growl that echoed and vibrated the glass barrier between him and his witnesses. His body was writhing wildly against the constraints, the gurney itself seeming like it was going to break apart under his violent spasms.

"*SHUT THE FUCKING CURTAIN!*" screamed the warden as he and the doctor watched Walter helplessly.

Walter pressed himself upward against his constraints as the guard inside the witness gallery stepped forward to pull the curtain back. Everyone's hearts sank at the sound of tearing as his restraints gave way. He shot up on the gurney, his legs still secured under unbroken straps. He stared at his witnesses with intense, crimson eyes, which pulsed like they were about to explode from his eye sockets.

"*LEAVE ISH ORPEN!*" he bellowed, his words slurred through pain as the veins in his body darkened and expanded under his skin.

"Leave it open..." Sarah said, her gaze fixed on Walter's manic, crimson eyes.

The warden looked at the guard who had begun to close the curtain in the witness gallery. He nodded, letting the guard know to leave it open. Walter slammed himself back against the gurney and continued to scream while tearing and scratching at his chest. His fingers clenched in and out, forming themselves into such rigid designs that some of them sent snapping sounds into the air as the bones began to break. Sections of the skin on his arm began to burn and peel away as trickles of blood forced their way through exposed veins and arteries. His screams bounced through the walls of the prison, rattling windows and terrifying the prisoners who were waiting for their own execution dates.

With a final wail and a gush of blood from his nostrils, it was done. Walter's bloodied and mutilated arms fell freely to his side, hanging like a limp marionette. His eyes remained open, bloated and red from the trauma of the failed execution. His body shuddered once more before he was completely still, sending drips of blood onto the freshly waxed floor.

*"WHAT THE FUCK HAPPENED?"* screamed Warden Crawford, grabbing the doctor by his white coat as the guard inside the gallery closed the curtain.

Everyone in the gallery stared mindlessly at the darkness of the now covered glass. The warden had begun to verbally attack the doctor when the microphone was shut off, plunging the room into utter silence.

"Folks, I'm sorry you had to see that. I honestly don't know what to say." The guard's words were small and soft as he struggled to comprehend what he'd just seen.

"It's over," Sarah said, turning and putting her arms around Hannah.

Stanley was standing, both his hands in his hair as he tried to hide the tears welling behind his eyes. Harvey stood with a smile on his face, clapping his hands together in applause.

"Good riddance," he said out loud. "Hope you got to see that from up there, David."

"You okay, kiddo?" Stanley asked, stepping past Harvey and placing his hand on Sarah's shoulder.

"Yeah, I'm fine. Are you?"

"I'll be okay," he said as he kissed the top of her head.

# CHAPTER FOUR

A year after Walter's execution, Sarah gathered a collection of text books from around her house and stacked them on the floor of her coat closet. There were seven books in all, collected during a failed attempt to go to the local community college. She had signed up, hoping that being busy at school would take her mind off Walter, but after a few months of struggling through classes that felt meaningless to her, she quit. She'd continued to look through the books on her own time, thinking maybe she'd still learn from them, but each of the books had ended up in different parts of her home as their subjects were abandoned one by one. She was more than content to stay locked away in her home, working on pieces of novels she hoped would be published someday.

After giving the books one last thoughtful glance before shutting the closet door, she poured herself a glass of wine and sat on the couch in her living room. She took a sip and placed the glass on the table in front of her before grabbing her laptop and settling into her comfortable couch. She turned on the television in front of her and grimaced as the screen illuminated images she'd become far too familiar with. There wasn't a day that went by that one of the major news networks didn't talk about Walter's crimes or his execution; the image on the screen in front of her was of Warden Crawford giving an interview and spewing information she'd heard dozens of times. To the surprise of everyone inside the witness gallery on the day of Walter's execution, the medical examiner and the Department of Corrections had determined Walter's execution had been a freak accident, chalked up to a host of small deviations in execution procedure. The general thinking by the public had been that Warden Crawford and the doctor who administered the injection drugs had conspired together to make sure that Walter's final moments were spent in agony, but at the end of the investigation, no wrongdoing could be linked to either of them. Sarah turned off the tv and tossed the remote onto the couch beside her, happy to enter into her own silence once again.

Other than a few interviews outside the prison on the day of the execution, she had been able to avoid having to talk to anyone about Walter's death. It had taken three months of declined interviews and meetings with everyone from nationally known news anchors to literary agents from New York City before the media realized that Sarah had no interest in speaking with them. The emails and phone calls slowly tapered off and her inbox didn't fill as quickly as the pace of her old life started to return. The entire town had gotten used to seeing news trucks parked near landmarks from the killings as reporters went about making their television specials, but as each day passed, there seemed to be fewer and fewer outsiders.

Rain began to pour heavily outside as she opened her laptop. A cursor blinked in front of her, waiting for her to begin typing another novel that would add to her growing collection of unfinished work. She placed her fingers on the keyboard as she waited for the words to come to her. The screen silently mocked her as she grabbed her wine glass and took a sip. She heard a car door slam and seconds later there was a knock at her door.

"Hey," Sarah said cheerfully as she opened the door to her aunt

Hannah. "Come in for a bit!"

"I wish I could sweetie but Robert's waiting in the car. We're heading home for the night. Can I come by tomorrow for a visit?"

"Of course!"

"I'm sorry for coming by so late but I wanted to drop this off to you. I think you should have it."

Hannah passed a shoebox through the door with her mom's name written in neat handwriting on the top. Sarah opened it to find it full of small knick-knacks and folded letters.

"What is this?"

"I had to stop by the storage locker today where we put a lot of your parents' things. I was looking for something your grandma had given to her but I got lost in all the memories. I found this and knew I had to get it to you."

"Oh…" Sarah said, looking down at her mother's handwriting. She hadn't seen it in years.

"Honey…are you okay?"

"Yeah, I'm fine." Sarah continued to stare down at the box as Hanna stood on her porch. She reached forward and placed her hand on Sarah's.

"Sarah, I'm worried about you. You've never really talked much about everything. I'm concerned you're bottling up too much."

"I'm fine, Aunt Hannah. Truly, I am. It's just hard to talk about is all."

"You know you can talk to me, right?"

"Yeah, I know." Sarah placed the box on a table beside the door and leaned forward and hugged Hannah.

"I'll be by tomorrow, donuts in tow!"

"I'm looking forward to it! Thank you for dropping these off."

"Anytime," Hannah said. She squeezed Sarah's hand one final time and disappeared back toward their car. Sarah and Robert shared a quick wave before she closed the door and picked up the box.

She sat back down on the couch and looked at her mother's

name, Laura Elizabeth Prince, scrawled across the top. Her mother's handwriting had always been impeccable. It ranged from simple and clean to elaborately beautiful. It was a skill that Sarah had never been able to acquire, though she'd spent a considerable amount of her free time trying. Sarah removed the top, not knowing what kind of memories or discoveries she was about to unearth. She reached inside and pulled out a small pile of pictures. Each of them had been taken on her first day of each school year, standing on their front porch with her backpack slung over her shoulders. She thumbed through them, allowing a tear to roll freely down her cheek when she realized the photos stopped after freshman year.

She placed the photos back in the box and continued to look through the collection of items. A lot of the things in the box had no discernable meaning for her but she could sense her mother with each one she touched. She found a ring that she'd never seen her mother wear, which she immediately slid onto the ring finger of her right hand. It was a simple, white gold ring with a small diamond in the center. She searched her mind for anytime she'd seen her wear it but came up with nothing. It didn't matter to her; the ring had been her mother's and now it was sitting perfectly on her finger.

She pulled out a small, oddly folded piece of paper from the corner of the box. She unfolded it and smiled, seeing it was in the shape of a heart.

*Laura, my love...*
*I'm so sorry for how distant I've been.*
*I'll try harder, I promise.*
*XOXO, Michael*

The note brought another tear to her eye. She knew her parent's relationship had been strained, mostly due to her father's work life, but she had always known they'd loved each other. She caught a whiff of something and raised the note to her face and inhaled the faded scent of her father's cologne.

"Hi, Dad," she whispered with a smile as she refolded the note and placed it back inside the box. She picked another note and unfolded it.

*Hi Honey,*

*Dinner was amazing last night! You're a wonderful cook. It's so great that Sarah will have you to look up to and learn from. Have you really thought about how much our life is going to change? Seriously, have you thought about it? In just a month we are going to have a little person to take care of! A little person, Laura!*

*XOXO Love you*

Sarah held the note in her hands as her eyes overflowed with tears. She'd loved her dad dearly, but she'd never had to time to bond with him in the years before the accident. When he wasn't at work, his time had been fully dedicated to her, but the fact remained that he wasn't there a lot of the time. It was the main reason he and her mother had experienced such a quiet, reserved relationship leading up to their deaths. She put the note back and stared at the open box as she dried her cheeks with her blanket.

She put the box down beside her and finished her glass of wine. The warm sensation relaxed her as good memories of her parents flowed through her slightly inebriated mind. She placed the empty glass on the table and went to put the lid back the box when she noticed a balled-up piece of paper sitting apart from the rest of the letters. She flattened it out and realized it was much crisper than the rest of the notes; it was newer. She began reading as a cloud of confusion settled over her.

*This is fucking bullshit. After everything we've been through...after everything you've told me about him, you are STILL choosing him over me. I see him everyday, running around that fucking gas station like a chicken with his head cut off...why the hell would you chose him over me? He can't be there for you. I CAN. I CAN BE THERE FOR YOU. I*

*LOVE YOU, LAURA. DAMN IT, I LOVE YOU!!! I don't care that
you have a daughter. We can live as a happy family, and I'll be there for
both of you. You know I can. You know this is what's best for you, don't
ignore me, don't freeze me out.*
*I'm not giving up.*

"What the hell is this?" she whispered before reading the letter a
second time.

There was no name anywhere on the page, no way to tell who
had written it. She read it a third time, and a fourth, until she
could no longer ignore the obvious truth that her mother had had
an affair.

"Mom, no…"

She put the note aside and rifled back through the box,
opening up folded notes that were all from her dad. There was
another balled up piece of paper, half the size of the one she'd just
read, wedged underneath a small stack of photos in the corner of
the box. She opened it in a hurry and began reading.

*Fuck you, Laura! Fuck you, fuck him, FUCK YOU!!! He came to my
house, did you know that? Did you send him? Did you send that
ASSHOLE husband of yours to my house? My FUCKING HOUSE!!!*
*You cowardly bitch, I can't believe you. I hope you fucking die. Fuck
you, I'm done. Enjoy your boring, sexless life. I'm so fucking done. You
broke my fucking heart. We BOTH knew what we were getting into that
night you came to my house. You told me you loved me, Laura. Do you
remember that? I remember it and it fucking hurts. You broke my heart.*
*I'll always love you but you broke my fucking heart.*

Sarah sat cross legged on her couch with the note in her hands,
dumfounded, trying to make sense of it. She thought back to
when her parents were still alive, trying to figure out when her
mother's affair had happened. Her mother had told her father
about the affair; that much was made clear in the note. Her dad
had known, and yet he'd stayed with her. She'd had no clue at all

growing up that this had ever occurred, meaning the two of them had done exactly what they were tasked to do from the day of her birth; they'd protected their daughter.

She put both the notes in the box and closed it before falling sideways onto the couch. She let the tears flow, sobbing softly into the silence of the empty house, wishing her mother was there but feeling incredible anger toward her.

"How could you have done that to dad?"

The tears stopped after about ten minutes as she pushed herself back into a seated position. She opened up her phone and dialed Hannah's phone number.

"Hi honey," Hannah said after a few rings.

"Why would you give these to me?"

"What? The box? What's wrong?"

"Did you know?"

"Did I know what?"

"Did you know my mother was having an affair with some stranger while my dad was working at the gas station?"

The silence between them seemed endless as she waited for Hannah to respond. To Sarah, the words she'd just spoken sounded foreign, or false, but the evidence was lying beside her in a small cardboard coffin.

"Sarah…"

*"Did you know, aunt Hannah?"*

"Yes. Yes, I knew. How did you find out?"

"You handed me their notes tonight. You didn't know they were in there?"

"Honey, when I found the box I only openned one letter. It was from your father. I didn't feel right looking at the rest of them. They were for you to read, not me. What did you find?"

"It was a couple balled up notes; one where he was begging her to choose him over my dad and the other was pretty angry, but sad. I almost feel bad for him. Did you know him?"

"No, I didn't. She kept him pretty secret. I never even knew his name. All I know about him is from what your mother told me.

She said he was very handsome, and kind, and caring. She was quite smitten by him, but she loved your father dearly. I remember the day she broke it off with him. She was very upset."

"I never knew…"

"No, you wouldn't have. Your mom and dad didn't want you to know what she'd done. Your dad loved her too much, Sarah. He wasn't gonna let her go. He was brokenhearted but he made sure to keep his composure during the whole ordeal. She never knew this but he used to pop in at my house every so often to just vent and cry. He didn't want her to know that because he wanted their relationship to heal. He didn't want her to feel any more guilt than she already did. Trust me, she was riddled with remorse."

"Rightfully so. I can't believe she did that."

"You have to understand honey that your dad just wasn't around. I know that's no excuse, and what she did was wrong, but at the time, she was *so* lonely. She had tried to get him to scale back hours for years, and he just wasn't interested. He just kept working harder and harder and it put a divide between them. He got it from his daddy; he ran that station hard and your dad was just doing what he knew."

"Did dad find out, or did she tell him?"

"No, she told him before he found out. She told him one night when you were at a friends' house and they fought. It got pretty bad, from what I can remember, but they needed it. Shortly after that, your mom started helping at the gas station and he began scaling back his time there."

"I remember when that happened," Sarah said. "It was nice having him around more."

"They loved you, Sarah. They wanted nothing but good things for you. Please don't dwell on these notes. They put it in the past and moved on and I'm sure they'd want you to do the same. She made a mistake, and trust me, she regretted it."

"Did anyone show up at their funeral that we didn't know? Do you think he was there?"

"I had my eye out. I figured that he'd show up and blend into the back, but I didn't see anyone I didn't know. Honestly unless he comes forward, we won't ever know. She was embarrassed; she kept it all very tight lipped."

"Thank you for being honest with me, Aunt Hannah. This is a lot to take in."

"I know, sweetie. Please don't dwell on it. Your mother and father would be devastated if they knew you'd found out. Just remember the good times you had with them and preserve that memory."

"I will. Thank you."

Sarah ended the call and slid her phone onto the coffee table in front of her. She rubbed her red eyes as a heart appeared on her lock screen; a simple, loving text from her aunt. She didn't know how she'd be able to get any work done, given what she'd just unearthed about her past, but Hannah had been right; dwelling on it wouldn't help anything.

She picked up a couple copies of her mother's books that she always sat near her when she attempted to write. They comforted her, as if her mom was there with her, helping her through the sea of thoughts and words. She placed the laptop back on her lap and stared at the screen for a half hour as the rain continued to pour outside. For the first time in months, it was clear to her what she needed to work on. She tapped out the title and stared at it for a moment.

*The Eighteenth*
*By Sarah Nicole Prince*

It was a manuscript that could have turned into a bestseller about the events of 2009; a manuscript that would be forever sidelined with the ring of her cellphone.

*My mommy died yesterday. She was in a car crash with a drinking man and she died. Daddy is sad and yelling a lot because the man lived and mommy did not. It is not fair that mommy is dead. I miss her so much.*

*I was scared last night because the thing was back in my room. I turned my lights on and didn't see anything but something kept touching my foot and scratching my bed.*

*Maybe it was Mommy? I hope not because that is scary. I do miss her though so maybe it would be nice.*

# CHAPTER FIVE

Nish Patel had been a senior at Valley Ridge High the year that Walter David Scott began murdering members of the student body. Like Sarah, Nish was on the lonely fringe of the school, choosing to spend his time in solitude as opposed to engaging with other members of the class. Neither one of them had been part of the group of students that seemed to garner daily ridicule and abuse, but they were also far removed from the upper-echelon of the school's social hierarchy. Each day, when first lunch shift would shuffle into the cafeteria, Nish would make his way to the school library and sit in one of the comfortable reading chairs with a book and a bottle of Pepsi.

Like clockwork, within five minutes of his first sip, Sarah would come in and sit across from him, open a bottle of Perrier, and begin reading her own book. The first few weeks of school, he hadn't so much as lifted his eyes from his book when she sat down, but as it became more of shared routine, he couldn't help but at least smile at her from time to time. It had started with just a glance and a smile, a slight recognition of their daily presence, but as time went on they began to realize they'd found a friend in each other.

Their first words came the day that Nish finally got around to taking *The Stand* by Stephen King off the shelf and check it out with his student card. He wasn't a chapter in before Sarah sat across from him with a tattered copy of *The Shining*.

"It seems we both finished our books at some point yesterday," Sarah said, twisting the cap off her Perrier before taking a sip. "I came in here today to check out *The Stand*, and here you sit across from me with the school's only copy."

"Yeah, I finished reading my other one last night," he had said with a smile, putting the book down on his lap. "I'd be happy to check out another, *but*…if you haven't read *The Shining* yet, it's a classic."

"No, I haven't read it…and no, you keep it. I'll read it after you and maybe we can compare notes."

"*Like a date?*" Nish thought to himself, surprised by the thought.

"Sure," he said with a sip of Pepsi.

The remainder of the lunches they shared started with a smile, which became slightly more flirtatious as time went on, but as more and more students were added to the list of the dead, their time together seemed to always be drenched in nervousness. The school board and parent association had discussed ending the school year early in order to better protect the kids. In the end, the board had voted to keep the school open as long as there was a police presence throughout the day and a mandatory town curfew of 7:00 pm. The police and the town were more than happy to help, and before they knew it, Nish and Sarah had a brand-new friend in the library each lunch period. He was tall, wearing a dark-gray police uniform with a gun strapped to his waist. Needless to say, he didn't spend too much time reading with them.

Sarah and Nish continued to slowly get to know each other, swapping books back and forth under the protection of the police officer. The day that Sarah had finished *The Stand*, Nish had been sitting alone, reading a magazine on computer programming.

Sarah tore into the library and ripped the magazine from his hands before sitting down and staring intently at him.

"I finished it," she said. "I finished it, and I'm *not* happy."

The two of them didn't even take the time to open their drinks that lunch break, but instead sat and discussed every part of the book. Nish defended it, saying it was a classic, while Sarah lamented on the Trashcan Man and her frustrations with the final act. It was that day, as Nish sat across from her, the eighteenth name on Walter's list, that he realized he desperately wanted to be with her.

The bell rang and they made their way to their separate classes, both of them with a new book that they'd agreed to exchange when they were finished. He spent the rest of his day thinking about Sarah and her intense rebuttal to his love of *The Stand*. He thought about the way her hands moved in frustration when he defended characters and plot twists, and the way her dark brown hair kept falling into her face before she would place it behind her ear each time. It was safe to say that after almost half a school year, Nish had become completely infatuated with Sarah Prince.

Nish spent the evening working up the courage to ask Sarah out on a date. A small, independent bookstore was having some locally famous authors in town for a signing and he'd decided that he was going to ask her to go with him. He sat in his room, thinking about all the different ways he could ask her to go with him. He'd finally made his plan, ready to go for the next day, when his mom and dad knocked on his door. That was the night that Nish Patel found out his parents were moving to D.C., a move they'd contemplated for years but had decided to make in the wake of the killings.

It was also the night Walter David Scott tried to murder Sarah in the Valley Ridge Public Library.

Nish didn't even have time to say goodbye to Sarah before his parents whisked him away to his new life in the nation's capital. His parents left Valley Ridge without waiting for their house to sell, although it would sell just one week after Walter's capture.

43

The Patel's were not the only family to leave the area after the murders. Michael Chan's parents left shortly after their son's funeral, leaving behind the house that had been the scene of Walter's house party massacre. Thomas and Helen Greene, parents to the deceased Kyle and Katie, left around the same time as well, packing only sentimental items with them and leaving their home fully furnished in their wake.

Walter's murder spree had ended in late April, meaning the school year was almost finished. Nish, like many of the students in the school, was allowed to end the school year early as his grades showed that he was on track to graduate. Graduation ceremonies were still held later that year, complete with a heartfelt tribute to the victims, but Nish had already left Valley Ridge behind and opted not to attend. He'd reached out to Sarah a couple times, but just like the everyone else in her life, she'd cut him out.

So Nish moved on, in the best way he knew how; he read...and he worked. From a young age, Nish had always had an interest and natural skill with computers, spending his free time between reading and learning to program. To his parent's dismay, he'd decided to forgo further schooling, instead spending his time in D.C. creating phone apps and virtual reality technologies. Within two years of leaving Valley Ridge, Nish was collecting money from multiple mobile games and photo manipulation programs he'd created. The photo applications were very similar to others already on the market, but different enough to set them apart from the crowd. His parents couldn't complain about his lack of further education, given the steady flow of income from his many projects.

By 2014, Nish's bank account was in the millions as cash continued to roll in with each and every successful application he uploaded to the public. His biggest success came in the form of a virtual reality application, setting the user against dozens of horror movie monsters and madmen. The user would connect through a virtual headset and try their hardest to escape whichever monster they'd chosen to face. Each landscape was known as a portal, featuring scenes and scenarios from classic horror movies. The application was called *Monsters & Madmen*, trademarked under his company's name, *V.R. Exodus*.

To the general public, V.R. simply stood for Virtual Reality. To Nish, it meant that as well, but it also stood for Valley Ridge Exodus, which is exactly what took him away from the small town where he'd once lived. Nish opened V.R. Exodus with one of his programming friends, Carlo Macasaet. Carlo was a few years older than Nish and brought with him an idea he'd been working on for a few years; an idea that he and Nish would introduce to the world in 2017.

It was a world-changing piece of technology, something Nish and Carlo could barely believe they were able to complete. By the time it was done, everyone was wanting their shot at utilizing the groundbreaking tech. With all the phone calls coming from people asking to get their piece of the pie, it was a single phone call that Nish made that brought him the most excitement.

Just a few weeks after the one-year anniversary of Walter's execution, Nish stepped onto the balcony of the Los Angeles high-rise hotel he had been renting for a week. It rang a couple of times as he stared at the water, listening as waves crashed against the beach below. And just like that, with a single word, Nish's life would take another drastic turn.

"Hello?"

Her voice hadn't changed at all. He hadn't talked to her in years and he figured she would have been an anxiety-ridden mess, but with that single greeting he could tell she was anything but. It was as if they were back in the library, sitting across from each other before Walter made his first stab wound.

"Who is this?" she asked, still sounding calm as ever.

"Hi, Sarah. It's Nish Patel." There was a moment of silence between the two of them, as if his words had taken the long way across the continent. "We were in school together at Valley Ridge."

"Nish, of course I remember you." He could tell she was slightly smiling...so was he. "Gotta tell you; I've got a few King books I need to discuss with you."

Nish chuckled a bit as Sarah's smile widened near the microphone of her cell. "I as well. How are you doing?"

"Good..."

Another period of silence.

"That doesn't sound so convincing. I always think about you when the anniversary gets closer."

"Really, I'm fine," she said. "Everything felt off at first, like some part of reality had shifted after watching him die like that, but it was a year ago. Things are better."

"I wish I could have been there to help you."

"Nish...I'm sorry. I always felt bad for what happened between us after you left."

"I just wanted to be there for you, Sarah, but I understand. I can't even begin to comprehend what you went through back then. It was hard keeping my distance, but I wanted you to heal, even if it had to be without me."

Another silence, interrupted by a roll of thunder on Sarah's end.

"We really missed out on something, didn't we?" she asked with a frown. "I guess I kinda ruined that. I'm sorry, Nish."

"Walter ruined it, Sarah. You did what you had to do. I can't blame you for that. I was a day away from asking you out though."

"Shut up!" she said, repositioning herself on her couch as her smile returned.

"Yep," he said as a seagull squawked in the air nearby. "The night he attacked you, I'd worked up this whole plan about taking you to this book signing in town. I always wondered what you would have said."

"I would have said yes," she said, a touch of the shy freshman girl from Valley Ridge creeping through.

"Of course," he said with a laugh. "Probably for the best that I wasn't able to ask then. I was a dork at Valley; probably wouldn't have been that exciting of a date."

The two of them let out a laugh in unison with another seagull's screech.

"Is that why you called me tonight, Nish Patel? To ask me out on another date?"

"In a way, maybe I am. I have something that I want to talk to you about."

"Is that so?"

"Have you ever heard of *Monsters & Madmen*?"

"Heard of it?" she said, looking at the black gaming headset with the V.R. Exodus logo sitting on her coffee table. "I was first in line! I play it daily. I love the Sasquatch Hunt portal."

"That's one of the only ones I still play!" He'd created the Sasquatch Hunt with Sarah in mind, remembering that she'd had a fascination with the lore back in high school.

"And you've come to me for new ideas for portals? You're only twenty-six, Patel; you can't be out of ideas already!"

"Very funny," he said in a mocking tone. "No, I have something else. Something like it…but much, much different. I was hoping we could actually meet in person to talk about it."

"That sounds suspiciously like a date. When are you thinking?"

"Well, I'm in L.A. for a couple more days, then I'll be back in D.C. Why don't I pick you up at 7:00 pm on Friday?"

"Friday works for me!"

"It's a date." Another roll of thunder as the line went silent again. "This is awkward now, isn't it?"

"Yes, quite," Sarah said as the two of them giggled together. "I'll see you Friday."

"See you then," Nish said, ending the call and looking out over the dark blue of the Pacific.

He went into the hotel room and took a beer from the fridge. Seagulls continued to squawk and screech outside the balcony as he stepped outside and took a long, deep sip of beer. He thought about the time to come and the uncertainty that had plagued him for the better part of a year. A shiver ran down his spine as a feeling of unease settled over him. Suddenly, the beauty of the ocean was lost on him as he closed himself in his hotel room and drew the shades.

There was something dark in his creation, something he couldn't quite decipher.

He would find out soon enough.

# CHAPTER SIX

There was a knock at Sarah's front door as she stood in front of her bathroom mirror, applying the finishing touches to her makeup. With a stressful exhale and final check of her appearance, she flicked off the light and walked quickly into her bedroom. A full-length mirror was fastened to the back of her door, waiting for her final inspection before she greeted Nish at the door. Her long, chestnut hair poured down onto the shoulders of a chunky, beige turtleneck sweater. Another knock came from the door as she slipped on a pair of tight but comfortable jeans and a pair of black and white Converse shoes. She took one last look at herself in her mirror before bounding down the steps to the main floor to greet Nish.

"Hold your horses, Patel!" she said as she opened the door with a smile.

A man she'd never met stood in front of her on her porch. He was dressed in an expensive-looking black suit, with leather shoes so shiny that they reflected the light from her porch.

"Mr. Patel is caught at his office," said the man in a soft, soothing voice. "He sends his apologies. My name is Thomas. I'll be your driver this evening."

"Driver?" She looked past him at a limousine parked on the road behind.

"After you," Thomas said with a smile as he stepped aside to let her pass.

Thomas appeared at her side as she stood in front of the expensive limo. He reached forward and opened the door, letting the smell of the vehicle pour out into the fresh air.

"Is this brand new?" Sarah asked as she inhaled the smell of the new car.

"It is indeed. Mr. Patel bought it yesterday for me to pick you up today."

"He bought it just to come pick me up?"

"Mr. Patel is a very particular man, Ms. Prince. Don't worry, he'll get ample use out of it."

Sarah slid inside and marvelled at the interior. She'd never been in a limo before but she could tell it was nicer than most. Normally, a blatant flashing of money would send her in the opposite direction, but something about the sentiment behind his gesture struck a chord. Thomas dropped into the driver's seat and adjusted his mirror.

"So did you come with the car or are you a rental?" Sarah asked as she adjusted her seatbelt.

Thomas let out a gentle laugh as he pulled the car onto the road. "I'm Mr. Patel's personal driver. He sent me to pick you up today on what he called 'an away mission.'"

"He would say that," Sarah said with a smile. She looked beside her on the back row of the limo and found a small present, wrapped in black wrapping paper with a silver bow.

"Mr. Patel asked me to put it back there before I got to your house."

"Well that's very kind of him, isn't it?" Sarah said as she ran her hand over the smooth wrapping paper. "Thomas, where are we heading?"

"Mr. Patel is meeting us at a restaurant in D.C. Have a good ride, Ms. Prince."

The privacy barrier closed, leaving her to her thoughts in the back of the limo.

"Mr. Patel," she said with a smirk. "How fancy."

Sarah ran her finger underneath of one of wrapping seams and gently tore the paper away. She couldn't help but smile as she looked down at a very familiar copy of *The Stand*. She opened to the inside back cover to find an index card taped to the inside. The name *Nish Patel* was written neatly, followed by *Sarah Prince*. She could still remember checking it out from the school library the day Nish had returned it. She flipped through the worn pages, catching phrases she hadn't read in years that brought back memories of reading in the quiet of the library. Her heart sank when she got to the back of the cover; staring back at her was a line, followed by a signature she quickly recognized.

*Sarah...hopefully this book finds you well – Stephen King*

"Unbelievable..." she muttered, fixated on the words staring up at her. Not only had he stolen the sentimental copy of the book they'd shared, he'd somehow gotten it signed for her. She sat speechless for the duration of the ride, watching the world fly by outside as the distance between her and the owner of V.R. Exodus drew smaller.

Once the limo hit the busy interstate that lead toward Washington, Sarah drifted off to sleep in the comfort of the warm limousine. The gentle, rhythmic shake of the vehicle had been like a lullaby, which was always the case whenever she was on a long car ride. It was a quick sleep and before she knew it, the car came to a stop as she jolted forward, the dark interior of the limo coming back into focus. Car horns blared in the distance, the sounds of city life echoing in her ears as she rubbed her tired eyes with her palms. She squinted through the dark tinted windows, trying in vain to see where Thomas had parked. The world outside was dark, but artificially lit by the bright shine of streetlights.

"Thomas?" she asked, surprised Nish's driver had yet to talk to her since stopping the car.

The privacy barrier rolled down slowly, much slower than when he had closed it originally. Thomas was sitting motionless, staring forward into the abnormally dark street. He turned his head toward her and her stomach turned as she realized it wasn't Thomas at all, but the dead, rotting face of Walter David Scott. His lips were a curled mess, split and cracked apart with decay. He smiled at her, revealing a mouth full of broken and cracked teeth. He watched her with a pair of cloudy, dead eyes, oozing with rot at the edges.

"Hey, sweetie…" he said, coupled with a gruesome version of his trademark wink.

*****

"Ms. Prince," said a voice from beside her. Sarah jolted as she stepped forward out of her nightmare. "Ms. Prince, we've arrived. Is everything okay?"

"Yes, everything's fine. I'm sorry Thomas, I dozed off."

"It's quite alright, Ms. Prince. It's a comfortable ride, for sure."

Thomas took her by the hand and helped her out of the limo. He shut the door behind her as she marveled at an old, beautiful building in front of her. The words "Old Ebbit Grill" spanned the top of three large archways, each elegantly lighting the space in front of the building.

"Mr. Patel is inside," Thomas said, gesturing to the revolving door in the center archway.

"Does he pay you extra to call him that?"

"That's between me and Mr. Patel."

The two of them chuckled together as they were greeted quickly by a hostess. Thomas disappeared outside as the hostess maneuvered the busy restaurant to where Nish was sitting. The table was full of plates of food, each steaming hot as they waited for them to dive in. Nish slid out of the booth and greeted her with a smile and a hug.

"I figured you'd be hungry so I took the liberty of ordering some appetizers," he said.

"Some?" she said, looking down at the table. "Don't you mean *all* the appetizers?"

"That's exactly what he means," said the hostess as Nish laughed out loud.

Sarah could hardly believe the amount of food spread out between them as they slid into the booth across from each other. Nish wasn't dressed overly fancy, which she was incredibly grateful for. She had seen when he'd stood up to greet her that he was wearing a pair of expensive-looking blue jeans, the waist hidden underneath a slim-fitting, black button up shirt. She admired his neatly coifed hair as the faint scent of sweet cologne clung to her after their hug.

"Please, order whatever you want to drink, eat whatever you'd like to eat. Nothing on the table is off limits!"

"Isn't this a bit much?"

"How do you mean?" he asked, picking up a shrimp taco and biting away half of it before taking a large sip of dark colored beer.

"The limo, the food, the book..."

"You didn't like the book?" he asked, finishing off the rest of the taco he'd started. She was amazed at his confidence as he stared at her while politely chewing.

"No...I mean yes," she said, stumbling with her words. "I'm sounding ungrateful, I'm sorry."

"I can send some of this food back, if you'd like. I mean these sliders are to die for but if they doth offend the lady, then I shall see to their disposal!"

"You're an ass," she said as the two of them laughed. "I'm sorry, let me start over. This is all lovely. I'm just not used to such..."

"Stick with me kid," he said before taking another long sip of beer. "It's not a bad way to live. I know I sound horrible, but it's true. I've worked hard, and dammit, if I want to spoil my friends with fancy food and drink, I'm gonna!"

"Well, in that case," she said, pulling a plate of grilled oysters to her. "These are mine. Hands off, *Mr. Patel.*"

The two of them ate, drank, and laughed long into the evening. The restaurant began to slowly empty as the evening wore on, leaving them mostly alone with the wait staff and a few other couples eating together. Nish stopped ordering alcohol halfway through the night, knowing he had important matters to attend to before the night was over.

"Care to tell me what it is you needed to talk to me about?"

Nish looked at his watch, which showed 11:15. He looked around the dining room, making sure there wasn't anyone listening in on their conversation before sliding out of the booth and ordering two whiskey sours from the bar. It had been their drink of choice for the evening and with the proposition he had in store for her, he felt they may need it. He slid himself back into the booth across from her and pushed one of the drinks toward her.

"That serious, huh?" she said, lifting the glass to her mouth and taking a sip.

"About three years ago I began work on an idea; something similar to Monsters and Madmen, but on a much larger scale." He stopped for a moment, gulping half his drink before motioning to the bartender for another. "The best way to describe it would be Monsters and Madmen...without the headset."

"I'm intrigued. How's it work?"

Nish finished off the remainder of his drink as the bartender placed another in front of him.

"Your *mind* is the headset. It's rather hard to explain, simply because there is nothing like this on the market."

"Try me," Sarah said, leaning into his words.

"What we've created is a totally immersive virtual reality experience. You aren't just experiencing it through a headset or video screen. Your mind, *your consciousness*, is alive inside the

Portal while your body sleeps in a V.R. Exodus facility. The programing, initially anyway, is the same as Monsters and Madmen. You plug into the game and your task is to stay alive as long as possible while you're pursued inside the environment. Obviously, there's a lot more involved with creating different portals and monsters, so for the initial launch we decided to stick to the basics."

"If I know you, I'm gonna guess it's an abandoned campground."

"You know me well," he said, finishing his drink. "The killer is something of our own creation, which we aren't revealing to anyone until they meet him inside the Portal. Once you're in and the match starts, his only goal is to find you and kill you. When nobody is in the system, he's dormant; just kind of stands there like an empty vessel."

"You call it *him*…"

"Yeah. It's a him. He's your classic psychopath."

"Can you watch from the outside when people are in the Portal?"

"Yes, but there's a delay. It's not a live feed. Basically, the entire scenario is recorded but it can't be uploaded to view until after the experience is complete. After that, we can view the footage from anyone's point of view that we want, even the killer's. The only time we can get a live feed inside the Portal is when nobody is plugged in. You're basically looking at a virtual environment, void of activity. It's kind of eerie, actually, watching Wallace just stand there by himself."

"Wallace?"

"Yeah, that's what we've dubbed him. What *I've* dubbed him, anyway. Carlo isn't so sure."

"Probably because it sounds a lot like Walter."

The two of them quieted when the waitress brought over another drink.

"I didn't make that connection until it was too late. Say the word and it's changed."

"It's okay, Nish. Leave it. You know people will probably make the connection though."

"Yeah, Carlo and I have talked about that. Could work for us or against us. I guess we'll find out soon enough."

"You want me to help you unveil it to the world," Sarah said, cutting to the chase before finishing the remainder of her drink.

"Yes. I've gone through this a hundred times in my head, trying to figure out a way to ask you that wouldn't seem inappropriate."

"You want me to take part because I'm the eighteenth. I'm the survivor."

"Yes. I know what I'm asking of you, and I know how it'll be perceived by the public. People are going to say it's grotesque, having Walter's only survivor as part of the unveiling. Maybe they're right, I don't know. Honestly, Carlo brought up the idea to me months ago. Initially, I said no. I didn't want to put you through that or subject you to the media backlash, but then I got thinking. You're a survivor, in more ways than one. You've been through a lot and you've got thick skin. I know you can handle it."

"I see," she said, her mind swimming with indecision.

"The Portal can accommodate eight people. We've already selected six and we wanted to offer you and a friend the opportunity to make the first run. You'd of course be compensated."

"Compensated…"

"I know the nature of what I'm asking of you. You could take a bit of criticism for being part of the launch, but having you involved would change the entire dynamic of the unveiling. I'm not sure if you realize it or not, but you're kind of a celebrity."

"I don't pay attention to any of that. I never wanted it."

"I know. Just think it over, no pressure at all. Honestly, show up, plug in, and leave with a million in your bank account."

"Excuse me?" The words grew and expanded in her head as she looked across the table at him.

"We're willing to pay you a million to take part in this. Honestly, it's a drop in the bucket compared to what this tech will mean to society. Take out the A.I. aspect, you still have the Portal itself, which is an unprecedented piece of technology. The police and military could use it for training exercises. Even bigger than that, terminally ill patients can live out the rest of their days in the comfort of a portal, leaving their pain in the real world while their mind enjoys whatever happiness they could conjure up. Even their family members could plug in and visit them in their paradise."

"One million? Wow...have you thought about the negative ramifications to all this? It's a moral dilemma, to say the very least."

"I know. Carlo and I have talked about this in length, many times. A portal could be used as a virtual brothel to fulfill all manner of disgusting fantasies, but V.R. Exodus owns the copyright on every piece of tech involved with this project. The only way anyone would be doing something like that would be with our blessing, which they obviously wouldn't get. There is one thing though..."

"Oh?"

"Things were going good, we were very happy with what we'd come up with, but something changed. Wallace started moving around when he was alone in the game, and eventually, it actually looked like he was trying to find a way to escape."

"Really? How has he been when the game is active?"

"When the game is active, he participates. He seems to still be bound by the rules of the Portal, but when he's alone he almost seems...sentient. I'm not sure exactly when, or how, but it looks like we've stumbled into artificial intelligence, or something very close to it."

"You seem very shaken when you talk about it," Sarah said, reaching across the table and placing her hand on his as it jittered slightly.

"It all started about eight months ago. I mean I've been

noticing little things here and there for about a year, but eight months ago I entered the Portal to do some in-game research. We were still working on the mechanics of the environment, making sure it looks seamless to the user. The best way to do that is to be inside and take note of any issues. Up until then we were able to make Wallace stay dormant while we worked, but on that day, he spoke to me."

"He *spoke* to you? What did he say?"

"*Where am I?*"

A shiver ran down Sarah's back at the sound of Wallace's simple question. For just a moment, Walter's last words echoed in her head; one of her favorite Robert Frost poems, perverted by the last utterings of a murderer.

"I can still hear it right now," Nish said, taking a drink from his glass. "*Where am I?* That's the moment I knew something wasn't right. Carlo and I are the only ones who know how to work the programming so we can only go in one at a time. We took turns going in, trying to talk to Wallace and figure out what had happened, but he hasn't said a thing since. He actually avoids us when we are inside."

"But you're still moving forward with the launch? Is it safe?"

"Yes, completely. Wallace is just a program and he's trapped inside the Portal. He can't physically harm anyone, self-aware or not. I won't lie; the A.I. aspect of this scares the shit out of me, but he's harmless. I wasn't looking to create it and now that we have it, I don't quite know what to do with it. Carlo and I aren't going to tell the public that he seems to be self-aware. Not until we understand it fully."

"This is a lot to think about, Nish."

"I know. I know you can handle it, but I have to ask...you can handle it, right? Post-traumatic stress can be a hard thing to deal with."

"I don't have PTSD. I have no doubt in my head that I could handle it. I just don't know if I want to subject myself to it."

"I understand. I really do, and if you say no, it's no problem. I could fill these spots, no problem. I'm offering them to you first because after everything you've been through, I feel like you could use a break."

"Are the others getting paid?"

"Not nearly as much as you, but yeah, they're being compensated. If you accept, I'm sure I can trust in your discretion."

"I'm not sure, Nish. I could, of course, use the money, but this seems dangerous. Mentally, I mean. And you're right…this will come across as grotesque by most people, namely the surviving family members of the seventeen."

"I know, Sarah. Trust me, I know. I've gone back and forth with this hundreds of times. I debated even coming to you."

"When are you going live?"

"November. I know it's soon but this is how we planned it. Announce it a couple months prior, that way the excitement is fresh." Nish looked at his watch as his face twisted with surprise. "Wow, time flies. I have to be on a flight to Seattle in about an hour. Sarah, please think about it. Whatever you choose, please just make sure it's the right situation for you. I do have to tell you one last thing."

"Oh boy, here it comes," Sarah said.

"I know you haven't talked to the press much since the execution and I understand why. If you're going to do this though, we're going to need to open a little bit to the public."

"I see…"

"I know it's not easy talking about what happened but part of having you involved is having you create a buzz about the release. I know it won't be easy, but that's partly why we're compensating you differently than the rest."

"It's not that I'm against talking to the public. I guess I just haven't cared to talk to anyone at all since everything happened." Sarah finished off the remainder of her last drink. "I'll think about it; I promise."

"Thank you. That's all I ask. I booked a hotel room for you here in town. It's a nice place, and I think you'll enjoy it. I actually booked it for a few nights, so please, stay as long as you want and Thomas will drive you home whenever you're ready...even if that is tonight."

"I love staying in the city. I'll at least stay tonight."

"Good! I'm glad. Room service is all on me, so please have fun."

Nish slid out of the booth and stretched his arms straight above his head, cracking and popping the joints up and down his back and arms. Sarah slid out of the booth too, almost losing her balance from the whiskey sours coursing through her system.

"I'll think about it, I really will," she said, stepping forward and putting her arms around him. He wrapped his arms around her too. "When are you back from Seattle?"

"I'm there for four days."

"I'll have your answer when you get back."

Nish was surprised when she took his head with both her hands and pulled him down to her. She placed her lips on his, tasting the whiskey on his lips as her head swam.

"Maybe it's the sours, but I've wanted to do that for years. Thank you for not giving up on me, Nish. I know it wasn't fair that I cut you out, and I'm sorry."

"How could I not?" he said with a smile, kissing her on the forehead and hugging her one last time.

Nish cleared the hefty tab before the two left together. Thomas was standing outside the limo with the door open while a taxi sat parked in front of it.

"I'm taking a taxi to the airport. Thomas will take you to the hotel whenever you're ready. Like I said, enjoy yourself. Can we meet up again when I get back from Seattle?"

"Of course," she said, hugging him again before he disappeared into the taxi.

"I trust you had a nice meal, Ms. Prince?" Thomas said as he helped her into the limo.

"I did, yes. Maybe a little too much to drink, Thomas."

"It's easy to do when you're around Mr. Patel. He likes to keep the drinks flowing, that one. I assume he talked to you about his proposal."

"He did, yes. Are you one of the participants?"

"Oh goodness, no. I don't have the nerves for that sort of thing. He did ask me, though, both my wife and I. Rebecca was somewhat interested, but I wasn't interested in the least. I do think Mr. Patel is onto something special though."

"Yeah, I do too..."

Sarah settled into the comfortable seat and was surprised when Thomas pulled the limo over after only a couple minutes. The building outside was the Grand Hyatt Hotel, which was just a few blocks away from where she and Nish had just eaten dinner. Thomas got out as he always did and helped Sarah out of the back of the limo.

"Everything is all set for you, Ms. Prince. The room is in your name so check in at the front. Do you need assistance getting inside?"

"Oh no, Thomas; I'm nowhere near that inebriated."

"Whenever you're ready to go back home, please give me a call." Thomas handed her his card and slipped back into the limo.

"Thank you, Thomas."

"Thank you, Ms. Prince. If you need anything at all, please let me know."

Sarah waved as Thomas pulled away from the hotel and disappeared down the street. The hotel wasn't a sky scrapper by any means but something about it seemed gargantuan to her. Maybe it was the decision looming over her and what the hotel room represented; the possible start of a new relationship with an old friend. She'd never been in a real relationship, and she was happy that Nish would be her first.

Sarah made her way into the hotel and checked herself in. She wasn't surprised at all that Nish had booked her stay in a grand suite, one of the more luxurious rooms available at the hotel. Almost every interaction with him since reconnecting had been drenched in expense and showmanship, something she would more than likely find less than appealing once the whiskey worked its way out of her system. Before taking the elevator to her room, she took a moment to wander through the hotel's atrium. It was enormous, raising high above her with its walls lined with the windows to guest rooms. Standing alone, looking at the high expanse of the atrium, she suddenly felt small and alone as she stared at the guests as they moved quietly through the beautiful, open space.

She quickly ushered herself to the elevators, her reflexes off slightly from the alcohol. The ride up to her room was a short one with no interruptions, which she was thankful for. She'd been to the city dozens of times, but never alone; she wanted to get to her room as fast as possible. Her keycard swiped with ease, unlocking the door to the room as she stepped into the comfortable, warm air. The space inside was one of the nicest places she'd ever seen, decorated in a modern, relaxed style. There was a note sitting on a table in the main living space of the suite.

*Sarah,*

*I've booked this suite for four days. Thomas will take you home whenever you're ready. Anything inside the hotel is on me, so please enjoy yourself. They know I've booked the suite, and they have my card on file.*

*Please, consider my offer. I know that pushing yourself into something like this won't be easy, especially after everything you went through in Valley Ridge, but I'll be there with you during every step. If you choose not to partake, I understand.*

*I know that your stay here was kind of unexpected so I had Thomas pick up a few sets of pjs for you. They're in the bedroom. I had to guess the size, I hope they're ok. What girl doesn't like new pjs, am I right?!*

*Your Friend Always, Nish*

Sarah smiled as she folded the note and placed it in her purse.

She made her way to the bedroom and flicked on the light; her smile widened as she looked at the largest, most comfortable looking bed she had ever seen. Laid out at the foot of the bed were four neatly folded sets of brand-new pajamas, each with a different color and pattern.

"You are right about the pjs, Mr. Patel," she said, taking a set of purple pajamas into her hands. They were soft, unlike any set she had at her home.

She changed quickly, choosing a pair of purple pajamas that were slightly too big, and crawled into the bed. She considered reaching over to the nightstand and flicking on the large tv hanging on the wall, but instead decided to close her eyes and fall asleep in the bed she would end up sleeping in for three more nights.

By the time she'd fallen asleep, she'd already made up her mind.

*I'm so fucking sick of this ghost in my room. I've told dad SO many times about it and he DOES NOT BELIEVE ME!!! I haven't seen it but stuff is always moving around in my room. Stuff falls off my dresser, clothes fall off hangers, stuff like that. I woke up the other night and my tv was on and I KNOW I turned it off because I remember turning it off after Buffy was done.*

*Last night, my blankets got torn off my bed like A HUNDRED TIMES!!! I ended up just sleeping with nothing and was scared out of my mind!!! I tried to talk to dad about it this morning and all he did was laugh at me. I don't know why he won't believe me but I'm SO over this.*

*I hate this house.*

*I can't wait to get out of here.*

*I miss mom.*

# CHAPTER SEVEN

Two months after Nish flew to Seattle, Sarah stood in her kitchen with a cup of tea in her hand, watching the morning world from her kitchen window. She sipped her green tea while hoping the caffeine would work its way into her system quickly. As per her agreement with Nish, she'd spent the last two months doing as many interviews Nish's publicist could book her. The media had been waiting years to speak with her so there was no real shortage of interviews. She had recorded her final interview two days prior to the unveiling, and even though she'd grown comfortable with talking about Walter, she was tired of doing it.

Her phone vibrated on the counter in front of her as Nish's name appeared on the lock screen.

*"See you soon! Check your bank account..."*

Sarah placed her cup on the counter and swiped her phone open. She quickly opened her bank account and stared down at the $800,000 that had been deposited that morning as she took another sip of tea. The numbers glared back at her, filling her with doubt over whether she had made the right decision. The banking screen disappeared as Stanley's face appeared on the phone as it vibrated. She smiled, knowing exactly why he was calling.

"Yes?" Sarah said with a touch of bravado.

"Sarah Prince, what did you do?"

"Whatever do you mean, Officer Wilkes?"

"Nish told me $10,000. Why am I looking at $200,000 in my account?"

"Stanley, we both know I don't need the money. $800,000 is more than I'll ever need. It means the world to me that you're doing this with me, and it's the least I could do."

"Sarah this is too much."

"Just shut up and accept it, you old curmudgeon."

"It's beyond generous. Thank you."

"You're welcome!"

"Are you sure you want to go through with this? It's not too late, you can walk away."

"I know. To be honest I've really been questioning myself all week. Am I doing the right thing, Stanley?"

"Honey, I can't answer that for you."

"I know that. I'm just so unsure. I was up until 3:00am last night talking myself out of calling Bethany Platt's parents. She was probably the only one of the seventeen that I talked to."

"Sarah, this has to be your decision. Not mine, not the Platt's—this is yours to make. I will support you in whatever you choose to do."

The line went silent as Sarah stared blankly outside. Her mind swam with doubt until she blurted out, "I'm gonna do it."

"I'm proud of you.. I hope you know that."

"I know."

"Just text me when you're ready and I'll come get you."

Sarah ended the call and finished her tea. She always felt better after drinking a hot tea, and speaking with Stanley made her feel more at ease. Sarah rinsed out her cup and walked upstairs to her bathroom. She peeled off her pajamas and stepped into the shower, letting the hot water soak her hair and run over her face. She smiled and felt butterflies in her stomach as she thought about Nish, whom she hadn't had time to connect with since he returned from Seattle. Between the V.R. Exodus launch and her exhausting interview regimen, their budding relationship had been left to texts and quick phone calls.

Sarah dried herself and spent the next hour getting ready. She dried her hair, thinking about everything from Nish Patel to Walter David Scott. She'd gone a long time without thinking about Walter but every day since agreeing to participate in the launch, all her thoughts seemed to circle back to him. She spent the rest of the morning cleaning and listening to music, trying in vain to push the thought of him from her head. It was like he knew what she was about to face, and he was taunting her from beyond the grave.

With a few final touches to her makeup, she picked up her phone and texted Stanley.

****

"You ready for this, kiddo?" Stanley asked as he turned into the V.R. Exodus parking lot that was filled with news vans.

"I'm not sure. If I have to do one more interview, I think my head might explode." Sarah made eye contact with one of the reporters as he prepared to pounce with his cameraman. "This is all the more tolerable with having you here. Thank you for coming along, Stan."

"Wouldn't miss it for the world."

Sarah watched the growing group of reporters make their way to Stanley's truck. "Let's get this over with."

Sarah opened her door and slid out of the cab, already hearing the questions the reporters were ready to pepper her with.

*"Did Walter's death bring you closure?"*

*"How's life been since the execution?"*

*"Did Walter have any last words to you before his death?"*

*"Isn't your participation in this event in bad taste?"*

Before she could even begin to start a dialogue with any of

them, Stanley swooped in front of her with their bags slung over his shoulder, his hands out in front of him to shoo away the approaching mob.

"Ms. Prince!" yelled an overly tanned reporter in the front of the group. "How do you think the families of Walter's victims feel about your participation in this?"

"Okay, come up with a unique angle, and I'm sure she'd be happy to speak with any of you," Stanley said, glaring angrily at the tanned reporter. "Until then, fuck off."

Sarah smiled as Stanley whisked her away, the reporters faces dumbfounded by the way he'd brushed them off so casually. As they made their way toward the V.R. Exodus building, two men walked up the sidewalk near them, holding hands and chatting together. Stanley watched them with a curious look, tripping slightly as he and Sarah moved from the parking lot onto the sidewalk.

"Everything okay over there, officer Wilkes?" Sarah said, pushing him playfully as they began to walk behind the couple.

"Don't start up with me, lil' lady. All my votes have gone to the democratic party, you know that. You just don't see that sort of thing that often in Valley Ridge is all."

Sarah thought back to her high school days and realized Stanley was right. It was almost as if the entire gay community in her little slice of Virginia had died out with Trevor and Scott. One of the men walking in front of them held the door open with a smile, his partner waiting inside silently.

"Sarah Prince! It's so nice to meet you," said the man holding the door. "I'm Daniel Reisman, but you can call me Dan. Just not Danny, or Danny-Boy. Just Dan."

Dan shook both Sarah and Stanley's hands as they walked into the building. He wasn't overly tall, stopping just below six feet with a slight belly underneath a vintage Star Wars t-shirt. He wore a dark gray beanie on his head, hiding strands of curly brown hair, which peaked out of the bottom. A pair of dark framed glasses matched his face well, with a smile hidden behind a soft, short-cut beard.

"Dan it is," Stanley said as he walked through the door behind Sarah.

"This handsome devil is my boyfriend, Billy," Dan said, gesturing toward the tall, clean-cut man standing in front of them. Billy didn't bother to look back, but simply continued to admire the building around them. He was as All-American as they came; a Washington Redskins t-shirt sitting overtop a pair of tighter blue jeans, framing his muscular and toned physique in a way that told everyone around him he had once been the quarterback of his high school team.

"He's not overly thrilled to be here," Dan said with a nervous smile.

"I'm not entirely sure I am either," Sarah said, returning a smile that matched Daniel's nervousness.

The foyer was exactly what she'd expected, given Nish's taste for the expensive and theatrical. The floor was a dull, glowing white, which left a hazy, colored footprint with each step they took. A receptionist sat behind a desk in front of them, watching them as they entered with a smile. The desk she sat behind seemed to have grown seamlessly from the floor; its base white but darkening as it rose, ending at the desktop as a solid, intimidating black. The receptionist, who wore a nametag that read "Stephanie," ushered them forward.

"Looks like everyone is here. Mr. Patel and Mr. Macasaet will be here shortly. If you could all step forward to make your identification badges."

Sarah, Stanley, Daniel, and Billy all stepped forward, as well as four other people who had filed in quietly behind them. A well-dressed older couple stepped up behind Sarah with a smile. She wasn't sure how, but she recognized the older man as they exchanged a quick glance. Following the older couple were two college-aged men. Sarah could tell from their facial features that they were brothers.

"If everyone could step forward onto the footprints," Stephanie said as eight pairs of footprints appeared on the floor in front of them. They each stepped forward as a digital whooshing sound echoed through the room. "All done!"

She opened a small compartment next to her computer and took out a pile of eight neatly laminated photo badges. She quickly threaded each of them through a fabric lanyard and placed them onto the long, black desk in front of her. Billy reached forward and grabbed his badge, complete with his newly taken picture and printed name.

"I don't think I'd even told you my name yet." Billy inspected the laminated badge in his hand. "That's slightly creepy."

"Oh, settle down," Daniel said, grabbing his and flinging it around his neck. "It's pretty cool, actually. Thank you, my dear Stephanie."

A door swung open from the back of the room as Nish stepped forward into the foyer. He was wearing a pair of white pants, as well as a white button-up, short-sleeve shirt. An old-fashioned gold watch hung from his wrist as a tightly woven straw sunhat sat atop his head. The group chuckled at his costume as he leaned against a walking stick made of bamboo, topped with a round piece of artificial amber.

"Oh my *God* he's John Hammond!" Daniel squealed, stomping his feet and leaving colorful footprints on the ground as he wheezed in a fit of laughter.

"Welcome...*to the Exodus Portal*," Nish bellowed, doing his best impression of the owner of Jurassic Park. "Please, if everyone can follow me."

The group walked toward him with smiles as Daniel tried his best to hide his ever-increasing wave of laughter. Each of them filed through the door before Nish closed it behind them. The door seamlessly disappeared against the wall, blending in perfectly except for a slight green glow that emanated from the door's edges.

"This place is unbelievable, Mr. Patel," said the older man, holding his wife's hand as he admired the hallway in front of them. Sarah looked at him again, not quite knowing where she'd seen him before.

"Spared no expense, am I right Mr. Reisman?" Nish said, tapping Daniel's leg with his cane and sending Daniel into a new fit of wheezing laughter.

The group continued to walk with Nish as Sarah admired his outfit. He was nothing like the quiet, reserved library friend she'd known back in Valley Ridge. She couldn't help but admire the sense of humor he'd developed over the years they'd spent apart.

"It is rather incredible, isn't it?" Nish said as he began to guide them down the illuminated hallway. "I can't really take credit for any of it, either. Carlo built most of the aesthetic tech here. He wanted the entire experience, from the front foyer to the actual Portal experience, to be something people will never forget. Seriously, the man's brain is a national treasure."

"When will you be open to the public?" Sarah asked, listening to the tap of Nish's cane as he led them toward a door at the end of the hall, illuminated at its edges, just like the one they'd entered previously.

"As of right now, the only people who have tested the software have been Carlo, Stephanie, and myself. Tomorrow, you will all be the first group to take part, and we'll start bookings the day after that."

"If this machine works the way you say it does, I don't think you'll have any problem keeping this place busy," said the older man.

Sarah got a glimpse of his badge, which said Kurt Saunders. It was at that moment she realized she'd recognized him from the back of some of the books on her bookcase.

"I'm sorry, I just realized you're Kurt Saunders," Sarah said. "I just finished reading *Final Flight*. It terrified me!"

"Thank you so much," Kurt said with a smile. "I'm glad you enjoyed it. Probably one of the few books I've released that I was a bit nervous about."

"I don't see why, it was fantastic! Seriously, I'm a huge fan."

Sarah reached out and shook Kurt's hand. "It's an honor meeting you."

"Thank you, Ms. Prince, but the honor is all mine. It's incredibly brave of you to take part in this, and I count myself lucky to be here to witness it."

"I met Mr. Saunders last year at a literary convention here in D.C.," Nish said. "I knew within the first few minutes of our conversation that I was going to offer him an invitation to the Portal."

"He hasn't stopped talking about it," said the woman standing with Kurt.

"This is my wife, Betsy. I'm the spooky one. She's the funny one."

"Nice to meet you," Betsy said, reaching forward and shaking Sarah's hand. "I followed the events of Valley Ridge very closely. I'm glad you're here today, safe and sound."

"I was on the fence at first in regards to participating today, but when Betsy found out you'd be here, there was no stopping her."

"That execution must have been something to witness," said one of the two guys from the back of the group. He was the younger of the two, but not by much. He was slightly shorter than the other, wearing an old pair of jeans and a t-shirt of a band she'd never heard of.

"You're an idiot," said the taller guy as he pushed his brother to the side. "I'm sure she's tired of talking about it all."

"It's okay," Sarah said, looking back at them as they all continued to follow Nish down the long hallway. "I'm not shy about any of it; not anymore, anyway. This whole Exodus experience has forced me to be a bit more open about it all."

"Still, it's none of his damn business. I'm Will Caldwell. This is my brother, Brad. He says dumb shit."

"*You are* a dumb shit," Brad said, clearly perturbed by his brother.

"I didn't have an ounce of sympathy inside me for Walter, but I wouldn't wish that death on anyone. It was horrific," Sarah said.

"Agreed," Stanley said as they stopped at the end of the hall.

"Here we are," Nish said. He waved his key card in front of the door as it released from its latch and swung open. "Let's go meet the wizard, as they say."

They each walked through the door after Nish and were immediately awestruck at the oval-shaped room in front of them. The entire area was dark, but bathed in a brilliant blue glow, which seemed to emanate from a sphere in the middle of the room. It hovered a few feet off the ground, sending strands of light and smoke into the air around it. The floor was completely black, but situated around the orb were eight cylinders, tall enough to hold a person of at least seven feet tall. Light glowed from inside, waiting for each of them to climb inside and descend into the Portal. At the front of the room was a massive, curved screen, comprised of hundreds of other smaller screens.

"Hello everyone," said a voice from behind as they placed their bags on the floor. Each of them looked backward to find a man sitting in a semicircular set of amphitheater style seats. He wasn't tall, shorter than Nish by at least a few inches, wearing a black suit as he sat with a tablet in his hands. The light from the tablet illuminated a face that was younger than his actual age as he smiled and stood to greet them.

"Everyone, this is Carlo Macasaet, the other half of this glorious project you see before you."

Carlo came down and shook the group's hands, using both hands to shake Sarah's. She'd gone above and beyond with her interview appearances leading up to the unveiling of the Portal, and he was beyond pleased with their investment.

"Thank you all for taking part in this project. Tomorrow is a big day, and you're going to be part of a fantastic technological leap forward."

"What exactly is the seating for?" Billy asked, looking at the ample seating where Carlo had been sitting.

"That's a good question," Nish said. "Simply put, the seating is meant for spectators. Every action, every move, every kill is recorded digitally while the eight participants are in the game. However, we haven't found an adequate way to live stream the environment while an experience is happening. After the match is done and everyone has been ejected from the Portal, our computers will splice the best angles and footage from the event and mold it into a short movie. For a much lower cost compared to actually entering the Portal, spectators can pay to watch the footage after the experience is done."

"Think of it like buying your picture at the end of a roller coaster," Carlo said.

Nish stepped apart from the group and motioned to the large screen that spanned the curved wall at the front of the room. "The footage is played on our screen and will be available for purchase after the match is complete."

"Well do we get to do a trial run today?" asked Brad.

"We'd thought about it but we decided we wanted your reactions to be 100% authentic when you are placed into the Portal. Trust me when I say we've done hundreds of simulations to make sure the Portal is ready for you."

"Tomorrow, you'll each be harnessed into the entry pods and be transported mentally to the virtual environment," Carlo said. "Your body will remain fully asleep in the entry pod while your mind will be fully alive inside the Portal. You'll be able to explore the Portal, search for Wallace, and even interact with each other while inside."

"When you first wake up inside, you're going to feel quite disoriented," Nish said. "You will more than likely deal with a little dizziness, tingling in your hands, and blurry vision, but it will go away after a minute or two."

"Any questions about tomorrow?" asked Carlo.

Everyone in the group stood in silence as they shook their heads. Feelings of nervousness and excitement flowed through them in equal parts as they marveled at the room around them. Carlo tapped his finger a couple times on his tablet and the screen in front of them illuminated. The scene was that of the parking lot outside, almost completely filled with news vans and reporters waiting for the group to leave the building.

"I'm glad all of you got our email last night about bringing your bags inside today," Carlo said with a chuckle. "We had a feeling this would happen."

"We've already received dozens of requests from celebrities to book experiences in the Portal," said Nish. "We installed a private entrance just for that purpose, which means we can get you out of here in peace."

"A limo will take you from here to the Grand Hyatt for the night. For tomorrow, breakfast and lunch have already been arranged for you at the hotel and the drivers will be back at 3:00pm to pick you up. You'll have a few interviews with the press before you enter into the Portal at 5:00pm, as well as after the experience is over with."

Carlo tapped a few more times on his tablet as a door appeared at the bottom of the screen and revealed a brightly lit hallway with a moving floor. The footage of the reporters continued while the door remained open.

"This hallway leads to an underground garage. There's a limo waiting to take you all to the hotel. Dinner reservations have been made at 7:00 so the driver will be back at 6:30 to get you."

"For now, go enjoy the city," Nish said. "I think most of you know your way around but if not, let our driver know. He can take you wherever you'd like. Ms. Prince, I would like a word with you before you head out."

"Go ahead, I'll bring your bag to the limo," Stanley said.

Carlo escorted the group through the open door as Sarah and Nish watched them leave.

"What's all this about, Mr. Patel?" she asked as the door closed and completed the video picture. Nish tapped his fingers on a tablet and it shut off.

"It's been a busy two months, and the next while is going to be even busier, so if I don't do this now I'm going to regret it."

He pulled her close to him by her waist and kissed her on the lips in the light of the glowing blue orb. Butterflies filled both of their stomachs as her arms wrapped their way around his back. Sarah pulled back slightly with a smile as they opened their eyes and watched the blue glow flutter across their pupils. Sarah tried to think of something witty to say but found nothing as she returned his gaze.

"Will you be at dinner tonight?" she asked.

"Of course."

"I'll see you then."

Her hands shook with nervous excitement as she turned and left him alone in the Chamber. Nish tapped his fingers on his tablet and the door swung open just as she reached it. She disappeared inside and turned around, both of them smiling at each other as Nish tapped a few more times and the door closed. The screen switched to a view of the hidden walkway as he sat down, watching Sarah enter the parking garage and disappear into the limo. He shut the screen off and sat in silence for a few moments before the door in the screen opened and Carlo walked through.

"Are you sure you're comfortable with sending her inside?" Carlo asked as the door closed behind him.

"Yes. I know that something is off with Wallace, but there's nothing he can do to actually hurt her. We're a little too late to hit the brakes now, anyway."

"It's never too late, Nishal. Let's push the release off a few weeks while we figure out what's going on."

"No. Carlo, we've run simulations inside dozens of times. It's going to be fine—and don't call me Nishal. You only call me Nishal when you think you're right about something."

The two stared at each other in the eerie blue glow. Even though he was outwardly confident in the Exodus Portal, secret, hidden doubts nagged at the back of Nish's mind,

"You're right," Carlo said. "I'm just exhausted and stressed about the first run."

"It'll be fine, buddy," Nish said, turning and leaving the

Chamber. "Tomorrow, we make history!"

Carlo stood alone in the Chamber with his tablet in his hands, his optimism fighting back against his nervousness.

# CHAPTER EIGHT

Nish and Carlo sat at opposite ends of a long table at the same restaurant where Nish had asked for Sarah's help. The table was lined with the eight Portal participants with empty plates and glasses between them. Nish sat with Sarah, their hands joined together under the table, hidden from the gaze of the rest of the party. Daniel, who had already had his suspicions about them, was able to figure out what was going on between them and drunkenly giggled at them as he continued sipping his wine.

"So how do all of you know Nish?" Sarah asked as she finished the last sip of a whiskey sour.

"I interned at Exodus for a while," Dan said. He took another sip of wine and broke into a fit of drunken laughter after making eye contact with Nish.

"We're on the same dodgeball team," Will said.

"Hold on...you play dodgeball?" Sarah asked with a skeptical eye.

"I live a very stressful life Ms. Prince. I take relaxation in many forms." The group laughed as Nish and Will raised their glasses to each other. "Kurt already told you how we met, and it's been well documented how I know Sarah."

"Too well," Sarah said.

Daniel spit out a mouthful of wine onto his plate, believing in his inebriated mind that what Sarah had said was the funniest thing he'd ever heard.

"On that note..." Carlo said, standing from the table.

"Booo!" Daniel heckled before wheezing with laughter.

"I think Carlo might be onto something. Why don't we call it a night and get some rest. We're making history tomorrow!"

The group stood and filtered outside as Carlo paid their bill. Thomas stepped out of the limo into the cool night air and greeted Sarah with a smile.

"Hello again, Ms. Prince."

"Hello, my dear Thomas," she said as she stumbled into Nish's arms. "I'm afraid I've had too much to drink."

"Please see that Ms. Prince makes it back to the hotel in one piece, Thomas."

"Of course, Mr. Patel."

"I'll see you tomorrow..." Nish whispered in her ear as he placed her in her seat. He discreetly kissed her on the cheek as Daniel released a high-pitched giggle.

"See you tomorrow," Billy said with a stern face before helping Daniel inside.

The rest of the group filed in as Nish watched from the sidewalk. Sounds of the closing dinner service echoed behind him as he watched his friends settle into the comfortable leather seats.

"*OH MY GOD IT'S SO FUCKING FANCY!*" Daniel screamed as Thomas shut the door with a laugh.

"Until tomorrow, Mr. Patel."

"Goodnight, Thomas."

Even though the group only required eight rooms, Nish had reserved an entire floor of the hotel to ensure the group were given proper privacy leading up to the Exodus Portal's first public showing. Once they'd gotten to their rooms, each of them were asleep within minutes as the alcohol from the restaurant worked its way through their systems. Sarah, however, found herself awake well into the night. She tossed and turned, falling in and out of alcohol induced nightmares, mostly revolving around Walter actually completing his list. She finally dozed off fully just after 3:00 am.

****

The group collectively woke up at 11:00 am when their room phones rang at the same time. Sarah sleepily grabbed hers as her eyes tried to focus in the soft light of the room.

"Hello?" she asked in a groggy voice.

"Good morning, Ms. Prince. Mr. Patel requested a wake-up call for each of you at eleven. Your lunch reservation downstairs is at twelve-thirty."

"Did we all sleep through breakfast?"

"I'm afraid so," said the soft female voice on the other end. "Our lunch menu is superb; you won't be disappointed."

Sarah spent an hour getting prepared for the day, still reeling from the kiss she'd shared with Nish the day before. She'd never been one to wear a lot of makeup, but knowing that she'd be spending a majority of her day with him meant extra time in front of her hotel mirror. As she finished up, a knock came at her door. She quickly finished her application and ran to open it, expecting to see Nish smiling on the other side. She flung the door open with a smile as Stanley stood in front of her.

"Oh…Stan, good morning."

"Don't seem so excited, sweetie," Stanley said with a chuckle.

"I'm sorry, that was rude of me. Please, come in."

"Don't mention it. I know exactly who you were expecting, little Ms. Obvious."

"How do you know?" she asked herself quietly as she latched the door. "I don't know what you're talking about, Mr. Wilkes."

"I hate to break it to you Sarah, but your drunken self isn't as smooth with her secrets as you'd probably hoped. Any anyway, you're old enough that you probably can afford to be less secretive about it."

"Oh lord..." Sarah's face was beet-red as she turned to face him. "I've never done this before, Stan. I don't know what I'm doing."

"It's okay. I think it's great. He seems like a swell kind of guy."

"Swell? Do you think he'll take me down to the malt shop tonight?"

"I'm old, okay? I use old words." The two laughed as Sarah took another look in the bathroom mirror. "Are you sure you're ready for today?"

"You know I am, Stanley Wilkes."

"I know you are, but I still need to ask. You've been through enough, and this whole thing could really turn things around."

"Well, I've recently come into some money so any therapy won't be a financial strain," she said. Stanley stood to greet her as she exited the bathroom. "Seriously, Stanley, I'm okay. I think I'm actually looking forward to it."

"I'm proud of you, you know. I'm honored you picked me as your plus-one."

"Wouldn't want anyone else."

The two of them hugged each other before leaving the room and wandering downstairs. The other six were already seated at the table, holding menus in front of them as Sarah and Stanley took their seats. The woman who had administered their wake-up calls hadn't lied when she said their lunch menu was superb. Each of them ate well, ordering everything from sandwiches to steaks as they each prepared themselves mentally for the task at hand.

"So, are Betsy and I the only nervous ones or are we just a couple of old scardey-cats?" Kurt asked as the waitress began taking plates away from the table.

"I'm right there with ya, old-timer," Stanley said with a smile. "This kind of thing really isn't my cup of tea."

"You can say that again," Billy said, finishing off a beer.

"Maybe I'd be nervous if my head wasn't pounding so hard,"

Daniel said, looking somehow rested and tired at the same time. He pulled out a small pill bottle and popped one in his mouth before taking a long drink of orange juice.

"Maybe if you hadn't drank *all* the wine last night, you'd feel better," Billy said with a condescending face.

"You must be terrified," Brad said, looking at Sarah from across the table.

"I swear you are so fucking stupid," Will said. "Just shut up and eat your chicken fingers, you child."

The group laughed as Brad picked up a chicken finger from his plate and stuffed the entire thing into his mouth with a grin.

"It's okay, seriously. But no, I'm not terrified at all," Sarah said. "Maybe a little nervous, but I'm mostly excited."

"We're all nervous, sweetie," Betsy said. "I hardly slept a wink last night. Stayed up watching that awful Jerry Springer."

"Okay so that wasn't just me then," Stanley said as they all laughed again.

The group ate their fill as they nervously contemplated the day. They retired to their rooms once more to freshen up and collect their bags as Thomas promptly parked outside at 3:00.

"Good lunch, Ms. Prince?" he asked, opening the back door for her with his usual smile.

"Delicious, Thomas, thank you."

They each slid into the back to the limo as Thomas shut the door and sat in the driver's seat.

"Hey Dan," Brad said, shaking a small bottle of chilled champagne at him as Thomas pulled away from the hotel.

"Go back to your chicken tenders," Dan said as he opened a bottle of water and chugged half of it.

"So, once we're in…do we all want to work together?" Will asked.

"Sounds good to me," Kurt said. "If I've learned anything from all the horror movies I've watched over the years, it's that separating is a terrible idea."

"I don't mean to sound rude but I think I need to tackle this thing on my own," Sarah said. "These past few months have really forced me to face the past, and even if Wallace gets me first, I need to face him alone. I'm sorry."

"Honey you don't need to apologize to any of us." Betsy reached across the limo and squeezed her hand. "It's incredibly brave that you're participating at all."

The parking lot was filled with news vans and reporters as Thomas pulled up to the building. The privacy barrier rolled away as he parked.

"I'm not ready for this part of the day," Sarah said as she watched the eager reporters readying themselves to pounce.

A pair of large, muscular men in black suits opened the door of the limo. One of them leaned down and stuck his head inside.

"Mr. Patel doesn't want any of you talking to the press right now," he said. "He and Mr. Macasaet have already conducted a press conference and wish to restrict your interviews to after the event."

"Thank the Lord," Billy said in a dry tone.

"Why not just take us in through the garage we left from last night?" Brad asked.

"They want to keep that exit a secret, I imagine," Will said. "That and the photo ops I presume. Even though we have to keep quiet right now they'll still want us smiling for the cameras."

"Please, follow us," said one of the guards as they all filed out of the limo.

The two men led the group of eight up the long walkway that led to the main entrance. The reporters levied questions from behind them, almost all of them directed at Sarah. Billy walked ahead of Daniel, distancing himself from him as Daniel posed and waved wildly at the press.

"Until after, boys and girls!" he yelled before waving them off. "Please, hold your questions until after the ride has finished!"

"Would you *come on*, dammit?" Billy said in a hushed tone.

"Oh, settle the down. What the hell is your problem anyway?"

"I hate this horror stuff, you know that, and I hate this kind of attention even more. Let's just get this over with so we can get out of here."

"Pleasant as usual I see, Billy?" Nish said, standing behind the reception desk with a smirk on his face. Their obvious distaste for each other had become more and more apparent with each meeting.

"Okay, let's not get into this right now," Dan said, moving between the two of them. "Nish has been more than kind to us since this started, so Billy, just stop."

"Yes, let's not have any kind of bad blood today," Carlo said, appearing at the hidden door. "If everyone could please follow me, we'll begin shortly."

The group filed into the brightly lit hallway as Nish joined Sarah at the back.

"You ready for this?" he asked.

"I really wish people would stop asking me that."

"You're right, I'm sorry. You're gonna do great."

The group moved into the Exodus Chamber and was greeted by the curious eyes of a full viewing gallery, filled with privileged spectators and members of the press. Nish guided each of the eight to their entry pods as Carlo tapped his fingers on his tablet from the front of the room.

"Thank you all for being here today, especially our eights guinea pigs," Nish said, manically wringing his hands together as the group from the viewing gallery chuckled. "You've all been told how the Exodus Portal works but now's the time for you to see it happen in real life."

"You're in for a real treat, ladies and gentlemen," Carlo said as he and Nish stepped forward to the eight entry pods.

"If the eight of you could please relax and lean back into your pods," Nish said, giving a wink to Sarah as she leaned backward into her pod. The pods reclined to a sleeping position as a soft whirring sound echoed in the room. Sarah's nerves jittered as she felt movement from behind her back as four electrodes snaked their way forward and attached to her forearms. They secured themselves along the inside of her forearms before the wires became lifeless and fell to her side. Two other electrodes crawled around her head before attaching themselves to her temples.

"Pretty rad, huh?" asked Nish quietly to Sarah. She returned a nervous smiled as he turned to address the crowd.

"Every piece of tech you see in this room was designed and built by us, specifically for the purpose of the Exodus Portal. The ten electrodes that you see attached to each of our participants are the gateway to the Portal itself. In just a moment, a pulse will be sent through these receptors that will put them into a deep sleep. When the sphere in the middle glows red, it means our group is connected and active inside the Portal."

"Once you're inside, you'll have about ten minutes to acclimate to your surroundings," Nish said. "You'll more than likely feel light nausea, some tingling of your hands, and maybe some dizziness. That will go away quickly, and then you'll have some time to soak it all in before Wallace begins his hunt. A horn will sound once he's become active.

"I can't believe I never asked this, but this experience is painless, correct?" Brad asked.

"That's a story in itself!" Nish said.

"It took quite a bit more time and research than expected but were able to block pain receptors while in the portal," Carlo said. "Things like temperatures, textures, smells; you'll experience them just like you would here in the real world."

"Completely painless," Nish said. "Just the fun stuff!"

"Granted, Wallace will do anything and use anything he can to kill you inside the Portal, but you won't feel a thing when he does. As soon as you've been eliminated, your mind will awaken inside your body, and you'll be back with us here in the Exodus chamber."

"There is a red sphere, similar to the blue one you see here, in the center of the Portal," Nish said. "If for whatever reason you need to disconnect, just touch the orb and it will end your time in the Portal, although our hope is that Wallace gets to you long before you lose your nerve. The experience will not end until Wallace has either killed all of you, *or* you kill him first. Now, like a lot of your classic movie monsters, Wallace isn't easy to get rid of, and while he's not omnipresent, there are checkpoints in the Portal that he can transport himself to at will."

"Well that's not fair at all," Billy said. "So, when I eventually hunt him down, he can just jump to one of these checkpoints to save himself?"

"I think you'll find Wallace a bit more challenging of an opponent," Nish said, hiding his irritation over Billy's arrogance. "That being said, he doesn't have the ability to do that. Once Wallace has engaged with someone inside the environment, he cannot disengage. He's not programmed to flee."

"I thought you had said this was a genuine artificial intelligence," said a voice from the crowd. "Shouldn't he be able to make that choice for himself?"

"It is an artificial intelligence, I assure you," Carlo said. "However, he still does operate inside the confines of the system we have created here. Humans can't fly; that's a fact. We just aren't programmed that way. Wallace can't use the checkpoints once he's engaged with a participant. Beyond that, there really are no constraints to what he can and cannot do."

"How do we kill him?" asked Stanley.

"He's flesh and blood, just like the rest of you," explained Carlo. "You won't find any firearms in the Portal but there are plenty of things available for you to make a stand."

"I think the best thing to do is to go ahead and send them on their way," Nish said, smiling mischievously at Carlo. "Is everyone ready to see what all the hubbub is about?"

The spectators clapped while the group of eight smiled with nervous anticipation. Nish stayed standing in the glowing blue of the orb as Carlo tapped his fingers on his tablet. A countdown appeared on the tall, curved video screen behind Carlo as the group of eight stared in anticipation. It started with ten and began to count down with a soft chime with each dissolving number.

"Good luck to all of you," Nish said with a smile as the countdown reached three. "We'll see you in the afterlife!"

The number one dissolved away on the screen as each of the eight felt a small vibration where the electrodes attached to their skin. Nish winked at Sarah with a smile as she closed her eyes and fell into a deep sleep.

# CHAPTER NINE

Sarah's stomach swam with nausea as she opened her sore, blurry eyes. She rubbed her face with tingling fingers as the sounds of songbirds filled her ears. Her head rested on a thick, fluffy pillow, cradling her perfectly as she laid on a decently comfortable mattress. She pushed herself up and to the edge of the bed as lights and shadows swam in front of her blurry eyes.

It took five minutes for her vision to clear and the nausea to subside, although the tingling of her hands lasted much longer than Nish and Carlo had said. She was sitting in a small, one-room cabin, with only a door, two windows, and a set of twin beds. The bed across from her was empty and the door was wide open, revealing unkempt grass outside, which led down to the shore of a lake.

Sarah opened and closed her palms as the numbness and tingling slowly dissipated. She stood and stretched her joints, letting them pop as she released a long, open-mouthed yawn. She grabbed a baseball bat that was leaning in the corner before stepping outside into the bright, artificial light. The grass and sand crunched under her feet as she walked toward the calm, glistening water. She stopped just short of the water's edge and inhaled the sweet smell of honeysuckle and pine that permeated the air around her. A butterfly fluttered and landed on her hand before flapping its wings a couple times and flying off.

"This is incredible," she whispered to herself.

In front of her was a wooden walkway that stretched all the way across the lake to a small island in the center of the water. All along the waterline were other walkways, each ending at the same small patch of land in the center of the lake. The island was mostly barren, except for a few large trees and the red glow of the exit sphere. She jumped as a loud horn blast echoed across the lake, sending dozens of birds from the dense woods behind her into the sky.

"Can you believe all this?" asked a voice from behind her. She gasped in surprise and stepped forward slightly into the water. "Oh my God, I'm so sorry!"

Sarah turned around to find Daniel standing behind her, hands on his mouth from the shock of accidentally startling her.

"It's okay, Dan, really," Sarah said, brushing herself off and standing up beside him as they surveyed the lake together. "This is going to change the world."

"You're right about that," Dan said, spinning an ax in the air and jumping backward as he accidentally dropped it onto the ground. He picked it up in a fit of laughter. "I know you said you wanted to do this alone, but I'm happy to tag along if you'd like."

"I think I need to experience this on my own, but thank you."

"No worries! If you need me, I'll be getting murdered in the woods."

"Have fun, Mr. Reisman," Sarah said as Daniel disappeared into the woods behind her with his ax resting on his shoulder.

With the baseball bat at her side, Sarah walked the wooden walkway to get a better view of the world around her. From halfway down the walkway, she could see Will and Brad move along the beach, both with an ax in their hands. Farther down the beach she could see Stanley come out of a cabin and look around with his hand above his eyes like a visor. He looked at Sarah, and they both waved at each before he disappeared into the woods behind the cabin. Seeing him made her wish that he was with her, but she pushed the thought out of her head. She was hell-bent on experiencing the Portal alone, without the help of any of the other seven.

She reached the island and stepped onto the soft sand of the shore that led to a covering of long grass. Other than the glowing red orb and a few trees, the island was nothing but a bare patch of land, sitting alone in the middle of the calm lake. The orb glowed a soft, whitish-red, mimicking the orb back in the Exodus Chamber. She moved closer to it, watching it spit flares into the air as it slowly rotated and hovered above the ground. Sarah placed her palm an inch away from the orb, feeling it radiate with a soft warmth. Flares shot up from underneath and intertwined in her fingers, warming them and making them start to tingle again. She had no intention of leaving the game before finding Wallace, but she had to at least feel the beautiful glowing ball of light in front of her.

"You're not leaving yet, are you?" asked Kurt as he stepped off one of the wooden walkways onto the grass.

"Not at all. I came over here to get a better view of the Portal."

"You haven't seen Betsy in your travels, have you?"

"I haven't. Just after waking up, I bumped into Daniel and I saw Will and Brad on the shore from here."

"I didn't know we would all be separated like this," Kurt said, stepping past Sarah and scanning the shore, which formed a complete circle around them. "I want to see this Wallace character for myself, but first things first; I gotta find my Betsy. Care to join me?"

"I'm on my own today, but thank you. I think I'm gonna check out the shore a little bit, see if I run into Wally."

"Wally," Kurt said, laughing as he patted her on the shoulder before moving down the walkway opposite the one he came from. "Good luck, Miss Prince."

\* \* \*

*****

Betsy watched from behind the trees as Sarah brushed off Kurt. She'd watched her do the same thing to Daniel, and she respected her all the more for it. After everything Sarah had been through since Walter's attack on Valley Ridge, she still wanted to take on the mystery of the Portal alone. Betsy admired her sense of strength and independence, something she'd never really had herself. She had married Kurt when they were both just turning twenty and the two of them had been attached at the hip ever since. If something were to happen to Kurt, she would have no sense of how to move forward on her own. The thought terrified her beyond measure.

Betsy could tell that Kurt was looking for her, but she didn't care at all. Sarah's resolve had inspired her, and she was set on experiencing the Portal alone. Betsy knew that she wouldn't stand a chance against Wallace if she encountered him, but that was beside the point; it was long overdue that she showed some sort of strength apart from Kurt Saunders. Before he could catch sight of her, she turned and disappeared further into the woods to investigate her surroundings. She couldn't believe how intricate and rich the environment around her was, considering that everything she was experiencing was nothing more than a digital illusion.

She stopped at a patch of honeysuckle and plucked off one of the white flowers. She pulled out the stem to reveal the small bit of yellow sweetness on the end, waiting for her to enjoy. She inhaled the sweet smell of the flowers as she placed the stem in her mouth and marveled at the taste.

"Spared no expense," she said with a quiet chuckle.

Betsy pulled a few other flowers from the bush and disappeared further into the woods, enjoying the honeysuckle as she continued her expedition.

*****

"Betsy!" Kurt yelled as he stepped off the wooden walkway and back onto the sandy bank.

A flock of birds erupted from the top of the tree line, fluttering into the air and breaking the peaceful Portal with their squawking.

"Where are you?" he asked himself as he scanned the trees.

He walked along the line of trees, poking his head into each cabin in the hopes of finding Betsy inside. He stepped into the last cottage and exhaled in frustration when it turned up empty.

"Betsy!" he yelled once more before ending his search at the edge of the water.

He and Betsy hadn't done anything apart from each other in the thirty years they'd been married. Kurt had been lucky when his first book, *The Dark Watch*, had quickly taken off in popularity. After that, each of his books had been met with critical praise and enthusiastic fanfare. He loved the fame and accolades, but the part he loved the most was that the revenue meant that they could afford for Betsy to remain unemployed and follow Kurt on his numerous book tours and events. She'd been with him every step of the way, and as he stood alone in the Portal, he realized that he didn't just want to find her; he needed to. Standing alone and fearful on the shore of the lake, he realized there was no Kurt Saunders without Betsy Saunders.

*****

Billy walked effortlessly through the thick woods as Daniel tripped on a dead log and fell face first onto the ground.

"I'll help myself, thank you," he quipped as Billy continued forward. Billy stopped and looked backward as Daniel fumbled to his feet.

"What do you want from me, Dan? I just want to get this over with."

"You're being a real asshole, you know that? This is the opportunity of a lifetime."

"Oh yes, the *great* Nishal Patel, opening doors for all of humanity."

"What the hell is your problem with Nish, anyway? He's literally never done a thing to you."

"I don't want to go into this right now, Dan. Can we just get through this?"

"No, I need an answer. I know you've never been a fan of his, and it doesn't make any sense as to why. The only reason I can think of is that he's *brown*."

"Oh, *fuck you*, Daniel," Billy said as the two of them made their way out of the trees and into a large clearing. "How dare you even go there."

"Is it that far of a stretch? I've heard some of the things your father has said when he didn't think I was listening. Not just about *'them browns,'* but also about *'them queers.'* You know, like you and I?"

"First of all, if you heard it, then he *meant* for you to hear it, and you know I don't give a damn what my father thinks. I gave up on getting his blessing years ago. Secondly, he's a nothing but a dumb redneck, we both know it, but *fuck you* for putting that on me. I'm allowed to just not like somebody, especially when they're a cocky, rich little shit."

"You don't even know him, Billy. You've spent zero time with him, so how would you know what kind of person he is?"

"It's starting to sound like you've got a little crush, Dan, which by the way, I've always suspected."

"Grow up, Billy. I've known him for years, and you know damn well it's not like that."

They walked quietly through the clearing, both of them holding a bat in front of them in anticipation of Wallace's arrival. In the center of the clearing was an old, run-down cabin with the words "NORTH CHAPEL" etched across a plank on the front.

"Look, I'm sorry. Nish is a good friend of mine, and it makes it weird for me when you're so openly irritated by him."

Billy stopped and exhaled before taking Daniel's hand. "I'll try harder, okay? It's no secret I'm not his biggest fan but I'll try."

"Thank you," Daniel said, leaning in and kissing Billy on the lips. "Now come on; walk me down the aisle."

Billy and Daniel walked into the chapel, their bats held in front of them with white knuckles.

*****

"That Sarah's pretty hot," Brad said, following behind Will as they walked across one of the wooden walkways towards the island.

"Yeah she's cute; she's not interested in you though," Will said with a smile.

"And how the hell do you know that?"

"Because I know *you*, that's why. You need to stop bringing up the murders to her, by the way. I'm sure she's tired of talking about them, and you're probably one of the last people she'd want to discus them with."

"She seems fine."

"She's being polite, idiot. She spent years avoiding the press about it all, so why do you think she'd want to talk to you?"

"I'd have better luck with her than you, *shit-stain*!"

"Okay, good luck with that," Will said, laughing as they stepped off the wooden walkway and onto the island. "Help me look around. Do you see him?"

The two of them scanned the tree line across the lake with their axes hanging loosely in their hands. Out of the entire group of eight, they were the only ones who had decided to actively hunt Wallace.

"What the fuck is Saunders doing?" Brad asked, looking at Kurt standing alone near the edge of the water. "He's asking to get axed!"

"Yeah, I'll have to agree with you on that. He seems pretty out of it."

"Should we partner up with him? Better chance of giving Wallace the boot."

"I don't think so. He doesn't even look like he thought to find a weapon."

"Get good, noob," Brad said with a smile.

"You're such an dumbass."

Will left his brother alone on the island and made his way down another walkway.

*****

Sarah stepped back onto the shore and scanned the trees, hoping to find any sign of Wallace. She caught sight of Brad and Will walking across one of the walkways as a rabbit scurried across her feet. She jumped backward, startled, as it ran up the shore and turned to look at her before disappearing up a walking path into the woods. The path was dark, most of the sunlight having been choked away by the thick tree canopy above. She snickered to herself as she imagined Alice following the white rabbit after it checked its pocket watch and loudly proclaimed to be late.

"Down the rabbit hole, I suppose," she said, figuring the walking path was as good a direction as any other.

The floor of the path was clear, covered only by the occasional grouping of leaves or fallen branches from above. Just enough light was allowed through the canopy to illuminate the pathway, which wound lazily through the dense wood that smelled of pine and bonfire. Breathing in the pleasant smell of the forest around her and listening to the sounds of wildlife hidden by the afternoon's shadows, it was easy to forget that a vengeful monster was hunting her relentlessly while she soaked in her surroundings. Every so often, she'd catch a view of the rabbit ahead of her before it would disappear around a bend in the path.

The trees opened up into a clearing with a small building

situated in the middle. The water-damaged, splintered slats running horizontally along the sides of the building were spaced apart haphazardly, letting light and air flow freely through the inside. The old, shingled roof had collapsed on itself in a few spots, letting further light into the open space inside.

She watched as the rabbit disappeared inside, passing under a crocked sign that read *"SOUTH CHAPEL."* A breeze blew a gust of leaves and debris into the open doors as a crow cawed from the dilapidated roof.

"Further down the rabbit hole," she said as she made her way toward the chapel.

She passed through the open doors and stepped into the eerie glow of the broken-down building. On each side of the chapel were rows of pews, most covered in moss and crusty leaves. She moved down the aisle, passing through a patch of sunlight as she gripped her baseball bat tighter in her fingers. The old floorboards creaked underneath her feet as she inhaled the musty smell of the building Nish and Carlo had created for her to explore. The sounds of cicadas in the distance fluttered through the empty walls as she came to a stop at the front of the pulpit.

She was suddenly aware that she was no longer alone as the sound of heavy boots on the floor behind her rattled the old wood building. Her back was facing whoever was standing behind her, and as prepared as she thought she was to face Wallace, she found herself completely frozen in fear. She heard the sound of an ax being dragged along the floorboards, bumping loudly between each busted floor slat as it fought for audible dominance with his boots. A raspy, familiar voice cracked her mind open in a way she wasn't prepared for, sending a severe, debilitating chill down her spine.

*"Well this, my dear, is a pleasant surprise."*

*It's been ten years since I first came into contact with that damn ghost, and today, I actually saw it for the first time. I guess I should say her, as opposed to it, because it was most definitely a woman. I'd just finished packing all my stuff into my Civic, which was so full that I couldn't see out of the back windows. Dad's not happy about it but oh well. He gave me a hug at my car and we both cried a little. Neither of us said anything, but I know he was thinking about mom, just like I was. I wish so bad she was still here. I like to think she's here in a spiritual sense, but I just don't know. It's been years since I've felt her presence.*

*Anyway, after dad's hug, I looked up at my old bedroom and there she was, standing in the window looking at me. Not mom, I mean the ghost. I want to say she was old, but there was also a softness about her that gave her a youthful, angelic look. Her hair had the body of a much younger woman, but the color was a solid gray. Her face was covered in wrinkles, but even from where I had been standing, I could tell her skin was baby soft.*

*I don't know why it took her so long to let me see her, but I'm thankful she did. I'm also glad that I didn't have to grow up watching her skulk around my room. I feel kind of bad that I'm leaving dad alone with her, but I don't think he's ever even had any contact with her. I stopped bringing it up with him years ago because he just wasn't interested in hearing it. Maybe now that I'm gone, she'll start bugging him instead of me. I'll never understand why he wouldn't talk about it with me. Maybe it had something to do with Mom? I dunno, I don't care. I'm off to better things. Off to be a big, bad police lady.*

*I'm gonna miss my dad.*

*I won't miss that damn ghost, though.*

*Fuck you, ghost.*

# CHAPTER TEN

The hovering orb glowed red in the Exodus Chamber as Sarah and the rest of the group of eight remained motionless in their entry pods. Nish continued to mingle with the press and onlookers, telling jokes and entertaining them as Carlo monitored the group's statistics from his tablet.

"Wallace has been active for just over a half hour, and our group is still hanging in there," Carlo said.

"Looks like we have a tough bunch here," Nish said as the group smiled from the gallery.

"Mr. Patel, I need to show you something," Carlo said with a pleasant smile as he waved Nish over.

"What is it?"

"Something is off. You did the simulations just like I did. Wallace is usually much more active and aggressive than this."

Nish took the tablet from Carlo and looked over the statistics on the screen. All eight of the group's heart-rate patterns were displayed across the screen.

"I haven't seen a change in any of their patterns. Not a single spike in their heart rate"

"That's very odd," Nish said, watching the green zigzags

bounce up and down against the black of the screen.

"This makes me a little nervous, Nish," whispered Carlo. "I told you I didn't trust the tech. We're playing with something we don't understand."

"Calm down," Nish whispered as he continued to monitor their stats. "He's just being a little shy today."

"That's bullshit, and you know it. In the dozens of trials we did, he's never once behaved this way. I'm pulling them out."

"You'll do no such thing," Nish said, sternly. "It's a big environment. For all we know he could just be overwhelmed with people inside. He's only ever seen us and Stephanie."

"*Where am I?* You remember that, don't you?"

"Of course I do. What exactly are you worried about? It's a virtual environment. The worst he can do is kill them, which would just wake them up here in the Chamber. You need to relax before the gallery sees you freaking out."

Just as he finished speaking, Sarah's heartbeat jumped on the screen in front of them. It bounced wildly as her heart beat excitedly in her chest.

"See," Nish said as he tapped on the screen. "Everything's fine. We have our first encounter, ladies and gentlemen! It looks like Ms. Prince just met Wallace for the first time."

"Nish!" called Carlo, his eyes wide with terror as he looked at the screen.

Nish rushed to his side and looked down at the tablet, showing all eight heartbeats in a complete flat-line. He watched for a moment in disbelief, waiting for a spike in activity that wouldn't come. The orb in the center of the room changed from red to blue as the two of them looked at the sleeping eight.

"*Get the hell out of my way!*" barked Carlo, pushing Nish to the side as he flew to the entry pods. The first person he reached was Betsy, lying still in the soft blue light of the sphere. "Nish, she's not breathing."

The two of them frantically checked the other seven as the group of spectators watched with horror from the gallery. Carlo began the process of waking them up prematurely from the game but in a sudden, unified gasp, the group woke as their pods returned to a standing position. The electrodes attached to them peeled away as they all fell forward, landing on the floor with a clatter. They each writhed on the ground, trying in vain to draw in breath before their airways finally opened. Daniel cried on his knees while Billy writhed on the floor beside him. He reached out and grabbed Daniel's hand as his breath began to come back to him. Kurt immediately pulled his wife to him and placed his arms around her as she cried loudly.

"*What happened?*" screamed Carlo, looking at the chaos around him.

"*Calm down!*" Nish yelled, taking the tablet from Carlo and tapping madly on the screen. Emergency lights on the ceiling bathed the room in a harsh, artificial glow. "Keep your calm until we get to the bottom of this. Stephanie, please help with the gallery."

"Please, everyone come with me," Stephanie said, escorting the nervous and curious guests through the hallway. A few of the reporters tried to stay behind but were effectively shooed away by Stephanie and her clipboard.

As the last of the gallery members left the Chamber, Sarah released an ear-shattering scream as tears burst from her eyes. Nish rushed to her side, kneeling down beside her with his hands on her shoulders as she knelt weakly on the ground.

"*Get the hell away from me, you bastard!*" she screamed, her voice cracking as she pushed him backward onto the ground. She tried to move away from him but stumbled and fell to the ground, crying thick tears from her red eyes as she struggled for balance. Stanley rushed to her side and braced her, looking back at Nish and Carlo with an angered, confused look.

"Get me out of here, Stanley, *PLEASE* get me away from him!"

"Sarah, what happened?" yelled Nish as Stanley guided her through the door that led to the main foyer. With the emergency lighting on, the floor no longer left colorful prints, but stayed a constant gray as they left in a hurry.

"Can one of you please explain to us what happened?" Carlo asked.

"I was hoping you could tell us," Billy said, rubbing his eyes as Daniel sat looking queasy beside him.

"Will and I were on one of the walkways leading toward the island when there was a huge flash of light," Brad said.

"I remember a horrible tearing sound before everything went black," Betsy said. "Was that supposed to happen?"

"No," Carlo said. "Not at all."

"Did any of you actually meet Wallace inside the Portal?" Nish asked, still looking down the hallway in hopes Sarah would come back to the Chamber. The group shook their heads.

"This is bad," Carlo said. "How did none of you see Wallace?"

"Sarah did," Nish said. "Right before the blackout, her heart-rate spiked. Did anyone see her inside the Portal?"

"I saw her shortly after waking up," Daniel said. "I asked her if she wanted company and she said she wanted to be alone."

"I met her on the island while I was looking for Betsy," Kurt said, rubbing his temples in an attempt to relieve the tension. "Why do we all feel so horrible? My head is pounding."

"Mine too," Will said, struggling to his feet as he rubbed his eyes.

"We don't know why, but your hearts all stopped for a few moments," Carlo said. "Right before the game ended, your E.K.G. readings went dead."

"*Pardon me?*" asked Billy, standing to a wobbly stance with a disgruntled look on his face.

"Sit down, Billy," Daniel said. "He wouldn't have subjected us to the system if it wasn't safe."

"That's correct," Nish said. "If there was anything of concern, we wouldn't have let any of you inside the environment. Carlo, Stephanie, and I did dozens of runs through the Portal without a hitch. Obviously, something happened that we haven't yet experienced."

"Let's watch Sarah's feed," Carlo said. "Maybe that will give us insight into what happened."

The screen at the front of the room illuminated with a brilliantly clear picture of the Portal. Carlo fast-forwarded through the footage of Daniel and Sarah, as well as her short conversation with Kurt on the island. Even though they knew the exact moment when her heart increased, Carlo let the footage of Sarah walking through the forest play as they watched with nervous curiosity.

"What happened, Sarah..." asked Nish to himself as Daniel patted him on the back.

"Whatever happened in there, she knew what she signed up for."

The screen showed Sarah finding the South Chapel, her footsteps on the old wooden floor echoing throughout the Exodus Chamber. They all watched as she stepped up to the front of the chapel and they collectively shared her fear at the sound of the ax being pulled along the floorboards.

*"Well this, my dear, is a pleasant surprise."*

The words sent a chill down everyone's spines, especially for Nish and Carlo as they stood in front of the large, curved screen. The voice wasn't that of the man that Nish had met while doing trial runs in the Portal. It was a voice he still heard sometimes in his deepest, darkest nightmares.

Sarah's view shifted as she turned her head to her assailant. The silence was crippling as everyone stared at the image of Walter David Scott.

# CHAPTER ELEVEN

Nish stood on the island inside the Portal, scanning the shore in the hopes that Wallace would step forward. In the two weeks since the event they'd come to call *the glitch*, Wallace had completely disappeared. The programming for the Portal had stayed the same, but Carlo had discovered small variations in the programming that ran Wallace. The first time they'd plugged in, they had expected to see him glitching or acting off program, but instead he'd just been gone.

"Dammit," Nish said, taking a final look back at the shore before touching the red exit sphere.

"Anything?" Carlo asked as the electrodes fell to Nish's side in the Exodus Chamber

"Same as always. Where the hell did he go?" Carlo ignored him as he lost himself in Wallace's programming. Nish stepped out of the pod and pulled his phone out of his pocket. He looked at the blank screen.

"Anything?"

"Nothing. She's still ignoring me, understandably so. I even reached out to Stan and haven't heard anything."

"Why don't you just go visit her," Carlo said before yawning and stretching his arms above his head. "Take the evening off and go visit her. Explain yourself; make her realize you had nothing to do with this."

"I don't think she'd hear anything I had to say. Wallace looked *exactly* like Walter; that's too much of a coincidence for her to overlook, even though I had nothing to do with it. She thinks I swindled her."

"She'll come around," Carlo said. "That reminds me, though; I have to step out for a while. I have some family matters that need my attention."

"You don't have to tell me, Carlo. I'm gonna spend some time here, though. Wallace...or Walter, couldn't have just disappeared. He's somewhere in the Portal, and I'm going to find him."

"You shouldn't be in there without me monitoring you from the Chamber. You know that."

"Don't worry about me," Nish said, taking out his phone again as a text message came through. "We've done dozens of tests since the glitch. I'll be okay."

"It's your call, but I think it's a bad idea," Carlo said, looking at his watch. "I have to go. Let's meet for dinner later."

"Whenever you're done just bring some takeout back here. I want to keep working through the night."

"Nish, you need a break. Let's meet at Ebbit's."

Carlo stood in the opening of the hallway that led to the foyer, watching Nish frantically search through data on the tablet. He could see the dark circles under Nish's eyes from where he stood, as well as the general look of fatigue and guilt that hung over him as he worked. Carlo left him alone, feeling exhausted himself as he walked down the hallway toward the foyer.

Carlo could hear the sound of the screen counting down as he exited the building, shaking his head in frustration as the doors closed behind him. Thomas pulled up in a black Lexus and opened the back door for him.

"All set to go, Mr. Macasaet?" asked Thomas.

"Yes, thank you, Thomas."

Carlo settled in against the warm, black leather seats as Thomas slid into the driver's seat. Calm, melodic music flowed through the speakers as Carlo closed his eyes, letting the exhaustion of the weeks since the glitch lull him to sleep.

"Take the long way, would you, Thomas?"

"Of course, sir."

He was asleep before the car was out of eyeshot of the Exodus building.

# CHAPTER TWELVE

The effects of entering the Exodus Portal had begun to take longer to wear off as Nish sat alone in one of the lakeside cabins. His hands tingled more than they ever had, and the nausea rolled over him in waves. His blurry vision almost bordered on blindness as he sat defeated on the uncomfortable mattress, waiting for his faculties to return. His mind was tired and hazy from the exhaustion of the last couple weeks, making the side effects harder to shake.

He stood up and stumbled out of the open door, falling to the dusty ground outside as his foot caught the lower ledge of the doorframe. Air coughed out of his lungs as he dry-heaved loudly into the dirt, sending small clouds of brown dust into the air around him.

"Fuck," he whispered as he rolled onto his back and stared up into the bright afternoon sky.

It took another ten minutes before he was able to regain his composure and stand up. He stumbled a few times as the remaining nausea and blurriness wore off, allowing him to view the enormous environment he and Carlo had created. All the sights, smells, and sounds around him were little memories from his childhood that he'd made part of the Portal, and given better circumstances, he would have taken the time to enjoy them.

Just as he always did, he scanned the banks of the lake, looking for any sign of Wallace, or possibly Walter. He strolled down one of the wooden walkways, searching as he walked for anything that seemed out of place. The slightest abnormality in the Portal's aesthetic could lead him to the cause of the glitch, but just like every other time he'd entered, he found nothing. He walked back down the walkway toward the shore and made his way to the forest path that lead to the South Chapel, even though he'd walked it dozens of times since the glitch. The chapel looked as it always did, drawing him toward its broken structure. He could still remember the day he'd built the south chapel, making it look as run down as possible without logic stating it should have fallen down. The woods around the island housed four chapels, and before the glitch they had been his favorite parts of the Portal. Now they were nothing but a reminder of he and Sarah's broken relationship.

The space inside the chapel was warmer than the outside, causing small beads of sweat to form on his brow while he moved to where Sarah had come face to face with Walter. The thought of Sarah believing he had deliberately placed Walter in the Portal was gut-wrenching, made worse by the fact that he'd not been given the opportunity to explain himself. He stood where she had, soaking in all the sights around him as he searched his thoughts for any clue as to what could have caused the glitch.

Nish turned, half expecting to see Walter as Sarah had, but found the chapel behind him as bare as when he'd entered it.

"What happened, Sarah?" he asked himself as a crow cawed in the distance.

No sooner than the words left his mouth, his fingers tingled for a split second before his world was swallowed in a deep, cavernous darkness.

*For as long as I can remember, I've wanted to be a cop, but holy-flying-fuck sometimes I hate this job. Being an officer was just a stepping-stone to possibly getting into the Bureau someday, but as each shift goes by, this just feels like a permanent placement rather than something that will take me where I wanna be.*

*My partner, Frank Morris, very obviously moonlights as a professional drunk. I don't think I go a shift without catching a whiff of alcohol, but everyone knows and keeps their mouths shut, so who am I to open mine? He was driving today when we got called to a house that we've known for a while for domestic shit. He's a good cop, but still, whenever he gets behind the wheel, I watch him out of the corner of my eye. So far, so good.*

*The house belongs to Willy and Aggie Ford. This was my second time going there just this month. Their neighbor had called us this time, stating she'd heard loud screaming and yelping coming from the small, two-room house. We parked our cruiser on the gravel driveway and made our way up the weed-covered walking path, listening to them bicker and yell at each other like they did every time we came for a visit. As usual, the second our knuckles touched their door, they quieted down. The door opened just like it always does and Willy Ford stood there in his stained wife-beater…just like he always did. He's fucking gross.*

*I don't even really remember what bullshit excuse he gave this time. His wife Aggie always defends him, as women in her position tend to do. It's sad. I don't understand how any woman could end up with an asshole like Willy Ford, but men like him always seem to have a punching bag of a wife to toss around. Sometimes I think about sneaking over there and giving him a taste of his own shit…beat his ass and get Aggie out of there, but that thought always gets pushed away the moment she opens her stupid mouth. That damn woman's got something against me, and I don't know why…probably just cops in general.*

*"Get on outta here, you pampered cunt!"*

*That's what she'd yelled at me today, among other things. She likes that "C" word, I tell ya. With tears in her red eyes, she wanted nothing more than to defend her horrible, shitty man. Oh well, not my problem. Like we always do, we warned his sorry ass and got back into our cruiser. We drove off, and while I'm sure things went quiet for a while after we left, I imagine we'll be back again soon.*

*Pathetic.*

*That wasn't even the craziest thing that happened to me today. I don't know why, but I feel like paranormal shit just flocks to me, like that fucking ghost in my room growing up. Even now, living far away from dad, I still always feel like something is watching me all the time. Maybe it's mom...I dunno. Even when we talk on the phone I feel like that ghost is listening to me through his receiver. Freaks me out. Anyway, as we were driving away from the Ford house, I saw this man walking on the sidewalk. He was wearing a long trench coat with a black top-hat... WAY too hot for summer. There was this gaudy, golden ribbon wrapped around the hat, holding in place a long, silver feather that stood high above his head. As we drove past, he smiled at me. It was a disgusting, creepy smile though. It's like he was saying "I know you see me. I want you to see me."*

*We drove past him, and when I spun my head around to get another look at him, he was gone. I'll never forget that smile; full of rotten, gold-capped teeth, pointing in every direction. I spent the rest of the day trying in vain to hide my anxiety from Frank as the image of the top-hat man spoiled my every thought. I'm not very good at hiding my mood when I'm stressed or anxious about something. Frank has been married for 21 years, which I find unbelievable given the fact that he didn't once ask me if I was okay. He has the emotional depth of a Mr. Potato Head. Probably for the best. Still, it would have been nice to talk to someone today. Guess that's why I have you.*

*Frank needs to retire.*

# CHAPTER THIRTEEN

The face of Walter David Scott, a man he'd never met before, flashed into Carlo's mind the second before he startled himself awake in the back of the Lexus. The cruel, slightly decayed face stuck in his mind for a moment before he rubbed the image away from his eyes with his palms. The world outside had grown dark, and he released a long, open-mouthed yawn as he looked out his window at Sarah's Prince's front porch.

"Bad dream, Mr. Macasaet?" Thomas asked, turning to address his boss.

"A rather quick one, yes, but a bad one nonetheless. I'm not entirely sure how long I'll be here, Thomas. Are you okay waiting?"

"Of course, sir. I'll be here when you're ready."

Carlo shot Thomas an exhausted smile before opening the door and walking up the path to Sarah's house. There was a small button for a doorbell on the right side of the door frame, but he chose instead to rap his knuckles on the cool wood of the door. He waited a few moments, hearing movement inside and feeling the eerie gaze of someone watching him through the peephole.

"Please," Carlo pleaded as he looked at the peephole. "Just talk to me. I only need a minute."

There was a momentary pause where he thought he'd be going back to the car before the lock unlatched and the door swung inward.

"What?" Sarah asked, standing defensively in the doorway with her arms folded across her chest.

"You need to know that what happened was not planned. I know how it must look from your point of view, but you need to believe me when I tell you that we have no idea what happened or how Wallace mimicked Walter's image."

There was another pause as Sarah looked past Carlo at Thomas, sitting behind the wheel of the Lexus. He gave her a small wave, which she returned before stepping aside and motioning for Carlo to come inside.

"He must have schmoozed you good to have you come all this way," she said as she closed the door behind him.

"He has no clue that I'm here. I've been urging him to come, but he's too nervous. The two of us have basically been living inside the Portal over the last two weeks to try and figure out what went wrong."

"It all seems too coincidental, Carlo. I've talked with the others, and I was the *only* one who had an experience with Wallace, or Walter; whoever the hell it was supposed to be."

"Sarah, please; at no time did we ever use any part of Walter's likeness in the Portal. I know you've heard it all before but we tested the Portal hundreds of times before any of you stepped into your entry pods. Our best theory is that Wallace recognized who you were and was able to extrapolate from the net what Walter had looked like."

"He can do that?"

"I'm not sure yet but it's our working theory. We think Wallace was able to access information through the net and that's how he knew who you were and what would rattle you. He wasn't designed to act that way at all, though."

"Isn't that the point of artificial intelligence? To be able to move beyond what it was designed to do?"

"Well, yes, you're right, but it still feels like quite a drastic measure on Wallace's part. I mean Nish had been in Valley Ridge during the murders too, so why didn't Wallace pull that with him when he was testing the game before the launch?"

"Well what about us getting booted from the Portal? What about the fact that our hearts stopped and I haven't been able to shake this damn migraine since?"

"We don't know. We've been working nonstop to try and figure it all out, especially Nish. I've never seen him like this. He's not doing well, Sarah. He's running on fumes trying to fit the pieces together and you ignoring him isn't doing any good."

"I dunno, Carlo."

"Just talk to him. He thinks the world of you and he just wants to make sure you're okay. I know that the two of you didn't get much time together leading up to the launch but if Nish wasn't talking about the Portal, he was talking about you. Quite frankly I was getting tired of hearing about you."

"I think that I know Nish wasn't behind Walter's appearance, but that doesn't change the fact that it happened. I don't know if I'm ready to go back."

"I don't think it was all that easy for him to see Walter again either, Sarah. You were the eighteenth and all, but Nish was there too."

"I'd never thought about that."

"I think that's partly why he's been working so hard since the glitch. He knows it's not possible but the thought that some part of Walter could be running wild somewhere frightens the hell out of him."

"As it should," Sarah said, followed by a moment of silence between the two of them. "Take me to him."

"Now?"

"Yes, now. Thomas is outside, and I doubt he'd care if I tagged along back to Washington. I shouldn't have let this go on for so long."

"Okay; well, pack a bag and meet me outside when you're ready."

Sarah quickly threw some clothes in a bag and freshened herself before stepping outside to join Carlo. Thomas smiled at her and opened the back door of a black Lexus. She slid into the back next to Carlo, and after a few pleasantries, the vehicle became silent as Thomas drove them back to the Exodus facility so that Sarah could make amends with Nish. The different ways the night could end swam through her head as she watched the world fly by outside her window, and before she knew it, Thomas was pulling into the empty Exodus parking lot. Last time Sarah had been here, it had been full of news trucks and reporters waiting to maul her for information,. She was more than pleased that wasn't the case this time.

She walked with Carlo toward the building, listening to the sounds of the city in the distance. The foyer was empty, and the hidden doorway to the Chamber was still open from when Carlo had left. As they entered the hallway, they could both see the Chamber was lit up with the harsh emergency lights.

"Something's not right..." Carlo said as he began to jog toward the chamber.

Sarah followed, her heart racing as they both crashed into the Chamber together. The entirety of the Chamber was bathed in the white of the emergency lighting above them. The screen was empty and the orb glowed blue in the middle of the room. Illuminated under the orb and leading to one of the entry pods was a thick, sticky pool of blood.

"Oh God!" Carlo said, looking at the pod with a horrified look on his face.

Nish's body was lying on its side in front of the upright pod, his intestines in a pile on the floor beside him. Sarah screamed as Carlo pulled out his phone and frantically dialed 911.

# CHAPTER FOURTEEN

The police stormed into the Exodus Chamber as Carlo sat in the viewing gallery with his arm around Sarah, both of them sitting in shock over the scene in front of them. Two officers immediately went to them while another set of officers and a coroner started to tend to Nish's body.

"Hi," Carlo said, standing up to great the officers with an outstretched hand. "I'm Carlo Macasaet; I made the call."

"I'm Detective Allison Carol, Metro P.D," said one of them, stepping forward and shaking his hand. She was tall and slender, with straight, shoulder-length auburn hair. "I assume you have security cameras installed here."

"Of course," Carlo said. "Let me get them queued up for you."

Carlo stood up with Detective Carol and tapped on his tablet a few times and the large viewing screen lit up, showing Nish fitting himself into the entry pod. Carlo paused the footage and looked down to Sarah, still sitting in the viewing gallery.

"I want to see," she said, wiping a tear away from her cheek as she stared at the image of Nish getting into the pod.

With a nod from the detective, Carlo started the video and they all watched as the electrodes crept around his arms and latched on. The orb in the center of the room turned red and cast a devilish glow over Nish's tired face. Carlo tapped a few spots on the tablet and the screen split in half, showing Nish's sleeping body on one half and his point of view from inside the Portal on the other.

"I remember hearing about this technology on the news awhile back," Detective Carol said. "I thought it was interesting, but I never imagined it would like this realistic. I imagine the military and police would be interested in this as a training tool."

"We've already had a lot of interest. Almost all the military branches and the FBI have reached out to us and I'm sure a lot of precincts will be following shortly."

The room grew silent as everyone present watched the screen, leaving their work until after the footage had ended. The camera that had recorded Nish's sleeping body was above the hallway door and showed the entirety of the Chamber in the shot. Just as Nish walked into view of the south cabin in the Portal footage, a shadow was cast across the ground in the security footage, breaking up the light being cast on the ground.

"There!" Sarah said, standing to her feet and moving onto the floor of the Chamber.

They all watched as the figure moved into the glowing red Chamber. The already quiet room entered into a new level of silence as a ghostly, cloaked figure walked into view of the camera. It picked up one of the control tablets and tapped a few times on the screen as the security lighting bathed the footage in a blinding, artificial glow.

"Oh my God..." whispered Sarah as her hand moved to cover her mouth in horror.

The figure moved in front of Nish's sleeping body, watching him from beneath a hooded, black cloak. The bottom of the cloak was tattered to bits, as were both of the sleeves. It was an outfit

Sarah and the rest of the world knew all too well.

It was the kill suit of Walter David Scott.

The figure continued to look at Nish as a large bowie knife slid from under its right sleeve and came to a rest in the palm of its black glove. The figure raised the knife and thrust it forward, the knife gleaming in the artificial light as the footage froze.

"That's enough," Carlo said, letting the image stay paused on the screen. He looked to the viewing gallery with tears in his eyes to find Sarah gone.

"I'm gonna need a copy of that before you leave tonight," the detective said, her green eyes still fixed on the screen in front of her.

"Of course," Carlo said, leaving the Chamber to chase after Sarah. He found her outside with Thomas, his arms around her as they both stood with wet cheeks. A police officer followed behind and stood at the entrance of the building, watching them from afar.

"*Can't we have a moment?*" Sarah barked, sounding much more harsh than she had intended.

"We're suspects, Sarah," Carlo said, giving a slight wave to the officer. "Me, you, Thomas; probably the seven members from the day of the glitch."

"That's insane," she said, crying harder into Thomas's chest.

"Of course it is, sweetie," Thomas said. "But Mr. Macasaet is right. They're going to look at all of us."

A small car pulled into the parking lot in a panic and parked sideways across two spots. Stephanie got out of the driver's seat and ran across the front grass of the building to them.

"I saw the lights when I was driving by! *What's going on?*"

Carlo explained what had happened, and by the end of his recollection, all four of them were hugging each other and crying softly as more police cars pulled into the parking lot.

## November 15th, 2017 – From the Personal Journal of Detective Allison Marie Carol

*Walter David Scott. Fuck me, what a case that would have been to be part of. I can remember doing my rounds with Frank, daydreaming about being part of that case. Like a doctor pines after some kind of crazy, unique surgery, THAT is the kind of case I'm after. Seems like I might have willed myself such a case, though.*

*Nish Patel was murdered tonight. He'd set up a new kind of virtual reality system, if that's what you could call it. It's so much more than that though. I don't even know how to describe it. From the way it was described to me by his business partner, it almost seems like it separates your mind from your body and sends your consciousness into some kind of horror movie experience. I can't even begin to imagine the usefulness for that damn thing.*

*Anyway, Nish is dead. His business partner, Carlo, found him with his guts hanging out. Sarah Price from the Reaper Grim murders had been with him. They'd been friends at Valley Ridge, and Nish had paid her to be part of the original run of the system.*

*Poor girl. Seems like this kind of shit just follows her around. I know the feeling.*

*Carlo put on the video footage of Nish's murder and I couldn't believe what I was seeing. I know it wasn't him, IT COULDN'T BE HIM, but I'll be damned if it wasn't Walter David Scott that murdered Nish. The video showed Nish's body asleep while his mind was exploring the gaming environment. In walks this figure, dressed in the EXACT kill suit that Walter wore. Sure, it wasn't the EXACT suit. We already confirmed the original suit is still in lockup, but fuck, it was damn close. It didn't bother me when I watched it at the crime scene, but when I watched the footage on my own, it freaked me the hell out. REALLY scared the shit out of me. Whoever that was that killed Nish just stood over him, staring down at his bleeding body for at least ten minutes. I'll never shake that image.*

*Standing in that room with Nish's body, I got that same feeling I had grown used to over the years. That eerie, ominous feeling, like something* was watching me. It was the same feeling I used to get in my bedroom growing up. It was the same feeling I got when I drove past the Ford's house, feeling that trench coat man's hidden gaze on me.

Ugh, I hate that feeling, but this is my case. This is the case I wished for, and I'm sure there are dozens of other detectives wishing they could have it. It's mine, but now that I have it, I'm not entirely sure I want it.

I miss my mom.

# CHAPTER FIFTEEN

Two nights after Nish's murder, Kurt and Betsy Saunders walked in their front door at 8:30 pm. Kurt held the door open for Betsy, as he always did, as she walked through with a paper bag holding their leftovers.

"I'm so full," Kurt said, closing the door and sliding the deadbolt shut. "I have a feeling I'll be sneaking some of those leftovers later tonight though."

"You'd better not, Kurt Saunders," Betsy said, putting the bag in the fridge as Kurt turned on some lights in their home. "I don't want to hear about your indigestion in the middle of the night."

"No promises."

Kurt kissed his wife on the lips before leaving the kitchen and sitting down on their living room couch. He turned on the television as Betsy disappeared into their bedroom to put on her pajamas. As usual, Kurt went right to CNN. He was a news junkie, starting and ending his days either by reading the newspaper or surfing the news channels. After Nish's murder, there was plenty of news to be had. On the screen in front of him were images from the Exodus Chamber, lit up with emergency lighting as Anderson Cooper went over the night of Nish's death, as well as what had happened the day of the glitch. He had heard the story replayed dozens of times, but each day he tuned in and followed the story diligently.

"Can we please watch something else?" Betsy asked, sitting down on the other side of the couch from him with a glass of iced tea. "I can't keep focusing on this. It hits far too close to home."

"I just can't believe it. I look at that money in our account, and I feel dirty for having it."

"I know what you mean, honey. I know that none of us did anything wrong, but I just don't feel right having it."

"I say we donate it. I'm sure there's lots of places out there that could use it much more than us."

"Works for me," Kurt said, refocusing on the television coverage as Betsy glared at him. He smiled at her and put on the last half of *The Shawshank Redemption*, which they'd began watching the night before.

By 9:30am, Betsy was asleep on the couch as Kurt snacked on his leftovers beside her. He'd switched the channel back to CNN the moment she'd fallen asleep to catch up on any updates on the investigation. He was surprised to see his and Betsy's photos on the screen, followed by the remaining six participants in the first run. A considerable amount of time had been spent focused on Sarah, which made sense given everything she'd been through.

"Poor girl," he said, watching her image on the screen before it dissolved to more images of the Exodus Chamber.

Every magazine and paper he'd ever written for had quickly reached out to him for his thoughts on the day of the glitch, to which he had politely declined. He, as well as the rest of the group, had decided to stay quiet until Nish and Carlo had figured out what had happened. With Nish's murder, Kurt had a feeling he wouldn't be able to avoid the press much longer. Betsy snorted loudly and sat up straight beside him.

"Go to bed," he said with a smile, kissing her on the cheek before she stood with a tired smile and disappeared down the hallway to their bedroom.

Kurt spent the rest of his night watching news coverage and connecting the dots in his head for a new story that had begun to take form. Ever since the glitch, his creative mind had been running at full capacity, and he was excited to see where it took him. He sat on the couch with a notebook, jotting down notes as he tried to keep himself from getting lost in the news on the television. Before he knew it, it was 2:30 am. He blinked his tired eyes and fell asleep for a moment before startling himself awake in a panic.

"Wow," he said out loud as he turned off the television. "I'm going to regret this tomorrow."

He placed his notebook on the coffee table in front of him before standing up and walking to his darkened kitchen. He placed his hand on the handle of his refrigerator and froze. He stood still for a moment, inhaling as deep as he could and exhaling quietly. His eyes focused in and out before a small, sly smile crept across his face. He opened the fridge and grabbed an almost empty bottle of orange juice from inside. He finished it in one exaggerated gulp as a trickle of juice ran down his bearded chin. The room returned to darkness as he shut the door and tossed the empty plastic container on to the tiled floor. It bounced and sputtered loudly on the tiles before spinning a couple times in the moonlight, coming to rest underneath their kitchen table. For a moment, Betsy stopped snoring in their bedroom down the hall before falling back asleep with a chorus of loud snorts.

Kurt stood at the sink, looking at his moon-soaked backyard. Normally, the image would inspire some literary dreamscape that would send him running to his notebook, but as he stood at his kitchen window, something inside him was different. He was seeing the backyard for the first time, a fact which thrilled him to no end. He turned and inhaled the smells of the kitchen, which smelled clean and tidy but definitely hiding the scents of food long since prepared. He opened the cabinets, leaving them open as he went along until his face lit up at the sight of a half-empty bottle of whiskey. He opened it and threw the cap to the ground before taking a long, laborious gulp from the glass bottle. The liquid warmed his core as he opened a drawer and pulled out a shining piece of cutlery and placed it in the pocket of his drooping housecoat.

"You'll do just fine," he said, patting the pocket as he took another drink of whiskey.

He placed the bottle on the kitchen table and walked down the hallway toward the bedroom that he shared with Betsy. He stopped at their bathroom, taking time to stare at himself in the mirror. He smiled, inspecting every inch of his tired face as his reflection glared back at him. Betsy's snoring continued to echo through their small house, chasing the smile from his face as repulsion crept over him. He found her snoring revolting; each snort hardening the grimace on his face as he stared at his reflection.

He turned the light off and made his way to their bedroom. He stared at the shape of her body underneath their shared blanket as the sound of her snoring boomed in the small room. He pulled back the blanket and slid in beside her, lying on his back for a moment before leaning over and spooning her gently. She stopped snoring for a moment, as she did whenever he wrapped his arms around her, and smiled. Her slightly flabby, wrinkled body made his skin crawl as he pressed himself against her. She had a smell that filled him with disgust as she pressed backward into him.

"Betsy," he whispered in her ear. "You're snoring."

"I'm sorry, honey," she said.

"You sound like a fucking cow."

"Excuse me?" she said, not recognizing the strange new tone of her husband's voice.

He reached into the pocket of his housecoat and pulled out the heavy kitchen knife. He wrapped his left hand around her throat and squeeze as tight as he could, cutting off her windpipe as he began thrusting the knife repeatedly into her lower back. Betsy writhed in agony, tears of pain and confusion running down her cheeks as the bed underneath her began to saturate with her warm, sticky blood. After six strokes of the knife, Betsy's struggling began to slow down. After eight strokes, she was dead. Kurt let go of her throat as a gasp of air rushed past her windpipes, releasing the last sound Betsy Saunders would ever make. He laid beside her lifeless body, feeling the warmth of her blood soak the bed beside him.

Betsy twitched slightly as he reached into a night-table beside the bed and pulled out a pad of paper and a pen. He wrote in the center of the page, creating a list in block form before tearing the page from the pad and throwing the pen to the floor. He dipped his finger into a growing pool of blood beside him and ran his finger nail across the page twice...

NISH PATEL

CARLO MACASAET

SARAH PRINCE

STANLEY WILKES

DANIEL REISMAN

BILLY SHAW

KURT SAUNDERS

BETSY SAUNDERS

WILLIAM CALDWELL

BRADLEY CALDWELL

# CHAPTER SIXTEEN

The sun began to set on their apartment on the outskirts of D.C. as Daniel stared at the text message he'd sent to Sarah two days prior...

*Sarah, I'm so sorry. I don't quite know what to say. Billy and I are here for you if you need us for anything xoxo*

He rubbed a tear away as he closed his phone and stared out the window as the sun softened outside. Billy sat in their living room, flipping channels as he patiently waited for Daniel to get ready for their dinner date. Billy had never been one to go out on dates, preferring to order in and watch whatever sport was on, but he knew Daniel loved going out and he was trying his hardest to help Daniel out of his depression. After minutes of trying to force himself up, Daniel finally pushed himself off the edge of their bed. He'd already gotten himself ready earlier in the afternoon in a fit of motivation and the last thing he needed to collect was a jacket. He searched through his cluttered closet as he looked for the perfect one.

"You need to come see this," Billy said as he appeared in the doorway.

Dan didn't say a word; he knew from the look on Billy's face that something was seriously wrong. Billy led him to their living room and guided Dan onto the couch in front of their television. Dan's hand involuntarily moved toward his mouth as he read the bulletin at the bottom of the screen.

### BETSY SAUNDERS, WIFE OF BEST-SELLING AUTHOR KURT SAUNDERS, FOUND MURDERED IN THEIR ALEXANDRIA HOME.

"They can't find Kurt," Billy said, standing with his hands on Dan's shoulders as he stood behind him. "They think he could be the one who killed Nish."

"That's impossible," Dan said. "You met him. Kurt was clearly still smitten with Betsy. I don't believe it. Not for a second, and he'd have no reason to kill Nish."

"They're saying that she was murdered a couple nights after Nish's death. All signs are pointing towards Kurt being the killer. They even did a height comparison with the Chamber footage and whoever killed Nish matches Kurt's figure perfectly."

"You don't think we're in danger, do you?"

"I'm not worried about Kurt Saunders," Billy said with a smile. "Let him come."

Billy kissed Daniel on the top of his head before walking to their foyer closet and sliding into a leather jacket.

"We can't go out after finding this out," Daniel said, looking backward over the back of the couch at Billy. "Come on, we can go out anytime."

"Daniel, get your ass up and let's go. Yes, it's awful that Betsy is dead, but that doesn't mean we're in any danger. I'll keep you safe."

"Oh, you will, will you?" asked Dan with an annoyed face. "I'm not worried about that, you ass. I just feel…*sad*."

"Look; get up, let's go get dinner, and then maybe we can go visit Sarah if she's up to it. I'm sure she's just as confused as you and I as to what's going on."

Daniel turned back to the television as footage of flashing police lights outside the Saunders' home filled the screen. He reached to the coffee table in front of him and hit the power button on the remote control.

"Fine. Let's go. I'm ordering dessert tonight."

Daniel quickly picked a jacket and dashed out the door as Billy held it open. The drive to their date was spent mostly in silence, interrupted every so often by Daniel asking questions about the murders that Billy had no way of answering. Daniel was nervous, that much was obvious, and although he would never admit it to him, Billy was as well. Since the glitch, two of the people involved had been murdered. Billy tried hard to chalk it up to coincidence, but it all seemed too calculated.

Their date started about the same way as the car ride, until their food arrived and Daniel's mood softened and became more light-hearted. Billy, as usual, ordered beer and fried calamari, both of which he finished almost as soon as they were placed at the table. Daniel started his night with a bowl of clam chowder and a glass of red wine, which he nursed until their meals arrived. Both of them ordered steak, which they both savored as they awaited the arrival of their desserts.

"*Holy shit-balls!*" Daniel said, placing his fork down beside his empty, chocolate-streaked plate. "That was *dyno-mite!*"

"Did Sarah message you back yet?"

"She sure did! She actually is having Carlo over later tonight so she told us to stop by."

"How is she?"

"She's scared," Dan said, using his finger to swipe as much chocolate off his plate that he could.

"That's disgusting." Billy reached into his back pocket to pull out his wallet, only to find it wasn't there. "Damn it. I think I left my wallet in the truck."

"Maybe if you didn't put it in the cup holder whenever you drive this wouldn't be an issue."

"Fuck you," Billy said with a smile as he stood up from the

table. "It's uncomfortable to sit on."

Billy left Daniel alone at the table and made his way to the front of the restaurant to retrieve his wallet. His breath escaped him in puffs of white vapor as he stepped outside into the cold November air. He'd left his jacket at the table, forcing him to cross his arms to keep warm as he made his way to his truck. As predicted, his wallet was sitting in one of the cup holders between the two front seats. He slid it into his back pocket, remembering all the times Daniel had razzed him about leaving it in the truck.

As he shut the door, something in the corner of his eye caught his attention. In an alleyway beside the restaurant, there was a person sitting against the cold brick with their feet straight out in front of him. The darkness of the alley kept him from fully seeing the person, but he could tell they were whimpering and reaching their hand out toward him. Without thinking, Billy took off down the alley, entering into the darkness between the buildings fearlessly.

"Hey! Are you okay?" he asked as he crouched down in front of the figure.

The figure's face was shielded by a thick, winter hood, hanging over the front part of their face. The figured looked up and slid their hood off, revealing a face Billy knew immediately.

"Hello, Billy-Boy," Kurt said as he placed a knife on the cold pavement between them.

*****

Daniel was sitting with the bill at the table as he worked on finishing a new basket of bread he'd asked the waiter to bring while he waited for Billy to return.

"I eat when I'm stressed, so sue me," he said as Billy sat across from him. "What the hell took you so long?"

"Sorry," Billy said, his face red from the cold as he reached for the black envelope the bill had come in.

"Find it?"

"Find what?" Billy asked, rubbing his hands together to bring back his warmth.

"What do you mean, find what? You're wallet, you dipshit!"

"Oh yeah," Billy said, feeling the wallet in his back pocket against the chair. "Yeah I've got it."

"You okay?"

"I'm fine, Daniel," Billy said, picking up the black envelope and examining the bill.

"What's the damage?"

"Just over a hundred."

"Oh, here we go," Daniel said with a smile. *"Daniel, you eat too much. Daniel, you always order the expensive shit on the menu. Daniel, you don't put out enough!"*

Billy sat for a moment as he put a credit card in the receipt holder and slid it to the edge of the table. "Not at all, Daniel; I'm glad you enjoyed your meal. You look really handsome tonight."

"That's not the kind of thing I hear that often from you," Daniel said with a flirtatious smile. "Keep it up and you might just get lucky tonight."

"Looking forward to it," Billy said with a wink as a waitress took their credit card and quickly returned with the receipt.

Daniel and Billy walked hand in hand out of the restaurant. An older couple sitting near the front of the restaurant looked at them with a grimace as they walked toward the exit. As they passed, Daniel swung his hand in an exaggerated manner and smacked Billy across the back of his blue jeans. Billy jumped forward slightly with a grimace as Daniel snorted with laughter.

"Dial it back, sailor," Billy said as the left the restaurant. He took a quick glance at the alley as they made their way toward his truck.

"Sailor? When the hell did you start saying *sailor*?"

"I dunno, seemed like a good enough nickname."

Daniel stood in the cold air, looking at Billy as he held open the truck door for him. "Okay what the hell is going on? I look *handsome*? You're holding the door for me? *Sailor*?"

"Just get in, Daniel. Let's go home."

Daniel took a moment before shrugging his shoulders and sliding into the passenger seat of the truck. Billy moved around the front, glancing into the alley again before climbing into the driver's seat and turning the ignition.

"What a good meal that was," Daniel said, thinking back to the chocolate cheesecake he'd devoured to end his meal. "We need to go back there more often."

"I would agree with you there," Billy said, driving away from the restaurant and pulling down a rural road.

"Where are you going? You know we need to go to Sarah's."

"Sarah's?"

"Are you okay?" Daniel asked, reaching over and rubbing Billy's thigh affectionately. "I'm serious. I'm starting to worry about you. You're acting really strange."

"I'm fine."

There was a coldness to Billy's voice that Daniel wasn't used to hearing. He took his hand back and looked out the window, watching the nightscape outside his window fly by. As he sank into his thoughts, Billy pulled the truck over to the side of the road and killed the engine.

"Where are we?" Daniel asked, looking over the dark, rolling field outside Billy's window.

"I want to show you something. Hop out, *sailor.*"

Billy stepped out of the truck as Daniel shivered at the word. Something inside told him to jump to the driver's seat and drive off, but before he could act, Billy had opened the door with his hand outstretched for him.

"Billy, what are you doing?"

"Daniel, I know I've been weird tonight. Please, just come with me. You won't regret it."

Daniel sat for a moment, looking at Billy with his outstretched hand. Billy smiled, and with that, Daniel took his hand and allowed himself to be led in front of the truck and into the dark field.

*"So this is why you've been so weird tonight,"* Daniel thought to himself, mentally preparing himself for Billy's proposal. They'd talked about getting married dozens times but Billy had never officially asked him.

"Stop," Billy whispered into Daniel's ear. "Close your eyes."

Daniel's curiosity overcame his nervousness as he smiled and closed his eyes. He felt Billy walk behind him and place a hand gently on his shoulder. He shivered at the feel of Billy's breath as he leaned toward Daniel's ear.

"I lied," Billy said. "You're most definitely going to regret this."

Daniel's abdomen exploded with hot, blistering pain. He looked down in the moonlight to find Billy's hand holding the handle of a knife that was buried deep inside his stomach. Daniel began to scream as Billy's left hand reached up and choked his voice away. Daniel's eyes filled with tears as his body shuddered against Billy's grasp. Billy removed the knife and dug it wildly into his abdomen over and over, twisting and turning it as Daniel fell to his knees. Billy crouched with him, both of them kneeling in the red, wet grass.

*"Why?"* muttered Daniel through the pain.

With one final stroke across his lower abdomen, Billy opened Daniel's stomach and let his intestines spill onto the ground. By instinct, he reached forward and caught them with his hands before falling forward and fading into darkness. Billy stood above Daniel's lifeless body, turning him to face the sky and inspecting his work in the moonlight. He reached into his pocket and pulled out his new list of victims and scratched out Daniel's name with the blood from his exposed abdomen.

Billy walked back to his truck and climbed inside. He started the engine and continued driving down the dirt road towards Sarah's house. Billy had walked Daniel far enough into the field that he wouldn't be found for days. Back at the restaurant though, the alley was alive with activity over the discovery of the corpse of Kurt Saunders.

# CHAPTER SEVENTEEN

Stanley Wilkes sat in front of his television with a bottle of beer as he tried to make sense of the news of Betsy's death. He couldn't help but feel worried and scared as he watched her smiling face on the screen next to footage of the Saunders home bathed in blue and red police lights. His cellphone vibrated on the coffee table in front of him. He grabbed it without taking his eyes off the screen.

*I'm sure you've heard about Betsy. Carlo, Daniel, and Billy are coming over tonight around 9:00pm. You should come too. I'm scared, Stan.*

It was Sarah. She was the first thing he'd thought about when the news had broken about Betsy's murder. Stanley had been one of the only people Sarah had allowed into her life after Walter's capture, and now that there were more murders happening around her, he knew he'd have to be there for her as much as possible.

\* \* \*

*Of course, I'll be there, sweetie. Don't stress. We will get through this.*

His phone showed 8:15 pm as he placed it back on the coffee table, just enough time for him to finish another beer before walking down the street to Sarah's house. He finished the beer in his hand and placed the bottle on the table as he felt a prick in the side of his neck. He swatted at it and felt a hand, but before he could turn to see who it was, hands on his shoulders guided him down onto the couch, unconscious.

\*\*\*\*\*

He woke up lying on his side, his hands tied in front of him with a shoelace. He could tell his feet were tied too as he wiggled himself up into a sitting position on the couch. It wasn't until he was sitting straight up on the couch that he noticed the figure sitting across from him. It was a figure he knew too well, with a black coat and a dark, hooded face.

"Hello, Stanley," said the figure. It sat across from him in a chair, watching him from beneath the dark hood.

"Whoever you are, you're not Walter, so just give up the act."

"Three years ago, we went fishing up at Lake Anna, just you and I. We were halfway through the day, without catching a damn thing, when you opened up to me about what happened to you as a child."

"Stop this."

"You told me what your father had done, Stanley. You told me he'd touched you."

*"You shut your damn mouth!"*

"Aren't you at all curious as to how I know that? You told me that day that you'd never told anyone before. I was pretty quiet the rest of the day, which I always regretted, but when we were back on dry land I put my arms around you."

"Stop," Stanley whispered as a tear ran down his cheek. The figure was right; he hadn't told anyone other than Walter David Scott his secret. "Please, just stop."

"It's me, Stanley," said the figure, removing the hood with both hands to reveal the face of Billy Shaw. "Well, kind of."

"Billy?" Confusion settled over him like a dense fog. "What the hell are you doing here? How'd you know those things?"

"Stanley, it's me. I can't fully explain it, but it's me—it's Walter."

"Billy, where is Daniel?"

"If it helps you to call me Billy, that's okay. I understand. It's a funny predicament we've found ourselves in."

"Where is Daniel?"

Billy looked at Stanley on the couch, knowing he wasn't understanding what he was trying to tell him. "He's right where he belongs, with Nish and Betsy and Kurt."

"Wait, *Kurt*?"

"I'm sure you'll be hearing about it soon enough. Daniel though, it'll be a while before anyone finds him I think."

"Billy, please, let me go."

"I'm sorry, Stanley, but I can't do that. I'm still bound by the rules of the Portal."

"What the fuck are you talking about, Billy? Either kill me or let me go. I'm not interested in listening to your bullshit delusions."

"Okay, you're not understanding this, so let me lay it out for you as plainly as I can. I'm sure you remember the day of my execution?"

Stanley sat still, not acknowledging Billy's talking. Billy leaned forward with his knife in front of him, raising is eyebrows as he awaited Stanley's response.

"Yes, Billy, I remember *Walter's* execution."

"Okay, well that day, let's just say my spirit took a pit-stop before headin' on down to the devil. Don't ask me to explain it to ya because I just don't know, but somehow I got all tangled up with that thing that Nish and Carlo created."

"The Exodus Portal?" Stanley asked, picking up on Walter's cadence in Billy's voice and shuddering a little.

"Yep, that's the one."

"That doesn't make any sense."

"Hey, you're telling me, big-guy. I didn't understand what had happened to me until all of you got kicked out of the system that day and brought me with you."

"What do you mean, brought you with us?"

"When all your minds left the game, I was somehow able to follow you. I'm inside all your heads, Stanley; yours, Billy's, Will's, Brad's; even Sarah's."

Stan glanced under the table at his cellphone, which had been knocked off the table at some point. He could see that it was 9:45 and Sarah had been texting him.

*9:15: Carlo is here. Where are you?*

*9:25: Seriously, you need to get here soon. Carlo thinks he knows what is going on.*

*9:40: Okay, Stan, I'm officially nervous. Carlo and I are coming to your place.*

"That's all good and fine but why are you killing all of us?" asked Stanley, hoping Sarah and Carlo would be at his door soon.

"I don't have a choice, Stan. Wallace's only goal was to kill everyone in the game. It seems that I'm still bound by that. Trust me, I'd love nothing more than to slice Sarah's pretty lil' throat and sail off into the sunset in Billy's body, but it's not that easy. It's like all that is left of me is completely focused on it, and I can't switch it off."

"Nish wasn't in the game that day."

"No, he wasn't. I still have a certain amount of freewill, and I wasn't about to have him figure out what was going on. I remember him back at Valley Ridge; I liked him. It was kind of bittersweet having Kurt kill him while he was in the Portal."

"You really are Walter, aren't you?" Stanley asked.

"Yes, old friend, it is I. I'm sorry, Stanley, I truly am, but you were in the game that day, and I have no choice. I haven't let anyone else know what was going on but I owed you that much before I put you down."

"Like an animal," Stanley said as Billy stood with his knife held at his side.

"Stanley, I didn't mean it that way."

There was a series of knocks at the door as Billy broke his attention and stared at the foyer.

"Stanley, are you in there? It's Sarah."

"*SARAH! GET OUT OF HERE, RUN!*" Stanley screamed.

Billy looked at Stanley with a surprised, wounded face. It was in that moment, as the two men stared into each others eyes, that Stanley knew that Billy had been telling the truth. The look of betrayal turned into a look of fierce anger as he lurched forward with the knife. Stanley rolled quickly off the couch and onto the floor, but not before Billy's knife cut deep into Stanley's left bicep. Stanley screamed in pain as the door flew open with a loud bang and Carlo and Sarah crashed into the foyer.

"*BILLY?*" Sarah said, confused at the sight of him wearing Walter's kill suit.

"*It's not Billy! It's Walter!*" Stanley yelled, still laying on the ground at Billy's feet.

Billy leaped over the couch and flew into the darkness of the house. Sarah and Carlo stood in shock over what Stanley had said as Billy disappeared out the back door.

"So, it's true," Carlo said, hurriedly turning on the lights around the home as Sarah untied Stan and held pressure on his arm.

"*You knew?*" yelled Stanley as Sarah helped him into the kitchen.

"I had my suspicions. What did he say to you exactly?"

Sarah dressed Stanley's wound as best she could as he explained what Billy had told him before his escape. Carlo listened intently, visibly shaken by what Stanley told them.

"I told Nish that this was a bad idea," Carlo said. "I told him, and he didn't want to listen."

"How could you have known this would happen, Carlo?" Sarah asked.

"I'm thinking back to the time around when Walter was executed. It was around that time that Wallace began acting funny. It wasn't long after the execution when he spoke to Nish."

"I hate that story," Sarah said, remembering Nish telling it to her over dinner.

"It makes sense now, though. Of course Wallace didn't know where he was because it wasn't Wallace talking to Nish; it was Walter."

"Let's go to the station and try and explain this to some of my buddies," Stanley said.

"Explain what to them?" Carlo asked. "That the disembodied soul of Walter David Scott is taking over our bodies and killing us one by one? Stan, nobody will believe us. We need to figure out what to do ourselves."

"Carlo, Stan's right. This is above us," Sarah said.

"Look, if I thought going to the police would help, I'd go in a heartbeat, but I don't think it will. If the cops were able to find Billy and throw him in a cell, who's to say he wouldn't just jump bodies and continue his plan."

"So we know for sure that this is Walter?" asked Sarah. "Is it possible this has been Billy the whole time?"

"He knew things about me that I only ever told Walter," Stanley said. He took a bottle of whiskey out of a cabinet above his sink. "When Billy talked, I was hearing Walter. Even the way he looked at me was like how Walter used to look at me. It's him, I know it. I don't want to believe it, trust me, but it's him."

Stanley took a drink of whiskey right from the bottle before offering it up to everyone. Carlo took it from him and took a drink. His face grimaced before he handed it back to Stanley.

"I stood idly by as Nish rushed us head first into this shit-storm and I'll be damned if I'm going to sit on the sideline again. We gotta get behind this quickly."

"Well what's your idea?" asked Stanley.

"Just give me some time. I'll think of something; I have to. Until then, I think we need to stick together."

"I need to warn Will and Brad," Sarah said, pulling out her phone to call Will's phone.

Her phone was already full of text messages and missed calls from both him and Brad.

# CHAPTER EIGHTEEN

Billy parked his truck in the field where he'd left Daniel's body. He stepped out and threw the keys as far as he could into a thick, overgrown area far off from the dirt road. The sun was starting to slowly rise as he sulked down the road, his hood pulled over his head while his kill suit swayed in the cold breeze. By the time he'd reached Daniel's corpse, the sun had risen and given the bloody field a soft, horrible glow.

Billy stood over Daniel's body as the winter sun began to warm the air around him. He looked down the road to see a couple of tall, muscular joggers moving toward him at a brisk pace, both of them wearing a pair of headphones whose cords bounced wildly as they moved. They were looking down, lost in their music and focused on their morning routine, too distracted to notice the darkly-clothed fiend they were approaching. Billy glared down at Daniel's face, looking up at him with lifeless, glazed-over eyes. Billy closed his eyes and inhaled a breath as deep as he could. He held it in for a few seconds before exhaling a puff of hot air into the cool morning air.

\*\*\*\*\*

\* \* \*

"What the hell?" Billy said, his eyes focusing in and out for a second before he was able to see the sight in front of him.

Lying before him was a large, sprawling Virginia field, coated with frost from the early November morning. The last thing he could remember was finding Kurt Saunders in the alleyway beside the restaurant; his mind was ablaze with confusion over how he ended up in the field. The sun had risen recently, slowly melting away the frost as it began its slow ascent toward the top of the sky, but Billy took no notice to any of that. All he could focus on was the mutilated, lifeless corpse of Daniel Reisman lying in front of him. Tears filled his eyes as he gasped, almost losing his breath while he gazed at his lifeless body.

"Daniel?" he whispered as the tears began to flow harder down his face as he silently stood above the corpse of his boyfriend.

He reached down and touched Daniel's face, only to retract his hand in revulsion at the cold, dead feel of his cheek. He looked off into the distance and caught sight of two joggers moving toward him, not having noticed him standing above Daniel's body. He went to call out to them when he noticed the black gloves on his hands, as well as the dark, hooded outfit that clung loosely to his body. He felt the unmistakable feeling of a sheathed knife on his right hip, attached to the belt he wore. He took it out and almost dropped it, realizing that somehow, in a way that he did not yet understand, that he had been the one who had killed Daniel. He placed the knife back in the sheath and felt his left pocket, confirming its contents were still there; a small, velvet box, holding a ring that would never be given to who it had been intended.

"Hey!" yelled one of the joggers as they entered into an all-out sprint toward Billy.

"*Wait!*" Billy said, holding his hands out in front of him but realizing there was nothing he could say to explain what they were seeing.

In a moment of panic, Billy took one more tearful glance at Daniel before breaking into a sprint and disappearing into a thick patch of woods nearby.

# CHAPTER NINETEEN

Will and Brad pulled into Sarah's driveway at 9:00 am. News had broken overnight about the discovery of Kurt's body in the alley beside the restaurant, prompting a manhunt for both Daniel and Billy as the restaurant owner confirmed to the police that they had been there for dinner around the time of Kurt's death. Sarah opened the door as they made their way up the steps, taking a look up and down the street before letting them in and locking the door behind them.

"This is all so fucked up," Will said as Sarah greeted him with a hug

"Trust me, you have no idea how fucked up it truly is."

"Have a seat, boys," Stanley said. "We have a lot to go over."

Stanley, Carlo, and Sarah explained to Will and Brad what they'd found out about Walter and the glitch. Stanley went into great detail about his experience with Billy and why he believed what Billy had said to him.

"It's not possible," Brad said. "This isn't the fucking Twilight Zone. You can't all believe this. Stanley, you're a lawman, you can't be buying this."

"I had trouble believing it at first too, trust me, but I was there

141

with Billy in my house. His voice, his manner of speaking, even the way he moved. I have no doubt that Walter was inside him."

"The timeline matches up perfectly," Carlo said. "Wallace began acting strange shortly after Walter's execution. Also, after the glitch, Wallace was gone. Nish and I both searched the Portal dozens of times, and he was simply gone. It doesn't make any sense at all, but it seems he left the Portal with one of you."

"So what you're saying is that Walter piggybacked his way out of the Portal and could be using any one of us at any time," Will said. "If he can jump from mind to mind, who's to say he's not listening right now?"

"You can't be believing this," Brad said as he shot a skeptical look at this brother.

"Why would Stan and Sarah lie? Also, how else would you explain Nish, Kurt, and Betsy's deaths?"

"Don't forget Daniel," Stanley said. "Billy said he killed Daniel and left him somewhere that would take awhile to find him."

"This is a mess," Will said.

"I know it seems crazy but given the information we have, it makes sense," Carlo said. "Walter was inside Billy last time we encountered him, but who knows how long that will last. Based on what Billy said, it seems like he left the Portal through Kurt."

"Kurt killed Nish and Betsy," Stanley said, rubbing the dressing on his arm. "Billy killed Kurt and Daniel, apparently."

"They found Daniel…" Sarah said, looking at her phone before flicking on the television.

The group watched silently as police lights flashed on the screen, each of them parked along the dirt road near the field where Daniel's body was found. Billy's photo was in the bottom of the screen near the constant scroll of headline news, most of it telling details about the murders and asking the public for tips on Billy's whereabouts.

"How do you suppose we handle this?" Sarah asked, her eyes glued to the screen. "There really isn't a logical way to explain this to the police."

"There's no logical way to explain this to anybody," Brad said. "I'm not even sure I believe it yet."

An abrupt knocking at the front door interrupted their conversation. They each looked at each other, wondering who it could be and fearing it was Billy. Sarah stood and made her way to the front door followed by Carlo and Stanley. She took a quick peek out of a narrow window that spanned the height of the door and felt relieved to see the detective from the night of Nish's murder.

"It's the detective," she whispered before opening the door.

"Good morning Miss Prince," Detective Carol said, her hair flowing straight on the sides of her face as always. She looked back and forth between Carlo and Stanley with a smile. "Nice to see the three of you again."

"We're all here, actually" Sarah said, standing aside and letting the detective inside.

"All?"

"Yeah. Everyone from the night of the glitch. Except Billy, that is. I assume that's why you're here."

"You assume correctly."

The four of them rejoined Brad and Will in the living room, who stood at the sight of the detective.

"At ease, gentleman," she said with a smile. "Have any of you had any contact with Billy Shaw over the past few days?"

"None of us have spoken to him since the glitch," Will said.

"I've kept in contact with Daniel a little, but that's the extent of it," Sarah said.

"I'm sure you're aware of what's happened to Daniel," the detective said, pointing to the muted television. "Billy was spotted earlier this morning by a couple joggers, standing over Daniel's body. We believe he's responsible for both Kurt and Betsy Saunders as well. Do any of you have any reason to believe Billy would be doing this?"

The group shook their heads in silence. They each knew exactly why Billy was doing what he was doing, but explaining that to Detective Carol was something none of them knew how to approach.

"Why are you all gathered here?"

"All the victims were people who were present at the glitch," Will said. "Seems pretty obvious we are all in danger."

"We were all talking last night when we found out about Kurt and Betsy," Sarah said. "We agreed to meet here today."

"Did you invite Daniel and Billy?" Detective Carol asked.

"Daniel texted me last night wanting to come over after their dinner, but they never showed up."

Detective Carol flipped through a small notebook as if she were looking for something to tell them before closing it and putting it on her lap.

"Everything okay with that arm?" asked the detective, motioning toward Stanley's bandaged arm, which had begun to show signs of leaking.

"Oh, yeah, it's fine," he said with a nervous laugh. "I was moving some 2x4s at my place this morning, and I jabbed myself pretty good with a nail."

"You should be more careful. I'll be in touch as much as I can. I think it's good that you're staying together. If he is coming after all of you, it'll be a lot harder with you together. If you hear anything at all from Billy, please let me know right away."

Detective Carol put a small stack of business cards on the coffee table before saying goodbye and leaving the house. Each of them sighed in relief as she left, most of all Stanley as he made his way to Sarah's bathroom to redress his wound.

"So, I guess we're all in deep now, lying to the feds and all," Brad said.

"Well we can't very well tell her about Billy last night without throwing him under the bus, can we?" Will said.

"Do we think we can trust her?" Sarah asked.

"I don't think we can trust anyone with the truth of what's going on," Will said. "Carlo do you have any ideas on what to do?"

"None," he said, rubbing his tired eyes with both his palms. "Not yet, anyway."

Stanley rejoined the group as they heard a door open and shut from the back of the house. The sound of footsteps filled their ears as Billy walked into the opening of the living room, his hands up in the air. He looked at them with red, tired eyes, exhausted from hours of crying.

"Please, help me," he whispered before falling to the ground in an unconscious heap.

# CHAPTER TWENTY

Billy woke up in the basement of Sarah's house, his feet and arms bound tightly with an old rope that scratched angrily at his agitated skin. He blinked his eyes hard, his vision blurring in and out until they finally focused on the image of Carlo and Stanley, sitting across from him with stern looks on their faces.

"Where am I?" Billy asked, grimacing at the feeling of the rope on his hands.

"Don't worry about that right now," Stanley said.

"I think I killed Daniel." The red shade in his eyes darkened as they filled with fresh tears.

"We know," Carlo said. "The police are looking for you. Do you remember killing him?"

"No! Daniel and I had gone out to dinner. I forgot my wallet in my truck so I went outside to get it. When I turned to go back in, I saw someone in the alleyway beside the restaurant. They looked like they needed help, so I went to check on them, and it was Kurt! He said hi to me and then I blacked out. When I woke up, I was standing over Daniel's body."

Carlo and Stanley looked at each other with concerned faces as Sarah, Will, and Brad walked down the stairs to join them.

"Do you remember anything at all after you found Kurt?" asked Stanley.

"Absolutely nothing."

The group sat in silence, not knowing what to say to the broken man in front of them. Billy continued to cry with a look of complete confusion on his face.

"Do any of you know what is going on?"

"I'll tell him," Sarah said, sitting down between Carlo and Stanley. "Billy, this is going to sound crazy, but I have a feeling it will clear up a lot of confusion for you. It's all crazy, so I'm just gonna say it how it is. When Walter was executed, somehow his spirit attached itself to the A.I. that Nish and Carlo created. When we all got booted out of the Portal, it seems that Walter attached himself to Kurt, and now he's able to jump between our minds and take over our bodies."

"He's still bound by the rules of the Portal, so he has to kill all of us," Stanley said. "He used Kurt to kill Nish and Betsy, then he switched bodies to you and killed Kurt and Daniel."

What little control Billy had on his emotions completely evaporated as the confirmation that he'd killed Daniel and Kurt settled in. His face scrunched, and he went into a complete sobbing fit as his shoulders slouched forward. Sarah stood to join him but was stopped by Stanley when he placed his hand on hers.

"It's okay," she said, brushing him away as she sat next to Billy and let him fall into her arms. "It's okay, Billy. This was Walter, not you."

"*Tell that to Daniel!*" Billy yelled through his sadness. "He had no idea this was happening! All he knew was that his boyfriend, who was about to *propose*, cut him open with a knife!"

"Billy, you have to keep it down," Will said. "The police are looking for you. We are all in deep shit if someone hears you down here."

"Maybe I should just turn myself in."

"Billy, you didn't do this," Will said. "It's really shitty that

Walter used you to kill Daniel, but if you go to jail, the murders will continue. Walter will just use another one of us to continue. We need to get that detective on our side."

"She'll never believe any of this," Brad said.

*"Well what the hell else do you expect us to do?"* Will yelled, pushing Brad slightly.

"Both you of, calm down!" Carlo yelled. "Brad is right. Outside of the six of us, there isn't anyone who would believe what's happening. We're on our own."

"We can't even trust each other," Sarah said. "How are we supposed to survive this?"

"I don't know," Carlo said. "He doesn't have access to my mind so maybe we can use that as an advantage. I think for the foreseeable future, we need to stay together."

"Everyone can stay here until we figure out what to do," Sarah said, pulling a small bottle of aspirin out of her sweatshirt pocket and shaking a couple pills into the palm of her hand.

*"Please* tell me you have more of those," Will said. "My head is pounding."

Sarah popped the pills into her mouth and tossed the bottle to Will.

"I wouldn't mind a couple either," Brad said, taking the bottle from his brother and popping three into his mouth.

"How long have you had your headaches?" Carlo asked.

"I've had mine since the day of the glitch," Stanley said. "I figured it was just stress. I didn't realize all of you were having them too."

"Daniel and I had them so bad that we couldn't sleep. We started playing board games in the middle of the night because it was better than just lying there in pain."

"So we've all had headaches since the glitch?" Sarah asked.

"With the way that Walter is moving between your minds, it seems the glitch made the eight of you into some sort of network," Carlo said. "Could explain the headaches."

"We're all here right now," Brad said. "Where's Walter?"

The group looked at each other skeptically, wondering if any of them were secretly housing Walter's spirit.

"All we can do is keep an eye on each other," Stanley said. "I tend to think we'll be able to figure out when Walter has taken over one of us."

"How can you be so sure?" Brad asked.

"He didn't need to sneak into my house last night. He could have just knocked on the door and I'd have let him in, no question. I think Walter knows he can't mimic our personalities, which is why he snuck into my house the way he did."

"Doesn't that make you his biggest conduit?" Brad asked.

"What makes you think that?"

"Walter doesn't know any of us so obviously he can't mimic our personalities but weren't you two fuck-buddies or something?"

"Everything you say is so damn stupid," Will said, punching his brother in the arm. "I'm sorry, Stanley."

"He's right, though," Stanley said. "Walter and I knew each other very well. If he could use any of us convincingly, it would be me."

"You're all at risk, not just Stanley," Carlo said. "I think you should all lay low while I try and figure out what to do. I'm gonna head to the Exodus building and do some research. I'll be back around dinner. Keep an eye on each other."

"Pizza's on me," Stanley said.

"Can I have a word, Sarah?" Carlo asked, motioning to the upstairs. She nodded and he followed her up the stairs into her kitchen. "Brad is right about Stan."

"I know."

"You know Stan the most out of any of us. I hate to put this on you but I need you to keep an eye on him."

"I know, Carlo. I'll keep my eye on him."

"If anything seems off with any of them, call me right away."

Carlo was surprised when she hugged him before he left the house to figure out a way to cut Walter out of their lives for good.

The group in Sarah's house spent the majority of the afternoon watching news footage about the murders. There were tributes to Kurt and his published works, as well as profiles on Betsy and Daniel's life. Billy was the prime suspect and his face never left any of the news broadcasts. Footage of roadblocks flashed on the screen as police officers examined the inside of cars, hoping to find Billy huddled in a backseat, but Billy was safe and secure where he was, tucked away in the last place anyone would think to look for him.

Stanley ordered pizza for the group as sunset approached. He paid the delivery boy a substantial tip, as he always did, before placing the pizzas on Sarah's kitchen table.

"Dinner is served," he said with a smile.

"I'm so hungry!" Brad said, flipping open a box and taking five pieces.

"Slow down, you jackass," Will said. "Stan didn't buy all this pizza for you. I really wish you'd let us chip in, Stan."

"Don't mention it. It's my treat."

They ate in relative silence, the small talk having long fizzled out earlier in the day. They'd watched the monotonous coverage for close to an hour after dinner before Stanley took the remote off the table and searched the guide until he found a channel playing a *Seinfeld* marathon. He put it on, and even though there wasn't much laughter among them, the mood was noticeably lighter.

"I've never understood the allure of this show," Brad said, taking his phone out of his pocket to distract himself.

"That's because you're an idiot," Will said.

"Oh whatever, *William*." Brad stood up and tried to walk away as Will grabbed his wrist.

"Carlo said we should stay together."

"Really?" Brad said, challenging Will with a pair of defiant eyes. "You'd better let go of me."

"Or what? You gonna run away again? None of your shitty friends are here to take you in this time, you dumb-shit."

"Fuck you, Will." Brad said with hurt in his eyes.

"Guys," Sarah said. "Dial it back. We don't need this right now."

The group watched the tension bubble between them before Brad relented and sat back down on the couch, completely checked out on his phone as he tried to hide the mounting tears in his eyes. They each mindlessly watched the television, knowing that danger lurked just below their consciousness. They all jumped as the front doorknob turned and swung open.

"I'm back," Carlo said, holding a white plastic bag at this side. "Anything happen?"

"Nothing," Sarah said, getting up and putting a plate of pizza in the microwave for Carlo. "Hope you're hungry, we have lots left."

"Starving." He dumped the contents of the white bag onto the table, revealing five pairs of shiny, new handcuffs.

"Whoa, this night is taking a turn for the weird," Will said as they all gathered near the table.

"Funny," Carlo said. "If we are going to sleep here, together, we need to make sure we are all safe. If you're all cuffed to something sturdy at night, I don't see how any of us can end up on the receiving end of a kitchen knife."

"Makes sense," Stanley said as he picked up a pair of the cuffs and inspected it. "You didn't have to waste money on these. I've got extra pairs in my cruiser."

"I think the more I do apart from all of you, the better. Who knows when, or if, he's watching."

"Makes sense," Stanley said, putting the cuffs back on the table.

"We'll split up between the second floor and the basement. We should keep the main floor open in case Detective Carol shows up again. Last thing we need is for her to peek in the window and catch a view of someone chained up in the kitchen."

"I'm sure Will would be pleased as punch if she did pop by," Brad said without taking his eyes away from his phone. "Did everyone see how he perked right up when she came by today?"

"Oh shut up," Will said, throwing a dishcloth from the table at him.

"No, he's right," Sarah said with a smile. "I don't know about the rest of you but it was pretty clear you've developed a little crush."

The group laughed together for the first time all day when Will's face blushed as he smiled. His smile was charmingly crooked, which showed his pearly white teeth underneath. His blue eyes sparkled as he tried to hide his attraction to the detective who didn't yet realize she was hunting Walter David Scott. The group retired again to the living room, sitting and watching the television together as Carlo finished his pizza. Stanley chuckled along as the *Seinfeld* marathon continued, saying some of the lines along with the actors with a subtle smile on his face. Other than him, nobody truly paid attention to what was happening on the screen; they were each lost in their thoughts, worried about the time to come.

Sarah was the first to let out a yawn, which spread like a wildfire through the rest of group. It was just after 11:00pm and each of them were equally tired and ready for bed.

"How do we go about this?" Sarah asked.

"Let's get everyone secured for the night," Carlo said. "Will, Brad, and Billy will take the basement. Myself, Stanley, and Sarah will take the upper floor."

"My face is all over the news," Billy said. "I guess I should just stay down there until this all blows over. Sarah, I might be moving in permanently."

"That actually brings up a fair point," Stanley said, leaning against the kitchen counter as he finished a cold slice of pizza. "What's going to happen to Billy at the end of this? Let's say that we figure out how to stop Walter; that won't matter to the police. Even if we get just one person in the police force or FBI to buy any of this, there's no way they'd be able to convince their higher-ups. This is all gonna fall on Billy in the end."

"And if he does succeed in killing all of us, he'll have to leave one of us alive at the end," Billy said. "That' doesn't necessarily mean it'll be me in the end. As a matter of fact, I'm the primary suspect, so why the hell would he leave me keep me to the end? If he wants to keep living after we're all dead, I doubt he'll want it to be with the police always chasing him."

"Let's just take it one day at a time," Carlo said. "I don't know how we're going to do it, but I think we're going to have to get Detective Carol on our side."

"Good luck with that," Brad said. "Are we at all worried that he'll eventually just make us all commit suicide?"

"No," Sarah said. "If I've learned anything about my experience with Walter it's that he is all about the theatrics. He wants to make a show of us. Me, especially"

"Not gonna happen," Stanley said, putting his arm around her and squeezing her slightly.

"If he's still bound by the rules of the Portal, I don't think it would be possible for him to do that anyway," Carlo said.

The group filed down Sarah's basement steps and found spots for Will, Brad, and Billy. Billy's arms were handcuffed around a thick drainage pipe, while Brad and Will sat on the floor across the room from him, both attached to metal beams from the floor to the ceiling. They were each far enough away from each other to not cause any problems if Walter decided to pay them a visit.

"This isn't going to be a comfortable night's sleep for any of us," Carlo said, helping Sarah hand the basement occupants pillows and blankets.

"At least we know we'll be safe," Will said.

The group said goodnight and made their way to the second floor of Sarah's house. Sarah, Stanley, and Carlo set up in Sarah's bedroom, with Carlo on the bed and Sarah on the ground, cuffed to a radiator. Stanley sat at a safe distance from her, sitting against the wall with his right hand cuffed to second radiator.

"I have no idea why I have that second radiator," Sarah said as they all settled in. "It's never worked."

"Good thing it's here though," Stanley said, trying to get

comfortable on the floor.

Carlo got up off the bed and sat on the opposite wall from them, using a pillow against the wall to comfort his head.

"What are you doing?" Sarah asked. "Use my bed."

"No, it's okay. You're all handcuffed and sleeping on the floor. It's not fair if I'm asleep on a mattress. Plus, if anything happens, I want to make sure I'm not in too deep of a sleep."

"That's quite good of you," Stanley said. "Let's all try and get some sleep. Who knows what's lying ahead of us."

Even though they were all filled with nervous energy, they each slowly began to fall asleep one by one. They would only be asleep for three hours before Walter David Scott would make another grand appearance.

# CHAPTER TWENTY-ONE

Billy, Brad, and Will laid on blankets on the cold concrete floor of Sarah's basement. Billy was in the middle of a horrible dream, imaging all the different ways he could have killed Daniel. He turned from side to side, trying to find comfort but not finding any. Brad was asleep across the room, snoring loudly as Will sat nearby, staring at him with an annoyed face. He took off his shoe and tossed it at Brad, hitting him in the head with a thud. Brad snorted loudly and woke with an alarmed face.

"*What the hell?*" he squawked.

"You're snoring. *Loudly.*"

"Fuck you, idiot," Brad said, turning to a different position before falling back asleep.

He still snored, but not as loud, allowing Will to close his eyes and fall asleep for the first time since being shackled in the basement. Upstairs, Stanley laid uncomfortable on the carpeted floor, struggling through a restless sleep as Sarah sat nearby. She was breathing softly, her back against the wall with her head cocked sideways onto her shoulder. Carlo had started his evening sitting like Sarah against the wall, but eventually sprawled out on the floor with his limbs spread comically in all directions.

Moonlight poured in through the window above Sarah's bed, casting a ghoulish glow across the room. Sarah's eyes fluttered for a moment before she opened her eyes with a yawn. She glanced at Stanley nearby, sleeping quietly in the moonlight, before a hazy feeling settled over her. Sarah closed her eyes and drew in a long, deep breath, and exhaled as her eyes opened wide. She blinked them open and shut a few times as she waited for her vision to return completely. The handcuffs pulled her down gruffly as she tried to stand. She looked down and grimaced at the sight of the cuffs before sitting back down and staring at Stanley. He was still fast asleep, unaware of the danger that had entered the room.

She looked at the plain, comfortable t-shirt she was wearing. A thought came into her head as she smiled and reached inside the back of her shirt and fumbled with her bra-strap. It took a couple attempts, more than it usually took for her, but she was finally able to remove it and let it fall limp under her shirt. She removed her ponytail and let her thick, brunette hair fall onto her slender shoulders. She tussled it slightly before turning her attention back to Stanley.

"*Stan!*" she whispered. "*Stan, wake up!*"

Stanley opened his eyes and propped himself up against the wall. Sarah was sitting in a similar fashion, staring at him with a scared look on her face.

"What is it?" he asked, looking over to make sure Carlo was still in the room. "Is everything okay?"

"Yes, everything is fine. I'm just really scared is all."

"I know, sweetie. We all are."

"I wish we weren't handcuffed right now. I need you."

"I'm right here. You don't have to worry about anything."

"No, Stan, you don't understand." She maneuvered herself onto her knees, facing him with her hair falling against the sides of her face. "I *need* you."

With her hand that wasn't cuffed to the radiator, Sarah reached under her shirt and lifted it up, revealing her breasts to him. He stared at her in shock as her shirt and bra slid down her left arm and onto her cuffed wrist. He couldn't take his eyes off of her; not because he was aroused or interested, but out of sheer shock and embarrassment over what she was doing.

"I want you to squeeze out of those cuffs and come *fuck* me."

"Carlo, *wake up!*" he yelled, breaking his confusion as he kept his eyes off of Sarah.

"Look at me, Stan!" She smiled and leaned toward him, rubbing her breasts with her free hand. "You know as well as I do that you want me."

"*CARLO!*" he yelled again as Carlo sat up in a panic. He stood to his feet to see Sarah on her knees in front of Stanley.

"Shit," he said, locking eyes with Stanley as Sarah began to laugh loudly.

"The bed's right here, boys. Let's make it a *threesome!*"

"*WALTER!*" Carlo yelled angrily. Sarah stopped laughing and looked at him with an amused look on her face. "We know it's you."

"You *do*, do you? Stan here has a loud fucking mouth, apparently. Spilled the beans on my little game, did you?"

Stanley stared at Sarah as Walter's words came spilling out of her. Sarah's soft, sweet voice was still present, but Walter's cadence had taken complete control.

"How long is this gonna go on for, Walter?" Stanley asked.

"*Fuck you*, Stanley. I was gonna give you an easy death back at the house and you went and fucked up my whole system! *You* were supposed to be the easy one!"

"Did you really think I was going to sympathize with you after you killed Betsy, Daniel, and Kurt?"

"We were friends, Stan."

"*Were* friends. Our friendship ended that night in the library."

"Well you can go to hell with the rest of them then." Sarah's face was twisted with betrayal. "I've got big plans for you, Stan."

"You have to stop, Walter," Stanley said. "This is your chance to atone for what happened in Valley Ridge."

"Atone? You really think that I need atonement? Hell, this is the *sequel*, you old sonofabitch! I'm having the time of my life!"

"Carlo, I need to leave this room," Stanley said, diverting his eyes from her as she began rubbing her chest again. "He's using her against me."

"Stan, I'm sorry, but I can't do that," Carlo said.

"Why not?" asked Stanley while Sarah began to giggle and toss her hair seductively.

"The moment I uncuff he'll just switch to your head and make a run at me."

"He's right, you know," Sarah said. "Carlo might not be on the official list but rest assured, he's gonna die too."

"What's your plan, Walter?" Carlo asked. "You can't kill us all. Logically, you'll have to leave one of us alive."

"Well I guess I just get my second chance then, don't I?"

"Not much of a life, if you ask me," Stanley said, still not looking at her. "Whichever of us you decide to leave alive will most likely be implicated in the murders."

"Hey don't you worry about my plan, *Stanley*. Why don't you just sit back, relax, and enjoy the show!"

Sarah let out another playful giggle as she slid her hand down the front of her shorts. She locked her eyes on Stanley with a sinister smile.

"Look at me, Stanley," she whispered. "I know you want to. Look at me and think about *fucking* me!"

Stanley looked up at Carlo with a weary, sad look on his face. They both knew there was nothing they could do as Walter used Sarah's body to perversely torture Stanley.

"Stan, I'm sorry," Carlo said. "He can't keep doing this forever."

"Fuck you, Carlo! I can go *all night long*!"

She began moaning loudly as Carlo sat back down against the wall, shielding himself with the bed between him and Sarah.

Stanley continued staring at Carlo, closing his eyes from time to time to try and numb the pain of what was happening in front of him.

"Stan, I gotta say, I always wondered what it would feel like to diddle myself as a girl; I'm pleased to report that it has exceeded my expectations."

"Walter, I'm not going to be paying attention to you anymore. I'm going to close my eyes, and even if I can't go to sleep, I'm not going to give you the satisfaction of watching what you're doing."

"You're killing my buzz, Wilkes!"

The room got silent for a moment as Sarah's head cocked sideways as if she were seeing some distant vision. Thinking it may be over, Stanley looked at her, making sure to keep his face locked on hers and nothing else.

"Hmmm," she said with a smile. "That's interesting."

Sarah inhaled as deep as she could and exhaled slowly before her eyes fluttered open. Stanley could tell Walter had left her as her face filled with embarrassed confusion.

"Stanley?" she whispered, covering her breasts with her free hand.

"Honey, your shirt is around your left wrist. Just pull it over yourself."

She pulled her shirt over her torso, feeling numb over not knowing exactly what had just happened. Given the fact that she was topless, she knew what Walter had used her for, and she felt horribly ashamed. She pulled her shirt on and fell to the floor crying as a wave of nausea cascaded over her. She threw up, filling the room with the pungent, sour smelling remains of her pizza. She laid on the floor for a moment and sobbed before pushing herself up into a seated position.

"Sarah honey, I'm so sorry," Stanley said, with tears running thick down his cheeks in the moonlight. "I didn't look, I promise."

"I know," she whimpered through her tears. "Stanley, I'm so

sorry. I'm so sorry he made you see that. We can't be in the same room anymore."

"He's using your relationships against you," Carlo said. "Kurt and Betsy; Daniel and Billy; You and Sarah."

"*HELP!*" screamed Billy from the basement, followed by a maniacal bought of laughter.

Carlo ran past Sarah and Stanley and made his way quickly to the basement. The sounds of Will's laughter echoed through the quiet home as Carlo made his way down the basement steps. Billy was still handcuffed across the room from Will and Brad, staring with wide-eyed fear as Will shook with glee between fits of laughter. Brad was sprawled out on the ground, a pool of blood slowly growing underneath his head as a bloody, rusted garden hoe sat wedged in top of his skull. His fingers twitched as Will continued laughing hysterically.

"Will's a tall boy, Carlo!" Will yelled through a sinister smile. "All I had to do was stretch out and use my foot to grab that bad boy. Looks like you should have measured better!"

Carlo looked under the stairs and found a collection of lawn tools. Will grabbed the hoe and pulled it out of Brad's skull, making a squishing sound as it pulled away. He threw it across the room, hitting Billy and leaving streaks of Brad's blood on his shirt.

"*BULLS-EYE!*" Will screamed, wailing with laughter as Billy began to sob.

*I was right. Something is for sure not adding up in regards to this Exodus Portal case. In the span of just three days, four deaths, all related to the first run of the Exodus Portal.*

**Nish Patel**

**Kurt Saunders**

**Betsy Saunders**

**Daniel Riesman**

*Billy Shaw is the main suspect, and as clear-cut as the case seems, it doesn't add up; it just doesn't feel right. Sure, the two joggers caught Billy standing over Dan's body, but what is his motive? By all accounts, Dan and Billy were good people. They'd been in a relationship for two years with no criminal charges against either of them.*

*What reason would Billy have to kill Daniel? He didn't just kill him...he gutted him. Dan's torso was covered in stab wounds and his abdomen was sliced clean open. It makes NO sense. On top of that, we have video evidence of Kurt Saunders sneaking into that alley beside the place Dan and Billy were eating. We have no logical reason as to why he was there.*

*I'm at a loss. I feel like I'm trying to piece together a puzzle but all the pieces are from different sets. I had hoped to get more information by talking with Sarah Prince, and when I went over to her house, the rest of the Exodus Eight were there...that's not what the media is calling them or anything but dammit I like the sound of it. I can tell they're all scared about what's going on. It's pretty clear whoever is doing this is targeting the eight of them. Grouped together, they'd easily be able to take on whoever came for them, but there was a hopelessness in their eyes, like they all felt their days were numbered. They're not just scared—they're terrified. They know more than they are letting on. I'm gonna go over again tomorrow morning and try and get some more information from them. Who knows what the hell I'm gonna walk into.*

*I have to say, seeing that Will Caldwell was a breath of fresh air. I might have to bring him in for further questioning...*

# CHAPTER TWENTY-TWO

The sun rose over Valley Ridge as the group sat in Sarah's basement with Brad's body sheathed in a white sheet. Sarah sat on her couch with her arms around Will as he stared at the sheeted silhouette of his dead brother.

"This is all my fault," Carlo said, closing his eyes and squeezing the bridge of his nose.

"I killed him, not you," Will said with a defeated voice.

"It's neither of your faults," Stanley said. "Walter almost broke Will's wrist stretching to get that garden hoe. Carlo, you couldn't have ever seen that coming."

"Doesn't feel that way," Will said, sitting up and rubbing his wrist. It was bruised, with deep scratches from struggling fiercely against the metal cuffs.

"Will, were you awake when Walter took over?" Carlo asked.

"Yeah, I was. I'd been in an out of sleep throughout the night because of Brad's snoring. When Walter took over, I was awake."

Carlo ran his hand through his hair with a concerned look on his face.

"Carlo what is it?" Sarah asked.

"Stan, I don't know if you heard it or not, but Walter revealed something last night. Right before he left Sarah's body, he said *'that's interesting.'* It wasn't but a couple minutes later when Billy started screaming."

"Wait, Walter had Sarah last night?" Will asked, looking to his side at her.

"Yes, but honestly I'd rather not talk about it."

"What do you think it means?" Stanley asked.

"I think he can see through all of your eyes without taking control of your bodies. I think he left Sarah in limbo for a moment to look through Will's eyes. That's when he saw the pile of garden tools within reach."

"My last thought was seeing the tools," Will said. "I remember thinking they were too close and that's about when I blacked out."

"He's one foot ahead of us at every turn," Billy said. "How the hell are we supposed to survive this?"

"I'll come up with something," Carlo said.

"Yeah? When?" quipped Billy. "Betsy and Kurt are dead! Daniel and Brad are dead! *He can see every fucking thing we are doing!"*

"Billy, shut the hell up," Stanley said. "It's not Carlo's fault."

"Isn't it though? If it wasn't for that fucking Portal bullshit, Daniel would still be alive, and Walter would be rotting in hell! I fucking *told* Daniel this was bad news! I told him and he didn't listen."

"Billy, you're right, okay?" Carlo said. "I knew something was off with the Portal, but I never imagined it would lead to this."

"How could you?" Will asked. "This is some science fiction bullshit that nobody could have predicted. It's not your fault."

"We can't do this alone, Carlo," Sarah said. "We need to tell Detective Carol."

"We tell her and we lose the little bit of control we have in this situation," Carlo said.

"What do you suppose we do when she finds Brad or another one of us? Are you gonna be the one to hide the bodies?"

"Sarah, I don't know," Carlo said. "I don't know what to do. I'm not into all this paranormal shit. I have no clue what to do right now, but I'm trying my hardest."

"I think Sarah's right," Stanley said. "Hiding the bodies will make us look like we've done something wrong, so it's just a matter of time before Detective Carol figures out that one of us is the killer."

"They're going to think you are covering up for me," Billy said. "That is exactly what they will think if we come forward with this. They'd arrest me on the spot and probably the rest of you for aiding and abetting."

"That's true," Stanley said. "Still, I don't see what we are supposed to do with Brad's body."

"Can we just call him Brad, please?" Will asked, still staring at his brother.

"Of course," Stanley said. "I'm sorry, Will."

"Look, if anyone can come up with a clear, concise way to convince Detective Carol about what's going on, let me know. Until then, I think we just keep this all to ourselves."

The sound of someone banging on the front door filled the house. Stanley went and discreetly looked through a curtained window to find Detective Carol standing at Sarah's front door.

"Speak of the devil," he said, slowly closing the edge of the curtain.

"Ignore her," Will said.

"We can't," Sarah said. "She was just here yesterday. She knows we're all here."

"Sarah, come with me," Carlo said. "Everyone else, stay quiet."

"What do we say to her?" Sarah asked as they went up the stairs. "We can't let her in here, it's too risky."

"I know," Carlo said. "But if she wants to come in there isn't anything we can do. Our cars are outside, so she knows we're all here. We have some time before Brad's body starts to smell, so we don't have to worry about her picking up on that. Unless she talks to you directly, let me do the talking."

Carlo opened the door with a smile as the detective returned one to him.

"Good morning," she said, shaking Sarah and Carlo's hands through the doorway. "How was your sleepover."

"Fun," Sarah said with a smile.

"Everything okay, Ms. Prince?" Detective Carol asked, noticing Sarah's red, heavy eyes.

"Yeah, I'm okay. It's just not easy, seeing all this happen again."

"We're all kind of in shock over it all," Carlo said.

"Well, that's why I'm here. We want to get to the bottom of this and end it quicker than last time. Would you mind if I came inside and had a few words with all of you?"

"Of course," Carlo said, stepping aside and letting the detective in. "The others are in the basement. I'll gather them up for you."

"*HELP!*" Billy yelled from the basement as Sarah and Carlo shot each other a nervous glance. "*PLEASE, DETECTIVE, HELP ME!*"

"That's Billy Shaw," she said, removing her gun from her holster. "*What's going on here?*"

"*PLEASE, HELP ME!*" Billy yelled, followed by the sound of struggling in the basement.

"Both of you, into the basement *now!*"

"Detective, please, let me explain," Carlo said, making his way down the steps with Sarah in front of him.

Detective Carol stepped onto the floor of the basement, her gun out in front of her as she watched Stanley and Will constrain Billy as he flailed wildly. She glanced quickly at Brad on the ground, still hidden by the white sheet.

"*Please*, detective, they're holding me against my will!" Billy screamed. "Stanley found me last night and they've been torturing me down here all night! They killed Bradley!"

"He's lying, detective," Carlo said, standing with Sarah far away from the struggle. "There's more going on here than meets the eye."

"*I need everyone on their knees, now!*" barked Detective Carol. "*Knees on the ground and hands behind your head. ALL OF YOU!*"

"I'm sorry, detective, but we can't let him go," Stanley said, still struggling with Billy.

"Please, let us explain ourselves," pleaded Carlo.

"Don't make me say it again," the detective said, adjusting her grip on her weapon.

Each of them slowly made their way to their knees, interlocking their fingers behind their heads as they stared at the detective. Carlo and Sarah knelt within a few feet of her as she reached into her pocket and pulled out her cellphone.

"I'm sorry," Carlo said before lunging forward from his knees and knocking her backward onto the stairs.

She hit the wooden steps hard, dropping her cellphone as Carlo grabbed her gun.

"*Stanley, help me!*" he yelled, pushing himself against the detective as Billy began to cackle wildly.

"Detective, I'm so sorry for this," Stanley said, grabbing her wrist and prying the gun from her hand.

"*Let me go!*" she screamed, thrashing wildly and kicking Carlo in the abdomen.

He fell away from her as Stanley scooped her into a tight bear-hug. Billy continued laughing hysterically through the chaos as Will punched him hard across the face. He fell sideways as Will grabbed his arms and pulled him to one of the metal support beams. He handcuffed him to the pole while Stan worked at subduing the detective. Billy spat a mouthful of bloody saliva into Will's face before falling to the ground, laughing through a wide, bloodied smile. Will wiped his face and got ready to land another punch before Sarah grabbed his wrist.

"You know it's not Billy," she whispered as she handed him a towel to wipe the remaining blood from his face.

"Sit her down, Stan," Carlo said, holding his abdomen and wincing as Stanley maneuvered her toward the couch. Carlo put a pair of cuffs on her and they sat her gently on the couch.

"My superiors know I'm here. If I go missing, this will be the first place they look."

"Missing?" Carlo said. "Detective Carol, we have no interest in hurting you. All we need right now is your attention."

"They've been waiting for you to show up," Billy said. "They've been planning to kill you, but not before Willy over there has his way with you."

"Walter, *stop it*," Will growled.

"He's got a *BIG*, horny crush on you, ya know."

"Why did you call him Walter?" she asked.

"That's why we had to do what we did just now," Carlo said. "There's no easy way to explain this, and it's not going to make any sense, but you need to hear it."

Carlo started talking to Detective Carol as Billy clanged his cuffs against the pole obnoxiously.

# CHAPTER TWENTY-THREE

Detective Carol sat on the couch in Sarah's basement with her hands cuffed uncomfortably behind her back. Carlo, Sarah, and Stanley sat on a couch across from her, silently waiting for her to react to what they'd told her. Will stood against the wall, his eyes moving between the detective and Billy, who remained handcuffed to one of the metal basement support beams.

"It's hard to believe, I know," Sarah said. "I had trouble believing it too until I witnessed it first-hand."

"She doesn't believe us," Will said. "Can't really blame her, really."

"It's a stupid story, that's why," Billy said. "Get me out of here, Detective, *please*! They're gonna kill both of us!"

"I believe you," she said. "Everything in my training tells me not to, but I've had a bad feeling about this case ever since I got called to the scene of Nish's murder."

"*Come on, you believe this shit?*" Billy yelled from the floor.

"I've always been more in tune with spooky stuff," she said. "I hate it, and I can't explain it, but I've always had a keen eye for stuff that sits outside of our reality. Outside of this investigation, I've never met any of you, but you don't seem like the type of people who would chain someone up and torture them, regardless of what they've done."

"They're lying to you!" Billy yelled, continuing to clang his handcuffs.

"And you," she said, turning sideways in her seat to look at him. "I don't need to have met Billy to know that you're *not* him. I read the personality profiles on each of you, and it doesn't take a genius to tell you're not Billy Shaw."

Billy's face turned sour with sadness as he looked at her, then at each of the people around him. Finding no sympathy, he let his sadness fade away as a sinister, devilish grin stretched across his face. He looked Detective Carol square in the eyes, sending an icy chill down her spine.

"You just made the list, you stubborn bitch."

Billy closed his eyes and inhaled deeply, followed by a long exhale before he fell to the ground. It took a second for him to regain his consciousness, but when he did he inspected his handcuffs and looked around the room.

"Me?" he asked. "Again? Why does he keep using me?"

"I know, buddy," Will said, unlocking his cuffs and helping him to his feet. "It'll be okay. We just filled Detective Carol in on everything. Carlo, take her cuffs off for God's sake."

"Oh, sorry," he said, leaning forward to uncuff her but stopping short for a moment. "You believe us, right?"

"Yes, I believe you. I'm not going to call anyone else in on this, and I honestly have no idea how to handle it, but I do believe you." She rubbed her wrists and looked at Stanley. "My gun?"

He awkwardly smiled at her as she stood, happy to be free. After a moment of nervous hesitation, Stanley handed the gun to her, which she quickly holstered.

"I believe you, but like I said, I don't know what to do. I can't very well bring this to the attention of my superiors, and I don't have many colleagues that would touch this with a ten-foot pole."

"You need to be careful around Will," Stanley said.

"Is that so?"

"Yes. I'm sorry, Will, but it has to be said. Billy wasn't lying when he said Will has a crush on you."

"Oh *God*," Will said, running his hands through his hair as he turned around to hide the red on his face. "What is this? Grade school?"

"I'm sorry but she needs to know. Walter has been using the people closest to us to target each other. Kurt killed Betsy. Billy killed Dan."

"I killed Brad," Will said, his shoulders noticeably slumped in sadness.

"So, you think Walter will use Will to come after me?"

"I would imagine so," Sarah said. "Fits what he's done so far."

"And he can hear us and see us at all times, even when he's not inside one of you?"

"Seems that way," Carlo said. "We aren't positive he can hear us, but he can for sure see through our eyes."

"I'll keep that in mind," said the Detective, glancing at Will with a smile.

"What do we do with my brother?" Will asked.

"I don't know. I don't know what to do about any of this. It's just a matter of time before the FBI takes over the case and they're gonna need to pin this on somebody. Billy, I hate to say it but as of right now, it's going to fall on you."

"I know that," Billy said. "I think that we should put Brad someplace where someone will find him, and then I need to go into hiding."

"No," Will said. "I'm not doing that to Brad, and you're not responsible for any of this."

"Will, I don't think we have much of an option," Detective Carol said. "Brad can't stay down here because he's going to start to decompose, quickly. I'm sorry to say it in such gruesome terms, but it's true. We can't just hide his body because someone is eventually going to start asking around for him. Billy, you know what this means, right?"

"Yes."

"What?" Sarah asked.

"It means he's going to be a fugitive. If Walter successfully kills any more of you, it's going to fall on Billy because he's the prime suspect of the current murders."

"I'm okay with this," Billy said. "I don't have much going on anymore without Daniel. I'll take the fall as much as I can."

"This isn't fair at all," Sarah said.

"This is how it has to be," Detective Carol said. "You're all very lucky I got assigned to your case. I'm about as close to Agent Mulder as you'll get around here."

"Thank you for helping us," Sarah said. "Although you're probably in the dark just as much as we are."

"You are right about that. You need to understand that I can only help you so much. If Billy ends up dead and the murders continue, the blame will more than likely shift to one of you. I'll be able to shield you from a lot of the spotlight, but at some point, my superiors are going to want answers."

"We understand," Will said.

"I think that you should drop Brad's body off near where they found Daniel's," Detective Carol said. "It's not a well-traveled area, but it's a place where he'll be found easily. Do it at night and get out of there quickly."

"We can all take my van, that way we stay together," Stanley said, as Detective Carol made her way toward the stairs.

"Good idea. I think you need to stay together as much as possible. Don't let each other out of sight. I'll be stopping by daily to check on all of you."

"Thank you," Stanley said as she made her way up the stairs.

"I'll be right back," Billy said, disappearing up the steps behind her.

Detective Carol spun around with her hand on her holster as Billy reached the top of the steps.

"Wait! No, it's me! It's Billy, not Walter."

"I'm sorry," she said, glaring at him to make sure he was telling the truth. "I would appreciate it if you all started calling me Allison, by the way."

"Okay, Allison. I don't know how this is going to end. I don't know if Carlo is going to find a way to stop Walter, but after he does, I want to take the fall for all this."

"That's very admirable of you, Billy," Allison said. "I don't think there's any way around it at this point. Once this is all done, I'll bring you in myself and make sure you're treated fairly."

"No, Allison. When this is all done, I want you to take me out. I want you to kill me."

"Billy..."

"I was going to propose to Dan the night Walter forced me to kill him and Kurt. I'm not interested in living on the run or in jail. Please, promise me you'll help me make this happen."

"Billy you'll forever be remembered as a murderer. I won't be able to protect your memory if we do this."

"I know that. I'm not concerned about my image or how people remember me. As long as mine and Daniel's family know the truth after the dust settles, I'll be content."

Allison smiled and nodded. She squeezed his shoulder softly before leaving him alone in the kitchen.

# CHAPTER TWENTY-FOUR

Walter stood at the edge of the lake inside the Exodus Portal, his feet only a few inches away from the waterline as he stared across the calm, unmoving water. If anyone had seen him standing there, they would have thought he was deep in thought, but upon closer inspection they would have realized that was the last thing he was doing. His eyes were solid white, twitching wildly as he stood lost in a vision. He was watching through Billy's eyes as he spoke to the detective, wishing against his frustration that he could hear what they were saying. He knew from his time controlling Billy that the detective knew he was the one responsible for the new string of murders, but the lack of total control rotted him to his core.

He clinched his eyes hard once and they returned to their usual light blue color. The image of the detective's smiling face still lingered in his head. "Bitch."

The sand and grass materialized into a large, comfortable throne underneath him as he sat backwards. After the glitch,

Walter had realized two things. Firstly, when he wasn't controlling someone's body, he was forced back inside the Portal. Secondly, he had complete control over anything inside the Portal. The weather, the landscape, the terrain; if it was inside the Portal, it was his to control in any way he wanted. For the first two weeks after the glitch, Walter had laid dormant inside the mind of Kurt Saunders. The night before Nish's murder, Kurt had been sitting at his desk, home alone, working late on one of his books. The headache they'd all shared after the glitch intensified for a moment until Walter's consciousness burst to life inside Kurt's head. He had yelled and toppled out of his chair, not sure what had happened as he laid on the floor. Walter forced himself onto his feet and stumbled through the house until he'd found the bathroom. He'd stood in front of the mirror above the sink, staring back at the image of Kurt Saunders in disbelief.

After he'd slightly come to his senses, Walter had gone straight to Kurt's liquor cabinet and drank himself silly. He'd drank the liquid fast, feeling the warmth quickly grow inside him. Walter had missed the feeling terribly, having not felt it since before Sarah had sent him to death row. As he laid on Kurt's couch, he noticed a window in the back of his mind. It was hazy and just out of reach of his view, but when he squinted his eyes he could tell it was a vision of the Exodus Portal. He focused on the image for a few moments and suddenly he was standing in the Portal at the edge of the trees, his inebriation left behind in the drunken body of Kurt Saunders.

Walter looked in awe at the Portal in front of him, still grasping for any understanding as to what was going on. He slowly backed himself into the trees as he caught sight of Nish across the water, wandering around as if he were searching for something. He had no idea what had happened to him, but one thing he did know was that if Nish or Carlo found him, they could possibly get rid of him. As he watched Nish search the Portal, he became aware of something else inside his mind. Just like he had seen the blurry vision of the Exodus Portal, Walter could see eight mirages in the back of his mind, each resembling a hazy, far-away window. It wasn't something he could tangibly look at or get a good look at, but more like something that he was vaguely aware of in the corner of his mind. Each window was a black, hazy vision, sitting just outside his mind's reach, though one of the images was a little less hazy than the rest. He focused his mind on it, and as Nish got closer to where he was hiding, Walter faded away in a blink and materialized in the comfort of a bed.

"This is fucked up," he'd said in a voice he instantly recognized. Walter threw back the covers and stumbled through the darkness until he found a light switch on the wall. He stood in the middle of the room, rubbing his eyes as he stared into a mirror as the image of Sarah Prince stared back at him. He stepped closer to the mirror, touching his face and gazing back at his new reflection. "I'm gonna have so much fun with this."

Within a day of finding out his new abilities, Nish Patel was dead. After Nish's death, Carlo stopped monitoring the Portal and spent most of his time with the participants of the glitch. The Exodus Portal had become Walter's personal playground.

Still feeling the sensation of Brad's skull breaking underneath the garden hoe, Walter stood up from his chair as the grass and sand fell into a pile behind him. He stepped to the edge of the water with a smile as his eyes turned once again a milky white.

# CHAPTER TWENTY-FIVE

Night fell over Sarah's house in Valley Ridge as the group stayed tucked away inside, each of them in the basement and handcuffed to the support beams. They'd collectively decided not to travel together to drop Brad's body, as they knew Walter would exploit them being out in the open. Carlo stood at the foot of the steps, having just handcuffed them all before double-checking that there wouldn't be a repeat of the previous night's events.

"I should be back in a couple hours, if that," he said.

"Be careful," Sarah said. "That road isn't always dead. What if someone sees you?"

"I guess Billy's off the hook then."

"Good luck," Will said, watching Carlo struggle to pick up Brad's cold, dead corpse.

"Thank you. I'll need it," he said, disappearing out of into the kitchen with Brad in tow.

"I'm really sorry, Will," Sarah said, watching him sit quietly with tears in his eyes. "I don't even know what to say."

"I'm not too sure what to say, either," he said, wiping a tear way from his eye.

*****

Carlo had pulled his car into the garage earlier in the day in anticipation of having to move Brad's body. He laid Brad on the cold cement and opened the door to the backseat of his Range Rover. He put on a baseball cap and gloves before spreading a blue, plastic tarp over the backseat and floor. He placed his hands under Brad's arms and pulled as hard as he could to get him into the back of the Rover. After five minutes, he was covered in a cold sweat, but Brad was secure in the seat.

"I'm sorry, buddy," he said as he slid into the driver's seat and hit the button to open the garage door. He felt nervous, fearing that anything could happen while he was gone, but also confident that they were each secure in the basement. It was a twenty-minute drive to where Allison had told him to drop Brad's body, but getting there would feel like an eternity.

*****

"What were you talking to her about when she was leaving?" Stanley asked Billy as Carlo made his way towards the field where he would drop Brad.

"Nothing, really. I'm just worried that some other cop will find me here but she says she'll take care of it. She still wants me staying here, though. Oh, and she wants us to call her Allison."

"I imagine being called detective feels weird when you're orchestrating the dumping of a body," Sarah said, looking at her watch. "He should be at the spot soon. I hope it's going okay."

"Oh, I'm sure it's going fine, you fucking cow," Stanley said, staring back at her with a sinister grin on his face. The group gazed back at him in shock. "So you have that stinky bitch detective on your side now. Big fucking deal. Do you think that's going to matter? You've just added another body to the pile."

"We've got a pretty good system going here," Will said. "You can't do much damage chained to that post."

"It's too bad, Willy Boy, that you can't remember killing your brother."

"Shut up," Will said turning his back to Stanley.

"I can still feel that rusty hoe coming to a stop in his skull. He twitched a few times while he bled out. Flopped—like a fish!"

"*SHUT THE FUCK UP!*" Will screamed as fresh tears filled his eyes.

"Oh stop it. Don't be so dramatic."

"Everyone just ignore him, please," Sarah said, turning away from him.

"Hey Sarah," Stanley said, unzipping his pants. "Wanna see Stan's cock? Seems only fair, given the little show we gave him last night!"

"Sarah, don't look at him," Billy said, turning away as Stanley pulled out his penis and waved it around toward Sarah.

"How about you, Billy-boy? With Dan in the ground, you're gonna need a new man to lay with."

"You're disgusting," Billy said as Stanley waved his penis at him.

They each turned their back toward him as he laughed as loud as he possibly could. They listened intently as the room got silent, hoping for any sign that Walter had left them alone. That hope faded away as Stanley began giggling again, mixed with the sound of struggling and grunting. Sarah pictured him sitting on his knees behind her, stroking his penis in the hope that she'd turn and look at him. As she squeezed her eyes tight to erase the image from her head, a series of snapping sounds filled the room, followed by more grunting and giggling.

"*Oh shit!*" Billy yelled.

Everyone turned to look at Stanley as he methodically began to pull his left hand through one of the metal cuffs. His fingers and wrist were mangled and bloody as he worked to pull his hand through the cuff.

"Sorry Stan," he said with a laugh. "This is gonna hurt like a bitch when you wake up."

Sarah reached into her jacket pocket with wide eyes and pulled out a set of four keys, each with their names scrawled across a small white tab. Sarah took hers and threw Billy and Will their keys.

"*How the hell did you get these?*" asked Will as he feverishly tried to unlock his cuffs.

"Carlo slipped them into my pocket when he handcuffed me," she said, slipping her key into the cuffs as Stanley finally managed to pull his bloodied, mangled hand free.

"*Oh did he now?*" Stanley yelled, smacking Sarah across the face with his broken hand. She fell backward with her face smeared with Stanley's blood.

Her key fell to the floor and bounced under the couch behind them as Stanley stood above her. He was on top of her in a flash, his good hand around her throat as her eyes bulged and began to burn.

"I've been waiting for this for some time," he said with a smile, squeezing her throat harder as his smile widened.

His hand was torn away from her as Billy tackled him. They flew to the ground beside her in a heap as she gasped angrily for breath. Will was still fumbling with his handcuffs as Billy pinned Stanley against the floor. As Sarah finally regained her breath in a loud, painful wheeze, Stanley let out a thunderous yell. Billy's eyes bulged in fear as he looked down at Stanley's face, twisted with pain and confusion.

"*NO! BILLY, WHAT DID I DO? SARAH? WHERE'S SARAH?*"

"I'm fine, Stanley, I'm fine," she whispered through her choked, agitated throat. "Billy, where is Will?"

"Fuck," Billy said, releasing Stanley and realizing that Will was missing. "What do we do?"

"Go after him, Billy! He can't get away," Stanley yelled,

wincing in pain as he maneuvered himself into a sitting position. "He pulled my hand through that damn cuff, didn't he?"

"He did," Sarah said as Billy disappeared up the steps. "Are you okay?"

"It hurts but I'll be okay. I think my ankle is broken." Stanley reached down and took off his shoe to reveal a puffy, swollen ankle. "What the hell happened while I was out?"

"We have a problem!" Billy said, standing at the top of the stairs. "*A BIG FUCKING PROBLEM!*"

Sarah and Stanley looked upstairs as the sound of crackling fire filled the basement. The doorway was illuminated with a warm, orange glow as the sound of Will's giggling mixed with the crackle of the fire.

"Billy, go after him!" Sarah yelled, helping Stanley to his feet. "Come on, old-timer. Let's get out of here."

The two of them made their way up the stairs as the fire grew rapidly on the main floor. Sarah paused at the top of the steps, taken aback by the sight of her kitchen being overtaken by flames.

"Sarah, I'm so sorry," Stanley said as she helped him into the kitchen. In a moment so fast that he hardly had time to react, Sarah grabbed a knife from a block on her countertop and plunged it into Stanley's gut.

"Don't mention it, *friend*," she yelled, her eyes filled with horrifying glee.

Stanley keeled over as the pain seared in his midsection. He looked up at her smiling, sinister face, and even though he knew it was not her, he couldn't help but feel a sad sense of betrayal. Sarah planted her foot into Stanley's chest and sent him flying down the stairs, tumbling a few times on the steps before landing on the concrete floor.

"She can see what's happening, Stan," Sarah yelled. "I wanted her to see you die, and more importantly, I wanted her to know *she* ended your life."

Stanley could feel his life begin to slip away as blood continued to pour from his stomach. He stared up at Sarah with tears in his eyes, knowing she'd be devastated when Walter left her.

"*Sarah*," he yelled, sending waves of pain through his body with each labored word. "*Honey, I love you! This isn't your...*"

Sarah slammed the door and disappeared into the flames.

\*\*\*\*\*

Carlo turned off his headlights as he pulled onto the road where the police had found Daniel's body. The moon was bright, giving just enough light to illuminate the road and make it easy for him to navigate with his headlights off. He pulled the car over and looked up and down the long, winding road, which was empty and dark in both directions. He got out of his car and opened the back door, sending a sheet of moonlight over Brad's silhouette. Carlo pulled him out of the back seat, making sure not to let him fall to the ground and cause further damage to his already broken body. He moved slowly, his arms underneath Brad's with his feet dragging on the cold grass.

Carlo laid him down on the ground and quickly made his way back to his car in a hurry, almost expecting Walter to possess Brad's dead body and murder him in the darkness. He bunched the sheet together with the tarp in a large ball and threw it in the back of the Range Rover, knowing he'd have to figure out how to dispose of it another time.

"I'll figure this out for you, buddy," he said, turning the car around and returning the way he'd come.

His eyes watered multiple times on the way back to Sarah's house; he could still feel the weight of Brad in his arms and the sound his body had made when it crashed into the grass. He racked his brain, trying to come up with a way to stop Walter. Like a spark of light in the dark, an idea started to grow in his mind, but it was quickly extinguished when he pulled onto Sarah's street. He'd seen the light from the flames even before turning down her street. Will and Sarah were standing on her front sidewalk, the entire house engulfed in a fury of bright flames.

"*What the hell happened?*" Carlo yelled.

Sarah was wailing wildly while Will held her in his arms.

"Where's Stan and Billy?"

"Billy took off when the flames got out of control," Will said. "He wasn't under Walter's control, but he knew the police would be here soon. Stanley's in the basement."

Allison pulled up shortly before the police and fire engines. Will explained to her and Carlo what had happened as the flames illuminated them with a soft, ominous glow.

"This is getting out of hand," Allison said.

"Can I speak to you for a moment?" Carlo asked Allison, stepping away from Will and Sarah.

"What is it?"

"I think I have an idea how to stop this mess but the three of them cannot know."

"Tell me."

"Do you have some place we can bring these two? Some place secret?"

She thought for a moment as she watched the firefighters start to work on Sarah's home.

"I do. What's the plan?"

# CHAPTER TWENTY-SIX

Sarah sat in the back row of Allison's SUV, her handcuffs secured through the headrest of the seat in front of her. Carlo followed close behind in his Range Rover with Will handcuffed in a similar fashion behind him. The two vehicles drove down a bumpy dirt road in a patch of thick, pitch-black woods. Carlo had to squint as Allison's brake lights illuminated when she came to a stop. She and Carlo got out of the drivers' seats and unlocked their prisoners before making their way to the porch of an old, darkened cabin.

"This is my family's cabin," Allison said. "We'll be safe here for a while."

She led them inside and turned on the lights. The musty smell of the seldom-used cabin surrounded them as she and Carlo guided Will and Sarah to separate parts of the room. Carlo secured Will to a sturdy wood stove while Sarah sat across the room, cuffed to a wooden support beam.

"I think I have a plan on how to get us out of this mess," Carlo said. "I can't do anything until I find Billy though. Hang in there, I'll be back as soon as I can."

Carlo disappeared into the woods in his Range Rover as Sarah's eyes filled with tears while thinking about Stanley.

"I'm so sorry, Sarah…" Allison said.

"I can't stop seeing it. I can still feel the knife in my hands."

"I didn't realize he could do that."

"None of us did," Will said. "She's the first one to remember anything while under Walter's spell."

"It's just not fair," Sarah said, leaning her head backward to stretch her neck. "I can't do this much longer."

Allison took a moment to look outside the front windows, her nerves so rattled that she was half expecting to see Walter himself standing outside. "Are the two of you comfortable enough?"

"Given that we're hooked up like a couple of convicts waiting for execution, yeah, I'd say we're comfortable enough," Will said.

"I'm sorry it has to be like this but you understand."

"It's okay," Will said. "It is what it is. Hopefully Carlo will have it all figured out soon."

"You really think Carlo's going to be able to stop me?" Sarah asked, smiling the sinister smile they'd all grown to hate.

"I hate this," Will said.

"Look, he's smart, but this is beyond him. What's he going to do? Shoot me? Maybe you should all look into an exorcist."

"He'll think of something," Will said, exchanging an exhausted look with Allison.

"Walter, what's your plan?"

"You're not the first person to ask me that, sweetie. It's almost over though; you won't have to worry about it much longer."

"You've got no power over us, Walter," Will said. "Look at us; we're chained up, and if you try anything, Allison is right there."

"You'll make a mistake eventually. You or Billy or Sarah; it's bound to happen. How do you think I killed the rest of you? It's all just a waiting game."

"Don't talk to him, Will. Honestly, it's pointless."

"Your life is pointless, you nosey bitch. I can't wait to take it from you."

"Good luck," she said, wondering if Carlo was having any luck finding Billy as she pulled out her cellphone.

\*\*\*\*\*

Carlo sat in the passenger side of his Range Rover as his secretary Stephanie maneuvered the vehicle onto Sarah's street. She'd been texting him nonstop since Nish's murder, and as he drove away from Allison's cabin, he broke down and called her. He'd explained everything to her; she was completely silent at first, not knowing what to say, but also not doubting what he said in the least. Carlo was, and always had been, the type to believe in more logical solutions. As crazy as the story was, she knew that if he believed it, then it must be true.

"That poor girl," Stephanie said as they pulled up in front of Sarah's burned down home.

"I'm sorry I had to drag you into all this, but Detective Carol needed to watch Sarah and Will while I looked for Billy. Quite honestly, I needed a familiar face."

"Mr. Macasaet, it's honestly no problem. I'm happy to help. Where are Sarah and Will now?"

"Steph, you can call me Carlo. I think we've known each other long enough."

"Okay then; Carlo it is."

"Detective Carol has them in a cabin her family owns. They're both chained up pretty well, so even if Walter tries something, it won't really matter. Allison's there to stop anything from happening."

Stephanie drove slowly away from the house, looking for anything that would point them to where Billy was hiding.

"Stop here," Carlo said as she drove near Stanley's house. His cellphone pinged in his pocket...

***Walter is here at the cabin. He's talking through Sarah right***

*now. Hopefully you can find Billy while he's here.*

Carlo and Stephanie stepped out of the Range Rover and made their way up the path to Stanley's house. "Allison says that Walter is using Sarah at the cabin. At least we know that Billy isn't possessed right now."

"Good. I'm happy to help, but I'd rather avoid seeing any of you possessed like that."

"I don't blame you," he said.

Stanley's door was closed but they could tell it had been forced open recently. Carlo pushed it open with ease, revealing splintered wood on the inside where someone had kicked it open. They stepped inside, keeping the lights off as to not bring attention to the house. They both felt uneasy, wandering through the dark house, hoping that Billy wouldn't lunge at them from the darkness.

"I have a feeling Billy could still be here," Carlo said, opening the door to Stanley's basement and making his way down the steps with the flashlight on his cellphone.

*****

"Billy's all blacked out," Sarah said after a couple moments of silence. "Weird. I wonder if he's dead."

"He's not dead," Will said, exhausted of hearing Walter talk through Sarah.

"Yeah, you're probably right, William. He's still open to me, but it's all black right now. When I lose track of someone and can't find their view, it usually means they're dead. Like seriously, right now, I'm trying to see through Brad, and I'm getting *nothing*."

"Will, ignore him," Allison said. "He wants you to react right now."

"She's right, Will. Come on—*react!*"

"Walter, I'm curious," Allison said. "Where do you go when you're not inside one of the eight?"

"I'm honestly surprised it took someone this long to ask. What's your guess, honey?"

"How would I know? This is new to all of us. My guess, though, is that you're always inside one of them but just dormant until you're ready to take over."

"Well that's a good enough answer; let's go with that."

"Is it the right answer?"

"Even if it were, do you really think I'd tell you? I've got a good thing going here, sweet-cheeks. Seems to me I've got three very healthy bodies to choose from."

"What the hell's that supposed to mean?" Will asked.

"He means that he intends to completely possess one of you once the other two are dead."

"Bingo!" Sarah yelled, pointing at Allison with her cuffed hands. "I don't think I have much of a choice, really. Stands to reason that I'd end up living in one of you permanently, once the rest of you are all dead; but who should I pick? I mean, I'm conflicted, especially when it comes to sweet little Sarah. On one hand, she's the eighteenth—the one that got away. Killing her would be a sweet, *sweet* feeling. On the other hand though, having her carry on my murderin' ways...well that brings a tear to my eye."

"Walter, whoever survives is going to be the primary suspect," Allison said. "How the hell do you think you're going to live that way?"

"Well I guess that settles it then, doesn't it?" Sarah said. "Nobody will suspect sweet, innocent Sarah Prince; not for a second."

"Walter, you're not going to get away with this," Allison said. "I'm the lead investigator in this case, and I'll be damned if you're going to get away with any of this."

"You're a world class piece of shit, you know that right?" Sarah said. "And for the record, you can't do anything if you're dead."

"Like I said before; good luck."

\* \* \*

*****

*"Billy?"* whispered Carlo as he and Stephanie reached the cold floor of Stanley's basement. *"It's me, Carlo."*

"Over here," Billy whispered, his voice hoarse and tired.

Carlo flashed his light across the empty, unfinished basement to find Billy handcuffed to an old radiator. He had a necktie tied across his eyes as he directed his face in their direction.

"How'd you find me?"

"I had a good feeling you'd stay close by."

"I threw the cuff key across the room. It's against the wall."

"You blindfolded yourself?" Carlo asked.

"I was thinking that Walter's never taken any of us over in our sleep so maybe he needs to be able to see through our eyes before he jumps in. I know I blacked out one point so I'm assuming he was inside me but he must have left after he realized I was handcuffed again."

"How'd you find handcuffs?" asked Stephanie as she used the key to release Billy.

"Stanley was a cop," Carlo said.

*"Was?"* asked Billy.

"Stanley didn't make it out of Sarah's basement," Carlo said. "Walter made sure of that."

"Fuck," Billy said, standing up and putting his hands back out for Carlo to cuff him again.

"Are you sure?"

"Neither of you are safe with me around. I need to be cuffed."

Carlo put the cuffs back on Billy's already red, agitated wrists. He and Stephanie lead him up the dark stairs. They quietly made their way to the front door as Carlo scanned the street from the front window, looking up and down the road to make sure nobody would be watching them.

"Okay, let's go."

The three of them hurriedly made their way across Stanley's lawn to where Stephanie had parked the car. Carlo opened the door and helped Billy inside before repositioning his handcuffs around through the passenger seat headrest. He opened the door for Stephanie as she put her arms around his waist and kissed him. His eyes stayed open for a moment of shock as she kept her lips pressed against his before he closed them and kissed her back.

"I'm sorry," she said, pulling away and sliding into the passenger seat.

Carlo closed the door for her, but not before exchanging a smile with her.

"You kissed, didn't you?" Billy asked as Carlo slid into the driver's seat.

"Mind your business, Billy," Carlo said as Stephanie chuckled softly.

"Where to now?" Stephanie asked.

"For everyone's safety I think it's best I don't' say. We have a long night ahead. Walter has no clue you're involved, so I'm gonna drop you off before he finds out."

"I'm glad I could help," she said. "I am relieved that my part is done, though."

They drove to Stephanie's apartment in silence as the dark world passed rapidly outside. Carlo pulled up in front of her apartment building and unbuckled his seatbelt but stopped when her hand found his wrist.

"No. You can't leave him alone. I'll be fine."

She leaned over and kissed him on the cheek before sliding out of the vehicle and bounding up to the steps to her building.

"Good luck," she mouthed to him before disappearing inside.

# CHAPTER TWENTY-SEVEN

Sarah was asleep while Will blankly looked out the darkened window. Allison's phone vibrated in her pocket, breaking her away from a daydream. She pulled it out and read the message alert without opening her phone.

*Found Billy. He's safe. Blindfold Sarah and Will and don't tell them anything. I'll be there soon.*

Allison slid her phone back into her pocket and paced for a moment. Will watched her with tired, exhausted eyes as she disappeared into the small kitchen. She came back quickly with a kitchen towel in both hands, making eye contact with Will as she made her way toward him.

"What are those for?" he asked.

"I'm sorry, Will, but I have to do this."

She tied the towel around his eyes tightly, making sure it was as secure as possible.

"Is that too tight?"

"No, not at all."

She reached down and put her hand in his. She squeezed them softly as he returned the pressure, feeling the softness of her skin on his.

"I'm scared," he whispered, in a way the sounded as if he were ashamed to admit it.

"I know. I am too."

Allison released his hand and gently woke Sarah. She opened her tired, red eyes and looked up at her as she immediately began to tear up again.

"I know this is hard. I have to do this, though."

Sarah looked at Will with the towel wrapped around his eyes as Allison began to wrap the towel around her eyes.

"That okay?" she asked, pulling strands of Sarah's hair from under the towel.

"Yeah, it's fine. Where's Carlo? Did he find Billy?"

"Don't answer her," Will said.

Allison stared at Sarah's now blindfolded eyes as she stared up at her, awaiting an answer. After a moment of silence, Sarah turned her gaze towards Will.

"Good call, Detective Fuck-Shit." Sarah turned her gaze back to Allison. "What can I say, he's a smart boy. He's got me pegged. So what's the answer, sweet-cheeks? Did Carlo find him?"

"How'd you know?" Allison asked Will as Sarah continued to stare and smile at her.

"I didn't. He's getting better at mimicking us."

"You're both no fun," Sarah said before letting her head fall forward in defeat.

"I can't do this anymore!" Sarah yelled, her voice broken with sadness.

"It's getting easier for him," Will said. "There used to be a loud inhale before he took over someone. He just jumped right into her right then."

A set of headlights illuminated the windows as Carlo's Range Rover parked outside. He walked inside and was greeted by Allison with her index finger raised above her lips.

"The less they know, the better," she said.

Allison released Will from his restraints and helped him out of the chair before handcuffing his hands behinds his back. Both she and Carlo maneuvered Will into the back seat of Carlo's Range Rover next to Billy.

"I'll get Sarah," Allison said, leaving Will with Carlo and going back into the cabin.

"Where are we going?" Will asked.

"You know I can't tell you."

"I know. Can't blame me for being curious."

"I have an idea on how to stop this. Just hang in there, okay?"

"Whatever you're planning, I hope it works," Allison said, shutting the door of her car with Sarah secured in the back. "Where are we going?"

"Just follow me. You'll see soon enough."

# CHAPTER TWENTY-EIGHT

Sarah was jolted awake in the back of the Allison's car as it came to a stop. She wiggled uncomfortably, her arms tingling with pain from being cuffed behind her back.

"Where are we?" she asked.

"I shouldn't say just yet," Allison said, staring at the V.R. Exodus building in front of her. She slid out of the driver's seat, and by the time she'd gotten to Sarah's door, Walter had taken over.

"Where the fuck are you bringing me?" Sarah screamed as Allison stood outside her door. "I can't fucking see a thing!"

"Shut up, Walter," Allison said as she opened her door.

"He was in Will pretty much the whole way here, singing gross limericks and trying to bite Billy," Carlo said, standing nearby with both Will and Billy cuffed in front of him.

"*There once was a man from Nantucket!*" yelled Sarah as Allison pulled her from the back of the car. "I should try to take a bite out of you, sugar-tits!"

"Don't listen to her," Carlo said. "Let's just get inside."

Sarah continued to fight backward against Allison as they made their way into the foyer of the Exodus building. Carlo grabbed a tablet from the front desk and tapped on it a few times as the hidden door opened. The security lights illuminated the hallway leading to the chamber, which was also lit by the harsh security lighting.

"Whatever we're doing, I hope it works," Billy said.

"*Whatever we're doing, I hope it works,*" scathed Sarah, mocking Billy's words in a whiny voice as Carlo and Allison maneuvered them into the Exodus Chamber. Sarah picked up on the change in her voice as it echoed inside the Chamber.

"I gotta hand it to you; Nish probably wouldn't have thought about this," Sarah said with a smile as she realized where they were. "You always were the brains of this operation, weren't you?"

"Shut up," Carlo said.

"You're a real piece of shit, Carlo. Whatever plan you've cooked up, it's not gonna work. Once your little experiment is done, I'm gonna carve those brains right out of your fucking skull! Maybe I'll have Sarah here take a bite, let her feel you swim around in her stomach a bit."

"I should have guessed," Will said as Carlo slipped off his and Billy's blindfolds.

"This has got to stop!" Sarah said, suddenly free from Walter. "Why are we here?"

"You're a stupid fucking twat if you can't figure out why we're here," Wills said, pushing away from Carlo and knocking him to the ground.

Will made his way toward Sarah with a furious, angry look on his face as Carlo flew to his feet and planted his fist across Will's face. Will fell sideways and hit the ground, dazed from the hit and free of Walter.

"Holy shit, Carlo!" Allison yelled. "I didn't know you had it in you!"

"Neither did I," he said, shaking his hand in the air. "Let's get them into the pods before he comes back."

"He's already back!" Billy yelled. He lunged at Carlo and the two of them fell backward to the ground. Billy landed a punch across Carlo's face before Allison took out her firearm and pistol-whipped Billy across the face. He fell to the side and before he could regain his stature, Allison and Carlo had forced him into a pod and cuffed him to side.

As Billy stood dazed in his pod, Will voluntarily placed himself into his and cuffed himself as Carlo quickly helped Sarah into her own pod.

"He's coming back," Allison said, watching Billy begin to open his eyes.

"It's me. He's gone."

"He's pissed off," Allison said. "You must be onto something, Carlo. What's the plan?"

"I'm curious if you going back into the Portal will sever your connection with him. Judging from his reaction, I think it may."

"So, what do we need to do?" Sarah asked.

"I don't know. I really have no idea what will happen once you're in there. First thing, you need to connect with each other. You're going to wake up at different points on the map so find each other quickly. Walter's going to know you're coming, so he's going to be ready."

"But he can't hurt us in there," Will said. "That hasn't changed, right?"

"No, you shouldn't feel a thing, however, Walter's gonna do everything he can to keep you from getting out. I think that the three of you need to find the exit point as soon as possible and try and remove yourself. If you can all get out, maybe he'll be trapped in there."

"Where is he right now?" Sarah asked. "Seriously, as soon as we were cuffed to the pods he stopped channeling through us."

"He knows you're coming," Carlo said. "He's probably preparing."

The orb turned blue as Carlo began tapping on his tablet. A few more taps on the screen and the electrodes crawled forward and attached themselves to Sarah, Billy, and Will.

"I don't know if I'm ready for this," Sarah said.

"None of us are," Will said, locking eyes with a concerned Allison.

"You'll do fine," she said with a nervous smile. "Just get in and get out."

"Here we go," Carlo said.

With a few more taps on his screen, the three of them fell asleep inside their pods.

*****

Sarah woke up in excruciating pain. The smell of burning wood and smoke filled her nose as she rolled out of her bed onto the floor. She couldn't see yet, but she knew from the searing pain that parts of her were on fire. She rolled on the ground, extinguishing the flames on her aching body. Her blurry, burning eyes were filled with tears; she blinked them hard through the pain as she tried to regain her eyesight. A bookshelf fell behind her as she pushed herself onto her feet and stumbled out of the cabin, falling to the ground as she made her way through the open doorway. Her eyesight returned to her as she stood and looked in horror at the entirety of the Portal.

The once beautiful blanket of green trees had been replaced with a sea of orange, which crackled and burned as she watched in horror. The island that housed the exit from the Portal was completely on fire, as well as the walkways leading there from the shore. The water around the island was boiling, sending pops of water into the air as each bubble exploded on the surface. Far down the shore, she watched as a figure made its way out of the woods; she could tell from its stature that it was Will. He moved sporadically, shaking in pain as flames licked up and down his body.

"*Will!*" she screamed, running toward him while dodging patches of flames on the ground.

She knelt down to help him to his feet but stopped at the sight of him; his normally tanned, clean skin had been charred to a black crisp. Wisps of smoke rose from his body as the fire from the woods behind her began encroaching toward her. She scanned the waterfront, looking for any sign of Billy before she took off down one of the floating pathways to the small, fire-soaked island. The water boiled and popped at her legs as she ran. She tried to avoid the flames on the walkway but they painfully bit at her legs as she moved.

She leaped from the flaming walkway and landed on the hot sand of the island. It looked the same as it did when she'd originally entered the Portal, except for a large wooden gazebo that stood overtop the exit orb. She could barely see the red glow of the orb as flames crackled fiercely around it. The sounds of screaming entered her ears as she turned around to see Billy fall while running on one of the walkways. He fell to the burning surface and instinctively rolled sideways, landing in the boiling hot water as the flames continued to lick at him as he tried to cling to the side of the walkway. He screamed wildly, not able to find any relief as the water boiled his skin and the wooden walkway charred whatever flesh was near it. It didn't take long before his cries of pain were extinguished as he slipped below the bubbling water.

Sarah turned with a tear in her eye and ran fast toward the gazebo. The flames seemed to intensify as she approached, creating an inferno that grew in size with each step she took. In one fast movement, she covered her face with her forearms and leaped through the wall of fire. She made it halfway through the wall of flames before she was flung backward onto the ground.

"You didn't think I'd make it that easy, did you?" Walter said, stepping forward through the flames.

He stood above her, his trademark, sinister grin etched across his face as he released a sing wink of his eye. The flames nipped at him and charred his clothing, but he seemed to be untouched by the heat. Sarah scrambled to her feet and ran, the smell of burning hair and flesh filling her nose as she left the burning gazebo behind. Walter jumped into the air, leaving a trail of smoke and fire in the air behind him. He looked down on her as he descended to the ground, his arms open wide and his teeth sharpened like a hungry vampire. He landed just behind, rattling the entire walkway as she struggled to keep her balance.

"The smell of your burned flesh is making me horny!" Walter seethed.

Smoke and flames billowed off of him as he gave chase, laughing wildly before placing his fiery hands on her shoulders. Sarah released a wild, unchained squeal as his fingers dug deep into her skin. The flames pouring off of him burned at her skin as he lifted her above his head with both hands.

"I hope you can swim, Ms. Prince, 'cause there's no lifeguards here!"

Walter threw Sarah high into the air. She screamed as she fell, seeing the bubbling water for a second before splashing into its boiling, horrible depths. She struggled to the surface as every inch of her body exploded with searing pain. She called for help, her body alive with pain as Walter laughed hysterically on the walkway. She began to swim to the walkway opposite the one she'd been thrown from but only made it a few strokes before the pain overtook her and she slipped beneath the surface.

The water continued to boil around her as she lost consciousness.

*****

Sarah woke up in her pod with a blood-curdling scream. Carlo was in front of her, his hands gently on her shoulders. She could tell he was talking to her but she could still feel the boiling water bubble on her skin.

"SARAH, IT'S OKAY! YOU'RE ALRIGHT!" he yelled, his tired

eyes filled with worry and fear.

"*I felt it!*" she yelled into his face. "*I felt every damn thing he did to me! Where's Will and Billy?*"

"Sarah, it's okay, we're here," Will said from the pod next to her.

Sarah let her body fall backward against the back of her pod as she began crying hysterically, still remembering the image of Walter standing on the walkway above her as she boiled in the water.

"He has complete control of the Portal," Carlo said. "I don't know how he did it, but he's able to control everything."

"Why are we feeling everything?" Billy yelled.

"I have no idea. It looks like the only thing he can't control is all of you."

"The orb was still in the same place," Sarah said. "I couldn't get to it, but it was there."

"The orb is located in the direct center of the Portal. It's the only exit point for the game so maybe he's unable to move it. You're sure it was there?"

"I'm positive. I made my way right to it but he was there waiting for me."

"We need to go back in," Will said.

"*Fuck that!*" Billy yelled. "I hardly made it out of my fucking cabin! I was burning before my eyes even focused!"

"Will's right," Sarah said, forcing the tears away from her eyes. "The orb was protected by the flames. He obviously doesn't want us getting to it. You may be onto something, Carlo."

"You're positive he can't remove it?" Will asked.

"If he could he would have already."

"Walter is all about the show," Sarah said. "If he has complete control over everything but the exit, it could get worse every time we go in."

"Okay, so what are we supposed to do?" Billy asked. "We just keep going in and dying horrific deaths until we all get lucky enough to touch the orb? Who's to say he'll ever let us near the damn thing?"

"We don't have a choice," Sarah said. "This is it, I know it is. He's not fighting back this hard for nothing. I'm ready to go back."

"You sure?" Carlo asked.

"I want to be done with this. Put me back in."

"Us too," Will said.

"This is bullshit," Billy said, leaning back into his pod with a sour face.

Carlo tapped on his tablet a few times and they each fell asleep.

*****

Sarah woke up the same place she did every time she entered the Portal, only this time she was cold and disoriented. Her eyes stung horribly when she opened them and her head swam with pain as she realized she was holding her breath. The world around her was nearly pitch black, giving hardly any form or shape to her surroundings. In a moment of panicked clarity, she realized she was underwater. She rolled off the bed and muddled her way to the open door as the cold water stung at her skin. The outside of the cabin was slightly brighter than inside, allowing her to see the silhouetted trees in the distance as they softly swayed with the current. The pressure inside her chest began to grow so she launched herself off the ground and began swimming upward to the surface. Her heartbeat rose wildly as she continued up, the air trapped in her lungs trying wildly to force itself out of her body. She knew she was moving, swimming up to wherever the surface was, but the frigid waters disoriented her and chased all feeling away from her body. She unexpectedly reached the surface and gasped harshly for breath as cold air stung her throat. A whirring sound filled the air, followed by a small splash in the water just beside her.

*"Ay, thar' be a slutty mermaid! Welcome to the surface, ye saucy lass!"*

Walter circled around her in a rickety pirate ship. He was dressed like a grizzled sea captain, with a long, black coat overtop a thick turtleneck sweater. A black captain's hat sat atop his head as he puffed from a wooden pipe, held tightly in his mouth by his teeth. Sarah had never known him to have a beard but there was a long, white, billowy beard on his face that hung halfway down his chest. An old-fashioned harpoon gun was strapped across his chest as he spun the wheel of the ship back and forth. A flash of lightning illuminated the ship, showing a black, tattered sail with the Jolly Roger crossbones in white.

Rain pelted her face as flashes of lightning continued to illuminate the seascape while the water tossed her up and down with each violent, stormy wave. A roll of thunder echoed across the top of the water as Billy surfaced with a gasp, much louder than Sarah's had been.

"*Billy, watch out!*" Sarah yelled as Walter straightened his ship and moved toward him. The ship cruised past Sarah quickly as Walter sang an old pirate shanty…

> *The worst old brig that ever did weigh,*
> *Sailed out of Harwich on a windy day.*
> *And we're waitin' for the day*
> *Waitin' for the day,*
> *Waitin' for the day that we get our pay!*

A bolt of lightning illuminated the sky as Walter aimed his harpoon gun and fired. The harpoon flew through the air with such speed that it had entered the back of Billy's skull before Sarah had a chance to warn him. Billy's body went limp and floated in the water as the tail-end of the harpoon struck straight up in the air like a shark's fin. Walter reloaded his gun and turned the ship around, facing Sarah as she wildly began to swim away from him. He begain to sing again, his voice clashing with the violence of the storm…

\* \* \*

*She was built in Roman time,*
*Held together with bits of twine.*
*And we're waitin' for the day,*
*Waitin' for the day,*
*Waitin' for the day that we get our pay!*

"*Will!*" she screamed frantically, looking in all directions for any sign of him.

"Ay, the lad's long gone, my lady," Walter cooed, smiling down at her from the side of the ship. "You'll be seein' em' soon, ya' scurvy wench!"

Walter pointed his harpoon gun down at her and fired. The harpoon shattered her spine, sending shards of pain through her entire body as her legs became immobile. She cried out in pain as she struggled to stay afloat. A gunshot rang out in the night as musket ball obliterated her right shoulder. She screamed loudly and struggled a moment more before slipping under the water.

Pain radiated throughout her entire body as she sank deeper into the darkness of the Portal. Her legs weren't moving due to the harpoon lodged in her spine and with only her left arm to swim, she had no more chance than a lead weight would have had. The panic began to overtake her as she sank faster and faster. When she could no longer hold her breath she inhaled a blast of frigid water, feeling like thousands of needles stabbing at her lungs. She sunk to the bottom, and before passing out, she saw the soft, red glow of the exit sphere.

*****

"*I saw it. I saw it. It was under the water but it was there!*" she yelled after a bought of coughing and heavy breathing.

"Wait, slow down!" Carlo said. "What did you see?"

"The entire portal was flooded. I made my way to the surface and he shot me with a harpoon and a pistol."

"He got me with the pistol right away," Will said. "I'd hardly made it to the surface when he shot me in the throat with that damn thing."

"He shot me in the spine with a harpoon and the shoulder with the pistol, so I had no way to stay afloat. As I was sinking, I looked down and saw a red glow. It was in the same spot. I think we're right; he can't move it!"

"We just have to get to it."

"I can't keep doing this," Billy said. *"I don't even like horror movies!"*

"Put us back in," Sarah said, settling back in to her pod and closing her eyes.

"Fuck!" yelled Billy before falling asleep.

*****

Sarah walked through the open door of her cabin as the sound of circus music echoed all around her. It was dark outside, but the Portal was filled with the glow of a lively circus where the lake used to sit. There weren't any people at all, but the sounds of joyful screams and laughter filled the air as she stood in the doorway.

"I hate carnivals," she muttered, listening as a group of voices screamed while a roller coaster entered into a loop above the bright lights.

"Sarah!" Will said, running up to her from the empty carnival. "This is fucked up."

"You're telling me. Have you seen Billy?"

"No, not yet."

"Let's find the exit sphere and get out of here."

The area surrounding the carnival was bathed in a deep, unending darkness, so the two of them quickly made their way toward the bright, heavy glow.

"That smells amazing," Will said as the aroma of cotton candy and fresh popcorn filled the air.

"I hate carnivals," Sarah said, looking at the empty midway

booths as phantom screams of joy echoed around them.

"I mean this carnival sucks, but in general, I love a good carnival. There is one near where Brad and I live that we used to go to every year."

"I guess they're not that bad," Sarah said, feeling the twinge of sadness in Will's voice as he thought about his brother.

Both of them froze in their place as a large, grizzled clown walked from between two carnival stands and came to a stop twenty feet in front of them. He wore a one-piece, red outfit, with three white, dirtied pompoms down his torso. His sleeves were baggy, hanging over his hands so that only his fingers popped out of the bottom. Around his neck were two frilly neck collars, each stained with brown and red splotches. He wore white, blotchy make up, except for his eyes that were messily painted black like a raccoon. He was bald, except for a small tuft of orange hair coming directly out of the top and laying limply against the front of his face in wet strands. His entire outfit was dripping wet, as if he'd just crawled out of a lake. The clown looked back at them with a smile, staring at them with a pair of glowing, crimson eyes.

"I hate carnivals," Will said, watching the clown start to move toward them, dragging a large, waist high mallet on the ground behind him. "It's Walter, right?"

"DING DING DING," yelled the Walter-clown, followed by a hoarse, gurgling laugh.

"*Fuck you, clown!*" Billy screamed as he appeared from behind a food stand and holding a mallet of his own.

Billy swung the mallet and connected with the top of Walter's head. The Walter-clown fell to the ground as the mallet skipped a few times and landed in a bloody heap next to them. Walter laid face down on the ground as blood poured thickly out of his crushed skull.

"Billy, *way to go!*" Will yelled as he and Sarah made their way cautiously toward him.

"Be careful," Sarah said. "He could still be alive."

"His head looks like a crushed cantaloupe, Sarah," Billy said.

"He's out for the count. Look…"

Billy reached down and turned Walter onto his back. The Walter-clown looked back up at him with a smile as he reached up and squeezed a flower attached to his chest. A flash of liquid sprayed from its center and splashed against Billy's face as he released a horrible scream into the air. Walter rolled to his side and made his way to his feet as Sarah and Will watched in horror. The left side of his head was completely caved in; his left eye barely sitting inside his broken eye socket as it rolled back and forth on its own accord. The entire left side of his body was covered in dark, sticky blood, as he picked up the mallet that Billy had smacked him with.

"*Ruhnnn,*" garbled Billy as Walter kicked him to the ground.

"Come on!" Will yelled, grabbing Sarah's hand.

Sarah watched as Walter swung the mallet in one swoop and planted it in the top of Billy's head. His face, which had already begun melting away from the liquid that Walter had sprayed him with, exploded as the mallet came to rest. Billy's body flailed a few times before becoming still as Walter cackled loudly into the night. He jumped into the air and landed on the roof of one of the midway games before leaping to the next one, and the next one, as he chased after Will and Sarah through the circus.

"*He's gaining on us!*" Sarah screamed, feeling the distance between them and the clown shortening.

Will turned a corner and pulled Sarah with him as they left the midway. Far ahead of them was a large circus tent with its entrance flaps opened and pulled away. The inside was pitch black, illuminated only by the red glow of the orb directly in the middle.

"*There!*" Will yelled, letting go of Sarah's hand as the two ran together.

Walter continued following them, running across the tops of the stands housing different carnival games and snacks. He growled and snarled as he followed them, showing a set of large, sharpened teeth with each violent wail. His tongue, which had been torn to shreds, hung limply out of his mouth, bouncing with every leap he made toward them. They had almost reached the opening of the tent when Walter leaped high into the air and landed on Will's back. Walter bumped into Sarah as he landed, knocking her down as he pinned Will to the ground. Walter looked like a rabid beast as he sat on Will's back; his eyes peering out of his mangled face with a fiery intensity. Sarah watched from behind as Walter turned his head backward toward her like an owl, the sound of breaking bones and joints filling the air. He smiled at her and winked as a stream of blood and pus oozed from the bottom of his left eye.

"SARAH, GO!" Will yelled.

Walter swiped at her as she turned to run and tore a deep gash down her back. Blood poured from the cut as she screamed, making her way into the tent as Walter cackled with glee. He turned his head back around and opened his mouth so wide that the bones in his jaw broke apart. He flung his head downward as Will yelled in fear, and in one swoop, bit half of Will's head and tore it away. He stood and spit what remained of Will's face into the air as Will twitched on the ground below him.

"Stop, BITCH!" scowled Walter, his words barely intelligible as they spewed from his broken mouth.

He began galloping behind her on all fours, sending clouds of dirt and dust in the air as he quickly gained on her. His broken jaw and tongue bobbed up and down as he moved, making crunching, slobbery sounds as he gained on her. She sobbed loudly as she ran, seeing the orb get closer to her as she ran but knowing that Walter was approaching much quicker than she thought possible. She mustered as much will as she could and began to sprint to the orb, screaming loudly in an attempt to drown out the sound of Walter's approach. She outstretched her hand, ready to touch the red, glowing orb as Walter crashed into her and sent her to the ground. He pinned her down on her back, sitting on top of her and looking down with his dark, vengeful, red eyes.

Sarah stared at the orb in defeat as the Walter-clown raised his hand triumphantly and slashed her throat with his long, talon-like hands. She tried to wiggle from side to side, still hoping to reach up and touch the orb as blood and air gurgled through the deep hole that Walter had dug into her throat. He didn't laugh, or smile, or taunt her; he simply continued sitting on top of her as she gurgled and gasped for air. In one final attempt, she reached her hand toward the orb before letting it fall to the ground in a small puff of dust and defeat.

*****

Will and Billy were yelling at each other when Sarah woke up in her pod. Carlo was standing in front of them with Allison, trying to calm them down as they yelled back and forth.

"Guys, calm down!" she yelled from her pod.

"*I can't keep doing this, Sarah!*" Billy yelled. "This is *bullshit*, I can't keep going through this over and over! He's never gonna let us anywhere near the orb!"

"We aren't going to get out of this at the same time," Sarah said. "We need to work together to get each of us out one by one. Let's find each other quickly and then get to work."

"*Fuck that, I'm done! Carlo, let me out of this fucking thing!*"

Carlo tapped on his tablet and the three of them fell asleep again.

"I feel bad for them," Carlo said to Allison as he tracked their vitals on his computer. "This can't be good for them, emotionally. I can't imagine what they're going through."

"We'll get them the help they'll need when it's done. Are your security cameras recording?"

"Technically, yes, but it's playing on a loop. To anyone who would watch it, it would just be an empty room."

"That's smart. Good thinking. There's no way in hell we'd be able to explain any of this."

"Have you given any thought to what happens when this is all over with? Let's say the three of them are able to leave the Portal and sever their connection with Walter; it's just a matter of time before the FBI steps in and they're gonna to need to pin this on someone."

"I have a plan," Allison said, nervously. "It's already in motion and it's gonna happen fast so I need you to get on board."

"Okay?" Carlo said, intrigued. "What are we talking here?"

"Get your checkbook ready, Mr. Macasaet."

# CHAPTER TWENTY-NINE

Harvey Braddock sat alone at a bar in Maryland, sipping a glass of whiskey and eating pretzels from a small bowl in front of him. His son David's name stared up at him from his left forearm, a bittersweet reminder of his son and the fact that he had been one of Walter's 17 victims. Harvey's life had undergone a drastic transformation in the years since his son was murdered. Once a decorated member of the Valley Ridge Police Department, Harvey had turned in his gun and badge after a bar fight that left a long, grizzled scar across the left side of his face. Shortly after, his wife had left him alone, leaving him alone in their empty home in a haze of cigar smoke and empty bottles of booze.

After a year of lonely binge drinking, Harvey had gathered himself together the best he could and began work as a privateer. He did all sorts of jobs, mostly under the table for law enforcement. Planting evidence, trailing a suspect, roughing up whoever needed to be roughed up; whatever he was needed for and whatever paid the most, he was game. It wasn't the life he'd imagined in his youth, but it was a life he'd grown to love.

Just as Sarah, Will, and Carlo were being ushered into the Exodus Portal, Harvey tapped his empty glass on the wooden bar to alert the bartender he was ready for another. The bartender, a woman named Cindy, was in her early fifties and looked much younger than her years. Her black hair was pulled back into a ponytail with a few strands hanging loosely on the sides of her face. She smiled as she poured, letting the glass fill more than she normally would as Harvey took a less-than-discreet glance at her cleavage. Harvey knew her well; she owned the bar and lived in an apartment above, and on more than one occasion she'd invited him to join her after she'd closed the bar for the night. The rueful smile she gave him as she returned the bottle of whiskey let him know that he'd be climbing the steps to her apartment soon.

He smiled back and took a sip of his whiskey as his phone rattled in his pocket. He placed the glass on the bar and pulled the phone out with quiet excitement. Other than Cindy, Harvey didn't have a personal life, so when his phone vibrated he knew it was a job. It had been awhile since he'd had any kind of work, so the thought of having something to do other than showing up at Cindy's bar with a condom in his pocket was exhilarating.

He took another sip of his whiskey as he read the message on his outdated flip-phone. He smiled, knowing he was set for a good time.

"Wife asking where you are?" Cindy asked, watching him smile from down the bar.

"She's a nosey bitch," Harvey said, knowing that Cindy knew he was single. "I told her I'm gonna be late tonight because I'll be fucking the bartender again."

Cindy laughed and blushed, excited for what the night had in store.

"I'd hate to turn down a good thing but I don't think I can tonight," he said, taking another look at his phone and standing to put on his jacket. He placed his money on the bar and took one last look at his phone before an idea formed in his head.

"Actually, Cindy; have you ever been to Nicaragua?"

# CHAPTER THIRTY

Sarah woke up much less comfortable than she usually did inside the Portal. She could tell that she was lying on the ground as opposed to the mattress she usually woke on. She pushed herself up onto her elbows and waited for her vision to return. The nausea was worse than ever this time, which she realized she hadn't really experienced the last few times inside the Portal.

"*SARAH*?" Will yelled as she forced herself to her feet.

His voice echoed all around her as her vision finally focused, revealing a large, dark expanse in front of them. It was bright enough for her to see Will and Billy running toward her, as well as the fact that the ground in all directions was gray, uninterrupted pavement.

"Look!" Billy said as the two of them came to a stop in front of her.

Sarah looked toward the middle of the Portal and saw the familiar, red glow of the exit orb. It was far away from them, but there was nothing to obstruct their path.

"It's too easy," Sarah said as Billy bent over and dry-heaved onto the ground.

"This nausea is for the birds," he said. "I can't do much more of this. I need out."

Billy took off toward the orb, running as fast as he could as Will and Sarah followed behind him.

"Billy, be careful!" Sarah yelled. "There has to be something we don't see!"

No sooner had she stopped talking, a car horn version of, "La Cucaracha," blared from behind them. They turned together and were greeted by a set of bright headlights.

"BEEP BEEP, MOTHERFUCKERS!" bellowed Walter from a speaker attached to the top of a large, hulking pickup truck.

"*Run!*" Will yelled as the three of them quickened their pace.

The song, "Flight of the Bumblebee" bellowed from the speaker on the truck as Walter put it into drive and sped toward them. Will looked back as he ran and was able to see Walter sitting behind the steering wheel with a red trucker hat and a cigar clinched in his teeth. A pair of reflective sunglasses sat underneath the brim of his hat as he smiled wildly on his approach. The words "FUCK YOU," were etched across the front of his red hat in white letters.

"*Spread out!*" Sarah yelled, distancing herself from Will and Billy. "*He can't get us all. One of us is leaving right now!*"

Will and Billy separated, putting distance between themselves as Walter quickly approached.

"You think I can't get all of you? Oh, that's *adorable!* I think I'll start with the *bitch* this time!"

Walter veered to the left and made his way to Sarah. Will started to run toward her, listening to Walter laugh through the loudspeaker.

"*Will, no!*" she screamed.

"Come on!" Billy yelled, grabbing Will's arm and pulling him toward the orb. "This isn't real, she'll be fine! Let's go!"

"La Cucaracha," continued to blare through the speaker, mixed with Sarah's scream as Walter hit her with his truck. She flew forward and smashed her face against the pavement before rolling over onto her back. Her face was a bloody mess as she looked up at Walter as he reversed his truck.

"Read the hat, sweetie," he said with a smile as he pointed to the white letters above the red brim. Sarah recoiled for a moment before sitting forward and spitting a mouthful of blood across the front bumper and grill.

"Gross," Walter said with a grimace before driving the truck over Sarah and squishing her like a bug on the pavement. He drove back and forth over top of her a few times, hooting and hollering out of the window each time he'd feel a squish or crack under his tires. By the time he had finished, Sarah was nothing but a smear of blood and gore under his tires. He rolled down his window and looked down at the pavement before grabbing the speaker to his megaphone. "Nasty! Must be that time of the month, boys!"

Walter pulled out an automatic rifle and began firing it wildly into the air as he turned the truck toward Will and Billy. He plowed into the back of them and sent them both flying forward as he exploded into a fit of laughter. Will landed on his chest on the ground, wedged underneath of the truck as Walter parked on top of him. Billy quickly got back to his feet and continued hobbling to the orb as Will screamed loudly behind him.

"Don't be so fucking dramatic," Walter said, stepping down from the truck and putting a bullet into the back of his head.

Walter looked up and panicked, realizing he'd let Billy get too far away from him. He opened fire, spraying bullets toward Billy. Billy ran in a zigzag pattern, flailing wildly in an attempt to dodge the bullets screaming past him. Walter screamed in frustration as a bullet intended for Billy's head struck the back part of his neck. The bullet exited the softness of Billy's throat, sending a splash of gurgling blood onto the orb as he landed on top of it.

*****

Billy awoke in his pod with a loud, laboured gasp.

"Billy, you're okay," said Carlo. "You're back in the chamber."

"I touched it!" Billy yelled, continuing to feel at his neck to make sure the wound was gone.

"*What?*" yelled Sarah and Will in unison, leaning out of their pods to see him.

"I touched the orb. The motherfucker shot me in the throat, but I was close enough that I just landed on the damn thing!"

"Do you feel any different?" Carlo asked.

"My headache is gone," he said as tears welled in his eyes. "It's gone, guys. 100%, it's gone. I think you were right, Carlo!"

"Send us back in," Sarah said.

"He messed up," Allison said as Carlo undid Billy's handcuffs. "He's creating all these scenarios because he gets a kick out of them, but he messed up. He won't screw up again."

"He's gonna be pissed," Carlo said. "Be careful."

"Send us back in," Will said. "Let's see what kind of fuckery he has in store for us this time."

Billy fell to his knees with tears in his eyes as Will and Sarah fell asleep.

\*\*\*\*\*

Sarah shook the nausea and blurriness away quickly and left the cabin. She hated going into the Portal, but something about waking up inside her usual cabin was comforting. The sun illuminated the landscape in the same exact way it did on her first time inside. She looked from left to right, listening to the false sounds of the wilderness around her and realized that everything was as it was supposed to be. The trees surrounding the lake were all in place, as well as the cabins that dotted the shoreline. Birds flew overhead and filled the space with their imagined songs as a fish jumped out of the water and landed with a splash. The long, wooden walkways still led from the shore to the island, and situated in the very middle of the abandoned island was the exit sphere.

"There's no way he's letting us go," Will said, jogging up to her from the sandy shore. "This is far too easy."

"Everything seems back to normal, right?"

"Seems to be, yeah."

They hardly had time to turn around before Walter sprung from the line of trees and smashed a baseball bat across Sarah's head. She fell to the ground, her hands on her head as she tried to regain her composure. Will grabbed at the bat and tried to pry it from Walter's hand but Walter simply removed a large knife from his side and plunged it into Will's stomach. Will keeled over immediately, feeling the stinging pain radiate through his abdomen as Walter kicked him to the ground.

"SARAH!" he yelled as Walter grabbed him by the foot and dragged him toward the water. *"What are you doing? Let me go!"*

Will felt his energy quickly depleting as he allowed himself to be dragged by Walter onto one of the walkways to the island. He left a trail of thick blood behind them as they moved, as if he were a paintbrush being dragged across a clean canvas.

"Where are we..." he said, his mind trailing back and forth from loss of blood. "Sarah!"

"Shut your damn mouth," Walter said, letting Will's foot fall to the ground. "I've had it with all of you. I'm done chasing you over and over again. This is not a kindness I'm doing for you; I just find you all so *fucking* boring."

Walter grabbed Will's hand and pulled him upward, sending another sharp wave of pain through his body.

"What..."

"Once you're gone, I am going to *destroy* her. She's going to feel like a fucking freight train derailed in her head."

"No..."

Walter heaved Will up off the ground and flung him onto the exit orb. Will's tired body hit the orb and disappeared in a cloud of wispy smoke.

*****

\* \* \*

Sarah's head rang with pain as she rolled on the ground, waiting for the pain to subside so she could get to her feet and run for the orb. She felt the back of her head where Walter had hit her and could feel a large welt, which seemed to be growing as the pain slowly marched throughout her skull.

"WILL!" she yelled, finally able to open her eyes and scan the area in front of her.

The light hurt her eyes, and her vision was blurred slightly, but it was clear enough for her to see what was happening. The walkway in front of her was streaked with blood, leading to the island where Walter was standing in front of the orb, holding Will slightly off the ground by his hand. Sarah could see Will's dark, blood-drenched wound as she clumsily pushed herself back onto her feet. She took two steps forward, ready to run to Will's aid, as Walter lifted Will completely off the ground and tossed him onto the orb. Her head swam with confusion as he disappeared into a puff of smoke. Walter turned and walked to the edge of the island, staring at her as a breeze blew between them.

"It's just me and you now, sweetheart," Walter said, his voice echoing in the empty Portal as they glared at each other.

# CHAPTER THIRTY-ONE

*"Send me back in!"* Will yelled as he woke up in his pod. *"She's all alone, she needs me!"*

"Hold on, Will, what happened?" Carlo asked.

"Just send me back, Carlo."

"I can't send you back in mid-sequence, Will. Nobody can go back in until she's out. Now tell me, *what happened*?"

Will's eyes filled with tears as he thought about what had happened. Before Walter had picked him up and tossed him onto the orb, he'd caught a glimpse of Sarah back on the shore. She was struggling clumsily to her feet as she tried in vain to get to him. As he sat in his pod, the image of her alone on the shore was all he could think about.

"The Portal was back to normal. We met up on the shore and were discussing what to do when Walter hit her with a bat. I tried to fight, but he stabbed me and dragged me to the island. He picked me up and threw me on the orb."

"*What?*" Allison yelled. "Why the hell would he do that?"

"He wants her alone," Carlo said. "She's the one who got away in Valley Ridge. She's the eighteenth."

"He's going to torture her, Carlo," Will said. "He told me so before he tossed me out. We have to do something."

"We have to give her a chance to escape on her own," Carlo said, tapping on his screen as the electrodes removed themselves from Will and snaked away behind him. "If it goes on too long, we can look into removing her, but if we take her out right now she's just going to ask to go back in."

"Well then I'll be able to go back in with her."

"No," Allison said, removing his cuffs. "No, you won't. You're free from him, and you're *not* going back inside. Sarah's going to have to figure this one out herself."

"She wouldn't want you to go back in, either," Carlo said.

Will stepped out of the pod and wiped away the tears from his eyes. He was exhausted and ready to collapse, but his headache was gone, and he knew he was free. Allison started to talk but he put his hand on the nape of her neck, and pulled her in for a kiss.

"Been wanting to do that for a while," he said.

"You're not going back in," she whispered. "Go sit down and relax while we wait for Sarah."

Will smiled at her before slinking over to the sitting gallery. He stretched himself out onto one of the rows of seats and exhaled as the exhaustion overcame him. He scanned the room as a look of confusion covered his face.

"Where's Billy?"

# CHAPTER THIRTY-TWO

Harvey sat in the driver's seat of his old cargo van with Cindy sitting in the passenger seat beside him. She looked uncomfortable, but overall, she felt excited over the adventure she had decided to take part in. She'd closed the bar and took all the money from the till before putting a CLOSED sign on the window, all the while not knowing when she'd be back to remove it. She was ready for a break and an exotic getaway with the handsome, grizzled man beside her was just what she needed.

Harvey pulled up to a barbed-wire fence and stopped beside a guard's booth with a younger man sitting inside.

"Good evening, Harvey," said the man as he slid his window open. "Where to this evening?"

"None of your damn business," Harvey said with a smile as he handed over a small envelope. The man opened it and thumbed through a pile of bills.

"Looks like all your paperwork is in order here, sir. Have a good flight."

Harvey rolled up his window as the tall, chain-link fence slid open in front of him. Inside the fence was a private airfield, complete with two runways and a small terminal in the middle.

"Are we going to get in trouble doing this?" she asked, nervously watching the airfield approach.

"No, not at all; I have a history with this place, they know me. Plus, I just handed Alex back there a handful of cash, so he'll make sure we're good to go. No need to worry."

Harvey pulled into an open hanger and parked his van in the back. The silence was eerie as he shut off the engine and took Cindy's hand in the dark.

"I'm very glad you said yes to this," he said, squeezing her hand and leaning over to kiss her. "I know it's probably a little more adventurous than you're used to but I promise to keep you safe. We won't run into any trouble, I promise."

"I think a little adventure is what I needed. I'm trusting you, Harvey Braddock."

"I know," he said with a smile as the two of them slipped out of his van.

Sitting idly in the dark of the hangar was an older-looking, single-engine plane.

"Is that yours?" asked Cindy as the two of them stood at the backdoors of the van.

"It is tonight," Harvey said, watching her face turn from stoic to complete nervousness. "I'm kidding! Yes, it's mine. My father's, actually; he passed it down to me when he died a few years back."

Harvey opened the doors of the van and handed Cindy the small duffle of clothes she'd packed before slinging his own bag over his shoulder.

"When do you think he'll wake up?" Cindy asked, looking at the sleeping figure in the back of the van.

"He'll probably be out for a little while longer. Let's get our bags loaded up."

Harvey and Cindy took their bags and loaded them into the

plane as Billy laid asleep on the floor of the van.

# CHAPTER THIRTY-THREE

Walter stood at the edge of the island, his feet just a few inches away from one of the wooden walkways. Sarah stood at the opposite end, staring back at him as a soft breeze slightly tussled her hair.

"What now, Walter?"

He didn't answer, but continued staring at her from across the walkway with a stoic look on his face.

*"What the hell do you want from me?"* she screamed, her voice echoing across the Portal. *"Why me? What did I ever do to you?"*

"She never told you, did she?

"Who? What are you talking about, Walter?"

"Why would she tell you? Of course, she didn't."

"Walter, I have no idea what you're talking about. Let's get this over with."

Sarah began walking toward him, thinking of ways to make it past him, as a familiar voice echoed from the trees behind her.

*"You are my sunshine, my only sunshine. You make me happy when*

*skies are gray."*

"Walter, stop it," she said, listening to the sound of her mother's singing as she stood motionless on the walkway.

*"You'll never know, dear, how much I love you. Please don't take my sunshine away."*

"Walter, STOP IT! *How are you doing this?*

"We're all connected, my dear. I have access to your mind, and you have equal access to mine."

"I want nothing to do with your demented mind," she said as the song continued in the background.

"Oh, I think I have a few things you'll want to be privy to."

"I want nothing to do with your memories, Walter."

"I'm afraid you don't have much of a choice, Sarah dear. Let's take a walk down memory lane."

Walter began walking toward her as she turned and ran as fast as she could. She left the wooden walkway and darted into the woods when a sudden, fierce wind began whipping the trees about as she maneuvered the thick patch of woods.

"Sarah, honey! Won't you slow down?" called Walter in her mother's voice as a tree branch smacked her across the face.

She fell backward onto the ground and landed in a muddy patch of ground as small traces of blood began to trickle onto the scratches across her face.

"Come on, then, let's go," Walter said, picking her up from the mud and slinging her over his shoulder.

Sarah kicked and punched as he walked, but it soon became apparent she had no power over him. Walter was taller and much stronger than her, and the harder she struggled, the harder he squeezed her against him. The wind stopped as he left the trees and entered into a still, silent clearing. He tossed her to the ground and she landed hard on the soft grass. She chipped a tooth as her jaw clamped shut on impact, sending a shot of pain through her head. Walter reached down and pulled her up to her feet by her neck and pointed her forward.

"Right where this all began," he said, the south chapel sitting abandoned in front of them. "Let's go on in and have some alone time, shall we?"

The pain in her mouth intensified as Walter guided her forward. She didn't try and fight it, but instead let him maneuver her with ease. She was nervous; he had something to show her, and the anticipation and fear shook her to her core.

"Have a seat," he said, forcefully pushing her into one of pews. He picked up a shotgun and cocked it before slinging it over his shoulder. "Don't bother running, either. You're gonna hear what I have to say, and if that means shooting out your knees so you can't move, so be it. I'd rather have this part be as pleasant as possible, but that's up to you, isn't it?"

Walter reached up and pulled a large, fabric screen to the floor. He wheeled an old projector to the back of the room and fiddled with a tattered, dusty film reel before getting it attached properly and turning it on. The screen illuminated as the light inside the chapel dimmed.

"Here ya go, bitch," he said, handing her a tub of popcorn and sitting on the pew across the aisle from her. "You're gonna love this."

The sound of the film running through the projector filled the small room as images began to flash on the screen. The first image was from Sarah's point of view, showing her mother and father singing her happy birthday as she sat in front of a cake with three candles.

"I thought we'd start off with something light before we got into the heavy stuff," Walter said, shoving a large handful of popcorn into his mouth.

"Cut to the chase, Walter."

"Oh, you're no fun," he said with a smile, throwing a handful of popcorn across the aisle at her. "Your call though."

Walter snapped his fingers and the images switched to something new that she didn't recognize. The footage was from the point of view of a man eating out of a bag of chips, crunching them one by one as he watched an episode of M.A.S.H. on the old television in front of him. The sound of someone knocking on the door interrupted the show as the man put his chips down and made his way to the door. Sarah glanced at Walter as the footage continued; his eyes were locked on the screen. He watched with no expression on his face, waiting for the door to be opened. The man on the screen opened the door to reveal Laura Prince standing on the other side.

"I've watched this part thousands of times," he said.

"What is this?" Sarah asked, only to be shushed loudly by Walter as he sat transfixed on the screen.

*"Hi, babe. I didn't know you were coming over."*

*"Hi, Walt. I needed to see you."*

"No..." Sarah said as a chill ran down her spine. "This isn't real."

"You bet your ass it is. Shocking, right?"

"I don't believe it. It's fake, *you're making this up!*"

"You think so, *do you?*"

"This might be some sick fantasy of yours, but I can tell you she would *never* have anything to do with you!"

"You stupid, dumb little girl. All you had to do is take a peak in one of your mother's yearbooks, and you would have had your first clue."

Walter snapped his fingers again and a photo appeared on the screen. It was from an old yearbook, showing black and white photos of people she didn't recognize. In the center of the screen was her mother's face with her name underneath:

*Laura Smith*

Her heart dropped into her stomach as she looked a couple pictures to the left of her mother:

*Walter Scott*

"Big deal, Walter. You went to high school with my mother."

Walter snapped his fingers again and the image switched to a picture of Walter and Laura sitting at a table in the school's courtyard. They were both holding hands and smiling at the camera.

"We didn't just go to school together, you idiot. We were in love."

"She didn't love you, Walter. For fuck's sake, you were kids."

"We were together for four years, Sarah. I proposed to her, and she said yes."

"Bullshit," Sarah said, analyzing the photo on the screen.

"Where exactly did you think that little ring you're wearing on your finger came from?"

Sarah looked down to her right hand to the ring she'd found in her mother's box of belongings. The diamond stared up at her, confirming to her the story that Walter had spun for her.

"She said yes. She said yes, then went off to college and met your deadbeat father. I'll never forget the day she told me our engagement was off. She came home and paraded him around town like some kind of prized piece of livestock—made me sick to my stomach."

"Walter, I'm sorry, but none of this matters. None of this warrants anything you did leading up to right now."

"What do you know about any of these things, you little bitch? You weren't there when your whorish mother broke my heart. I'm sure you can imagine my delight when she searched me out that day, wanting back in my life. I was a fool, thinking she'd leave him for me. I couldn't help myself."

"Don't flatter yourself, Walter." Sarah took off the ring and let it fall to the ground. It spun a few times before coming to a stop on the aisle between them.

"*She* searched *me* out, *girl*! I was doing just fine on my own until she pranced back into my life. That woman broke my heart *twice,* and you sit here as if I'm the heartless one!"

Walter snapped his finger again and the image switched to the image of Laura Prince on her back, moaning as her breasts moved up and down while Walter moved against her.

"What do you think about that? *Huh*?"

"*STOP IT!*" Sarah yelled as she stood up to leave. Walter stood in a flash and grabbed her. He threw her back against the pew as her mother continued to moan in the background.

*"YOU SIT DOWN AND WATCH, YOU LITTLE BITCH!"*

Laura leaned up and kissed Walter on the screen as he snapped his fingers again. The image switched to that of Michael Prince, pushing Walter backward onto his porch steps before planting three quick, hard punches against his face.

"Your father knew how to throw a punch, I'll give him that. Most assholes do."

"My father wasn't an asshole, Walter. *You are.*"

"Your father broke your poor mother's spirit. She begged him for attention, and he only gave it to her after it was too damn late."

"It wasn't too late, though. She chose him, *not you.* They were at their best when they died."

Walter looked at her with a face as cold and hard as stone. He snapped his fingers and the scene switched again.

"Pay close attention. I think you'll want to know this."

Sarah watched the screen, which showed Walter's point of view as he stared at her parent's gas station in the dark. He was waiting, watching as a car filled up its tank and drove off before he walked casually up to one of the pumps and inspected it methodically. After looking for a few moments, Walter pealed back a piece of paneling on the side of the pump, revealing a small space beneath filled with wires and dust.

"What is this?"

"I think you know," Walter said, tossing a single piece of popcorn into his mouth with a smile.

On the screen, Walter placed a device the size of a cell phone into the open panel and flicked a small switch on the side. A light on the front of the device turned green just before he replaced the panel and walked casually away from the pumps.

"No…"

"Oh, yes, my dear," he said as Sarah's eyes filled with tears. "I loved her, Sarah. I loved her, and she broke my heart."

*"SO YOU KILLED HER? YOU KILLED HER FOR NOT*

*LOVING A PSYCHOPATH?"*

"I wasn't always this way, you know. I had my life planned out perfectly! Me and your mother were going to run away together, and you were going to come with us!"

*"LIKE HELL I WAS! YOU'RE DELUSIONAL!"*

"I couldn't give a flying fuck if you came with us or not, whore!" He stood from his pew as his shadowy presence seemed to fill the entire room. The pressure in Sarah's head grew as if she were ascending the sky in an airplane. "She loved me!"

"Well she loved my dad more, prick! Is this what all the killings have been about? Just getting back at my mother?"

"Yes. No? Yes? I dunno. Your mother woke something inside me that I kinda knew had always been there but nobody had ever seen. The day she broke it off with me, I knew she had to die. Your dad too, and once they were gone, *you* had to go too."

"That's not what you did, though, Walter. You killed seventeen other kids that had *nothing* to do with what happened between you and my parents."

"Eighteen weeks. That's how long me and your mother's engagement lasted. Eighteen fucking weeks before she strolled back into town with your father."

"I think I'm going to be sick."

"Oh please, they were a bunch of assholes, and you know it. Scott and Trevor, those dick-breathed silly boys? That horrible bitch Marissa, and that smartass James Lampton? Each one of them was a gross little miscreant. It was all supposed to end with your guts laid bare in that library, but you put an end to that plan. You're a resilient little bitch, I'll give you that."

Walter's eyes returned to the screen as Sarah reached beside her and picked up an old piece of wood from the wet, moss covered pew. She swung it as hard as she could and smacked Walter across the face with it. He fell sideways with a yell as Sarah leaped from the pew and took off out of the chapel.

"Run all you want, girlie! I'll find you, and then the real fun will begin!"

Walter stepped out into the sunlight of the clearing and scanned the trees before walking into the darkened path that led back to the lake. Once he was in the trees he hurried, dragging an ax behind him as he moved. It didn't take him long before he was at the end of the wooded path that spilled out onto the grassy beach. He wrapped his hands around his axe, ready to hurl it through the air as she ran toward the orb. He stepped forward from the woods and was surprised to see that Sarah was nowhere in sight.

"Interesting," he whispered to himself. "You better make sure to have hidden yourself really fucking good, Sarah Prince, because when I find you, I'm going to torture the living *shit* out of you!"

*****

Sarah burst from the trees onto the beach to find all the walkways to the island gone. The water was boiling again, popping and turning as she hid behind a large, overturned tree. She looked across the water in frustration, watching the orb stare back at her, almost mocking her as if it were in league with Walter. Kneeling in the moist dirt, she watched him walk out of the trees with a smile on his face, an ax dragging in the dirt behind him.

"You know, Sarah, all I have to do is snap my fingers, and I'd know exactly where you're hiding. I could light these trees on fire in the blink of an eye and burn you out, but I'm not gonna do that today. You see, I'm feeling adventurous today, so I'm gonna drag this here ax around with me until I find you the old-fashioned way, and when I do, you're going to be in a world a pain."

She continued to watch him as he walked around the beach, kicking in the doors to the cabins as he went. After he'd leave, he'd snap his fingers, and the cabin would burst into flames. He was getting closer to her with every step, dragging his ax with him and illuminating the water's edge with every cabin. She scanned the beach for any idea what to do next and spotted a knife in the sand, it's handle standing straight up in the air. He'd neglected to remove the random weapons laying around the portal, knowing they really posed no threat to him inside the virtual arena. She stared at it as an idea started to formulate in her head. She wasn't sure if it would work, in fact she didn't expect it to, but it was the only thing she could do aside from getting to the orb. She sprung from behind the fallen tree in a flash and flew toward the knife. She dove to the ground and landed in front of it with her back towards him.

"Whoopsies!" he yelled with a laugh. "I thought you were more graceful than that, Ms. Prince."

Walter placed the ax on his shoulder with a grin as he made his way towards her. She gripped the knife tightly in her right hand, clinched her teeth, and ran the blade across her left wrist. She let out a muffled gasp as blood began to pour quickly from the cut.

"Okay, Ms. Prince, on your feet," he said, getting closer to her with each step. "What's wrong, bitch? Sprain your ankle on that fall?"

Tears filled her eyes as she grabbed the handle with both hands and planted it deep into the soft flesh of her throat. Pain erupted from the wound as she twisted the knife once before falling forward as blood flowed wickedly from her wounds.

"*NO!*" Walter screamed as he realized what she'd done.

He ran to her in frustration and raised the axe above his head. He flung it forward, sending it toward her as it turned end over end. Sarah laid motionless as the last moments of her life in the Exodus Portal began to slip away. It all seemed to be happening in slow motion as Walter continued sprinting toward her. Sarah closed her eyes and felt her life slip away as the ax sliced through a poof of wispy, curling smoke that was once Sarah Prince.

# CHAPTER THIRTY-FOUR

Sarah woke up in the Exodus Chamber and exploded into tears, but for the first time in a long time, they weren't from fear or sadness. She cried a loud, blubbering cry, all the while smiling as the tears flowed thickly onto her face.

"It's done," she said.

"*What happened?*" Carlo asked as he raced to help her out of her pod.

"I killed myself."

"You *killed* yourself?" Allison asked.

"I grabbed a knife and I killed myself with it. It was the only thing I could think of to try. He wasn't going to let me anywhere near the orb. He wasn't happy when he saw what I did."

"And your headache?" Will asked.

"It's gone! I mean it's still there a little but it's getting better by the second."

"So when you were stabbing yourself, what was he doing?" Allison asked.

"I had my back to him so he couldn't see; I didn't want to give him a chance to kill me before I did it myself. Once he realized what I was doing though, he lost his mind. I think he knew I'd beat him."

"So it's over?" Carlo asked. "You're sure?"

"I think so, yes," Sarah said, smiling through her tears as Will and Allison pulled her in for a hug.

Sarah released herself from their hug and put her arms around Carlo.

"Thank you," she whispered.

"You're sure it's over?" he said, holding her in front of him by her shoulders. She nodded with a smile as he pulled her in for a long hug. "Are you okay?"

"He said some really terrible, true things about my past that I didn't know about. It's gonna take some time to work through it all, but yeah…I think I'm okay."

"We should watch the footage," Allison said, handing Carlo his tablet as he released Sarah.

He tapped on the screen a few times and fast-forwarded to when Sarah began with the knife. They all slightly cringed, watching her make a bloody mess of herself. Allison gasped slightly as the ax reached the puff of smoke where Sarah had been.

"You weren't kidding," Will said. "A second more and we would have had to send you back in."

They watched as Walter screamed loudly into the air when Sarah disappeared. The boiling lake sent blasts of water high into the air as the trees ignited into flames. Walter walked to the shore of the lake and stood silently, staring intently over the burning landscape in front of him.

"It's like watching the devil himself," Allison said as Walter screamed into the burning portal. Carlo paused the footage and sent the room into an eerie, calm silence.

"What now?" Allison asked.

Carlo looked down at his tablet before taking a long look

around at he and Nish's grand design. His eyes fixed on the pod where Nish had spent his last moments, alone with the possessed body of Kurt Saunders.

"Onward," he said, tapping on his tablet one final time as the screen shut off and the blue orb extinguished itself.

- One Year Later -

# CHAPTER THIRTY-FIVE

Sarah stared at the psychiatrist in front of her, just as she had monthly since leaving the Exodus Portal for the last time. She stared at him with as much of a smile as she could muster while he stared back, notebook in hand.

"I'm fine," she reiterated.

"You don't seem it, Sarah. We've been seeing each other here for a year and we've had hardly any progress. I'm worried about you."

"Seriously, doctor, I'm fine. I know you're probably getting sick of hearing it from me but it's the truth."

The doctor took of his glasses and scratched the bridge of his nose, trying to suppress his frustration. He put the notebook down on a table beside him and leaned forward.

"Sarah, listen. Carlo's a good friend of mine. He trusts me, which is why he brought you to me and told me about what happened with Walter. Trust me when I say that I found the situation with Walter's spirit much more believable than your assertion that you're okay."

Sarah looked out of a window, watching a pair of birds fight over a small tree branch while she avoided the doctor's gaze. After a moment of waiting for her response, he glanced at his watch and sat back in his chair.

"I'm afraid that's all for today, Ms. Prince. Please check in with Margie at the front desk to schedule our next session."

"Actually, Doctor, I think this is going to be our last visit. I'm glad you've enjoyed the gory details of my life but I can't keep showing up every month to be told that I'm not okay when I know I am."

"That's not fair, Sarah," the doctor said, standing as she walked to his office door. "It's never been about that for me. I'm just trying to help you."

"Thank you for your help but I think this is the end for me."

Sarah left the office and was greeted by Carlo and Stephanie, sitting in the waiting room. She greeted them with a smile as they stood.

"All done!"

"Right on time, as usual," Carlo said. "Gonna book another appointment before we split?"

"No, I meant for good. I'm not coming back."

"What?" Carlo asked.

"Carlo, I appreciate you trying to help but this isn't helping at all. I'm fine, and I'm sick of people treating me like I'm broken. I've lived through two of Walter's killing sprees; I'm kind of numb to it all at this point."

"Sarah, I get that, but…"

"Leave it alone," Stephanie whispered into his ear.

"We just want what's best for you, Sarah."

"I know," she said. "Can we get out of here?"

"Sure," Carlo said, opening the office door and letting Sarah and Stephanie leave first.

They walked across the parking lot to Carlo's new Ranger Rover. It wasn't long after they'd gotten rid of Walter that he donated his old one to try and numb the memory of Brad's body in the back seat. Sarah slid into the back as Carlo and Stephanie got into the front seats.

"What time are we meeting Will and Allison?" Sarah asked as she buckled her seatbelt.

"We're supposed to be meeting them at noon but I think we'll probably be a little late," Carlo said.

"You going to tell her?" Stephanie asked Carlo with a smile.

"Tell me what?"

"Well I guess I don't have a choice, now do I?" Carlos said with a smile. "I sold the patent to the Exodus Portal to a medical research company in Boston."

"Really?" Sarah asked. "Congratulations!"

"Thank you. Sold it for much less than what I could have but after everything that happened, I just want to see it go to good use. They're going to be developing it for use with terminally ill patients."

"That's really nice, Carlo. I think Nish would be proud."

"Nish would be pissed," he said with a chuckle. "I could have easily sold it to the Army or Navy for more than triple what I did to this place."

"One of the stipulations for the sale was that they keep him on as a board member for the company," Stephanie said.

"I'll be able to make sure the tech never falls into the wrong hands or goes down a path we don't want it to."

"That's fantastic, Carlo, seriously."

"That's not even the best part!" Stephanie said.

Carlo reached over and pulled a small, leather envelope from the glove compartment. He opened it and pulled out a cheque and handed to Sarah in the backseat.

"I'm splitting the money I made from the sale between all of us."

Sarah looked at the cheque in her hands, her mind struggling to comprehend the $2,000,000 amount he had scrawled across it.

"Carlo…"

"Stop. Just take it. I sold it for just over $12,000,000. I don't need it all and honestly, it's the least I can do, considering what happened."

"None of what happened was your fault, Carlo," Sarah said. "But thank you. It's beyond generous."

"You're welcome."

"I think I may have been a little rude to your doctor friend. Apologize for me, would you?"

"Of course," Carlo said with another chuckle as he pulled the car out of the parking lot.

\*\*\*\*\*

Will stood and waved the three of them over to their table at the Grand Hyatt Hotel. Sarah felt an eerie feeling settle over her as she made her way through the main floor of the hotel, just as she had the night Nish had asked her to take part in the Exodus experiment. They all greeted each other with hugs and smiles before sitting down at the table and grabbing menus.

"Same table..." Sarah said, sitting in the same spot she had the morning of the Portal's first run.

"Yep, the very one," Will said, looking around at the empty seats where Nish, Daniel, Billy, Kurt, Betsy, and Stanley had sat. Everyone at the table took a moment of silence, feeling the empty spaces between them.

"We should make this an annual thing," Will said.

"Agreed," Carlo said.

The group ordered and ate their food, sharing stories of the past year before Carlo reached into his pocket and pulled out the leather envelope full of cheques. He explained the sale to them and handed out the cheques. The table was eerily silent before Will stood and hugged Carlo while Allison sobbed.

"Is that a ring on your finger?" Sarah asked, looking at a diamond engagement ring staring back at her from Allison's finger.

"I completely forgot," Allison said, letting a small laugh escape through her tears.

"Not the biggest surprise of the day, but yeah, I popped the question yesterday," Will said, sitting back down and kissing her on the forehead.

Carlo, Stephanie, and Sarah all stood and congratulated them with a collective hug.

"We're making a scene," Stephanie said, sitting back down with a smile as they all sat back down.

"Thank you, everyone," Will said. "I just wish Billy was here. Any word from him?"

"Well, if you'll allow it, I have one last surprise for you all. Stephanie and I are flying down to visit Billy in two days and we want you all to come with us. I think we could all use a getaway."

"Wow!" Will said.

"Is that going to be an issue for you, Allison? I wasn't sure if you'd be able to get away from Metro."

"Actually, I'm not with the department any longer."

"What?" Sarah asked, leaning forward in her seat.

"I resigned a month ago. All I every wanted was to work on a case like yours, but after everything that happened, it just didn't make sense any longer."

"Allison I'm sorry," Carlo said.

"Please, don't blame yourself. I fought it for months but at the end of the day, it was no longer right for me. I've been writing a lot, I'm much happier than I thought I'd be."

"That's fantastic," Sarah said with a smile.

"So what does everyone say?" Carlo asked. "Nicaragua?"

"It sounds great, Carlo, but I haven't renewed my passport in years," Will said.

"Don't worry about that," Carlo said, waving the waitress over to pay the cheque. "The way we're going, we won't need passports."

*****

Harvey Braddock handed a yellow envelope through the window of his van to the young man standing in the booth outside the airstrip. The man smiled and nodded at him before opening the gate and granting him access to the airstrip once again.

"We're in business," Harvey said, reaching over to the passenger seat and taking Cindy's hand with a smile.

"This makes me nervous," Stephanie said with a weary smile, sitting in the back seats with Will, Allison, and Sarah.

"It gets easier each time," Cindy said with a laugh.

Harvey pulled into the same hanger he had when he'd had Billy unconscious and tied up in the back. They each got out and looked at the plane in front of them, much bigger than the one he'd last flown.

"Okay, this one is for sure not yours," Cindy said.

"You are correct," Harvey said.

"You know how to fly something this big?"

"Only one way to find out," he said as he opened the side door of the van to let the group out. "I'm sure I'll figure it out once we're up there."

"Very reassuring, Mr. Braddock," Cindy said with a smile, opening the back door and handing everyone their bags.

After a six and a half our flight, Harvey landed the plane smoothly on a private airstrip a half hour outside of San Juan del Sur, Nicaragua. Harvey quickly secured a taxi-van and had them loaded and on their way to Billy's Nicaraguan safe house. The two-level home was nestled in a bunching of trees at the edge of a beach forest, with a small cliff overlooking a private beach on San Juan del Sur Bay. Its roof was made of red clay tiles, with a balcony that spanned the entire second level. Just outside the front door was a large sitting area, overlooking a small pool with a comically large inflatable duck floating inside. Harvey paid the taxi driver as the group removed their bags from the back of the van.

"Wow, Billy really hit the jackpot down here," Will said, looking at the gorgeous home in front of them.

"I'm glad," Carlo said. "Money well spent."

The front door opened and Billy walked into the sunlight. His skin was perfectly tanned as he stood smiling at them. His usual clean-shaven face was hidden behind a beard, mixing in with the hair he'd grown out.

"Hi," he said with a smile as the taxi drove off.

Sarah put her arms around him and burst into tears, relieved to see again. They all stood in the sun, hugging and laughing after a year removed from each other.

"We've got some catching up to do," Billy said with a smile as they all disappeared inside with their bags.

# CHAPTER THIRTY-SIX

Sarah walked to the edge of the cliff as the sun began to rise for the third time since they'd joined Billy at his hidden Nicaraguan home. She felt the warm morning air on her face as a breeze slightly tussled her hair. She inhaled the sweet morning air and watched the waves crash against the beach below. It was a beautiful morning, which she knew would lead to an even more beautiful day.

She looked back at Billy's home, still basked in morning shadows while the sun began its slow ascent to the top of the sky. She smiled, looking at the dark windows before turning back toward the bay. She reached into her pocket and pulled out a small piece of paper, folded a few times and crumpled slightly. She unfolded it and looked at the words running down the middle of the page, each competing with bloody finger prints that dotted the blank space of the white paper...

Allison Carol
William Caldwell
Billy Shaw
Carlo Macasaet
Stephanie Reynolds
Harvey Braddock
Cindy Paulson

She folded the paper again and placed it back into her pocket. When she pulled her hand out, she brought with it a small ring with a tiny diamond situated in the middle of the shiny white gold. She slid the ring onto her left ring finger before turning and going back into the dark house.

# About the Author

Tim Gabrielle is a married father of three amazing kids living in Ontario, Canada. He grew up in Loudoun County, Virginia, and a lot of the settings in the this book were created from an imalgimation of the areas in which he was raised. Tim's first book, This Land of Monsters, was published by Ink Smith Publishing in October, 2018.